A VIRUS CALLED DOG

DOG

BY WARWICK RENTON

This is a work of fiction. Names, characters, places, and incidents are products of the author's imagination or are used fictitiously and are not to be construed as real. Any resemblance to actual events, locales, organisations, or persons, living or dead, is entirely coincidental.

Editing by Liz Butcher & Heather Haunert

ACKNOWLEDGMENTS

Thank you to everyone along the way who listened, laughed and sometimes cried. For your patience, understanding and support – I thank you.

To my children for their honesty when something didn't sound right. To Liz for your help with the manuscript and Heather for your keen editorial eye.

And for your patience Oprah, as you eagerly await your next great read – please understand it took nine years to complete.

Warwick Renton

WARWICK RENTON

PROLOGUE

N othing would have happened the way it did if it wasn't for the crowd of blue, grey and green one-eyed aliens that gathered at the spaceport on a small planet far away. Each spoke in a different language, and not a single one could understand the other, but they were excited all the same. And the organisers of the "Competition to Discover the Most Absurd Thing in the Universe" were happy because as far as they could tell, everything was going according to plan. Many years before, the whole thing started when a tall, skinny alien with a big bald head and luminous skin discovered a new planet spinning around a distant sun. Minding his own business and looking through the lens of his lookoscope (which was an advanced type of telescope for looking at the stars), the alien searched for anything interesting when he saw an otherwise undiscovered, small blue-green planet far away. He planned to keep his discovery to himself until it occurred to him that he had found a way to fulfil his dying grandfather's final wish. A prolific and decorated explorer of distant stars, his

6

grandfather had concluded that most of what he'd seen in his life was absurd. The problem was, not being great with words, the old alien never took the time to write it down. In his honour, the elders of the planet, always excited at the idea of something new, agreed to stage the "*Competition to Discover the Most Absurd Thing in the Universe.*" And the first prize was a publishing deal and free publicity for the much-anticipated first volume of *The Chronicles of the Absurd*.

And so, amidst a fanfare of alien instruments that no one heard because these particular aliens had evolved beyond the need for ears, the competitors blasted off. The skinny alien with the big bald head, armed with the coordinates of his recent discovery, set course for the small and undiscovered blue-green planet, far away. And it was an extraordinary piece of luck that a devastating and unexpected meteor shower did not obliterate him. From the platform of the spaceport, the elders watched the carnage and quickly decided that the competition was over before it began. Every competitor was assumed dead once everything quieted, and not a single spaceship could be seen. To lessen the tragedy and the awkward silence that befell them all, the elders passed around a hat, accepting donations to fund an elaborate ceremony of final rites and flowers—and to pay for the vapours of a locally made tincture that, when inhaled, caused frequent and bizarre hallucinations. Sometimes for days...

On an even smaller brown planet just a couple of light-years away, a gathering of little blue beings with heads far too large for their bodies huddled in a circle and rocked from side to side. Their hands hung loosely by their sides and their eyes focused on the centre of a circle where the holographic image of a blue-green ball floated in space. It spun slowly at a tilt of twenty-three and a half degrees.

Now and then, the beings, who were mostly content just to watch life pass them by, took it upon themselves to lend others a helping hand. With no riches to bestow and wishing neither to alarm nor to offend, they sent their gift of peace out to space. Their first transmission identified itself as a species called Dog. It was mostly a voice, but sometimes it appeared as a short-haired canine with a shiny black coat, a long pink tongue, and carried a red rubber ball.

The little blue beings watched as their transmission reached a planet far away. They cocked their heads to one side with a fascination similar to a child watching a cat unravel a ball of string. They were the masters of suffering and joy, and joining their hands, they rocked from side to side and watched with mild amusement, waiting for what might happen next.

Somewhere else in the depths of space, where stars are just pinpricks of light, Aachoo, a different alien altogether and not very nice at all, stood on the bridge of his shiny spaceship with one arm behind his back. Commander of the warring fleet of Quadrant Delta Three, he was afflicted by a swathe of unsightly green warts and clothed himself in a ceremonial robe of purple and gold with tasselled shoulders to remind everyone of his position.

Aachoo lowered his other arm, which in the language of war was an order for destruction. He tried to smile but was distracted as he scratched at a wart that had become infected with age. Aachoo wiped the yellow and green pus on his sleeve and looked back out to space. He was comfortable with his decision to destroy the planet, which, as far as his outdated charts were concerned, had no name. Hoping to impress his young, beautiful, and most recent girlfriend of eleven days, Aachoo was adamant about winning her heart. He needed her to know that he, commander and creator of wars, could still hold his own against younger, richer, and far more attractive aliens who made no secret about staring at his girlfriend's voluptuous green and multi-nippled breasts that were not really breasts at all.

Aachoo rocked backwards on old, green spongy heels and looked out to space with a mellow grin.

A door opened on one of the artillery ships in Aachoo's fleet. There were a series of mechanical clunks and whirs, followed by a flash of yellow light that tore through space and disappeared.

"Well then, what do you think of that?" Aachoo asked his girlfriend, who perched on a metal stool at his side. With her three legs crossed, she had not bothered to look up for quite some time. For what could be more important than filing an obstinate cuticle that detracted from the beauty of her otherwise perfect claw?

"What?" she asked.

Aachoo clenched his yellow fangs. "What do you mean 'what'?" he said. He pointed out to space and raised his eyebrows in a secret and desperate search for approval.

"That's nice, Archie," his girlfriend said, flinching as her file slipped and stabbed her claw.

Aachoo puffed out his chest. "Millions will die," he said, and then, for effect, he added, "Because of me!"

There was a moment's silence, and then, clearly oblivious to the consequences of Aachoo's act, his girlfriend said, "Think we might get something to eat?"

Almost instantaneously, Commander Aachoo's beam of destructive yellow light ran into something with a flash and a bang. No one saw it coming, and anyway, for them, it was too late.

For everything.

PART ONE

MENTORIA

1. THE DOG WITH THE RED RUBBER BALL

On a not-so-distant, massive central sun, a storm raged, shooting spurts of molten fire into deep space. It was the storm season, after all, and a bad time for anyone travelling between the stars. The effects of the storm were felt far and wide, causing stomachs to turn, beings to topple over, and spacecraft to crash. And in a somewhat premature and dramatic end to the season, a spectacular pulse of fire and light ripped a new hole in the fabric of space.

Whilst the pulse of light started at break-neck speed, eventually, it slowed and ran out of steam. And it just so happened that Dog, an adventurer and seeker of good times, was minding his own business and sniffing a garden of small yellow flowers in his own little patch of space. When he noticed the beam of light, Dog forgot about the flowers and looked up. Far more interested in the idea of something new, he seized the opportunity and hitched a ride before the light was gone.

Sitting at attention, his head held high, Dog slobbered all over the red rubber ball he held firmly in his mouth. As he rode through space, his ears flapped backwards, and his fur flattened, as he hoped with all his heart that somewhere within the expansive universe, someone wanted to play.

Despite being a firm believer that the past should stay in the past, Dog was aware of a series of not so nice rumours circulating about him in recent years. And he did all he could to ignore them, even if some of them were true.

Why should it matter? Everybody makes mistakes—even dogs with red rubber balls. What's done is done.

Because as far as he was concerned, in his heart of hearts, Dog never really meant anyone any harm—despite the fact that sometimes things went terribly wrong.

A happy traveller on the beam of light, he reminisced about that fateful afternoon when he chanced upon a band of merry children playing "hit the ball with a stick." And compelled by any opportunity to play, Dog hopped off the beam of light.

Having long ago mastered the art of invisibility, and because he mostly travelled as a hologram of light, the children didn't realise Dog was there. So, when he arrived on that particular afternoon, Dog was little more than a shadow on the wall. But as the children continued to play, he did what was in his very nature to do. Over-excited, Dog ran in circles, chasing his tail and captivated by children's laughter; he gradually shifted from a hologram into his physical form.

As would be expected, the children were frightened at first to see a big black dog appear out of a shadow on the wall. But soon enough, the children sensed that Dog was a happy mutt and definitely male, which was confirmed as they watched him cock his left leg to pee on the wall.

For the rest of the afternoon, Dog—regal, medium-sized, shiny, and black—licked the children's hands as they giggled gleefully. He ran in circles, barking as the children encouraged him to pursue his tail. And as the children chased the ball, Dog chased them while skilfully avoiding the holder of the stick. But the laughter stopped when, playfully wrestling with the youngest boy over the slimy red ball, Dog accidentally bit his hand. But what did it matter? Everyone was having far too much fun to let a little bite get in the way. Nonetheless, what the little boy thought was a mere nip, turned out to be something far worse, and by the following day, the boy succumbed to a deadly fever and dropped into the deep waters of delirium. The boy's father, distraught by the sudden turn of events, set out to the fishmonger's stand at the market where the black dog was sound asleep.

Oblivious to the consequences of their game, Dog slept, symptom-free with his head on his front paws. That was until the large boot of the boy's father connected with his chest and wrenched him from his sleep. Dog yelped and sat up with wild, darting eyes. The man accused him of infecting his son, and whilst it made no sense to Dog, he knew he had no choice but to run.

Later, beneath a canopy of heavy stars, Dog licked his wounds, twisting to ease the pain of two broken ribs. Bemused at how quickly life could change, Dog sat with his sadness. That was until he remembered that the past is in the past—that what happened with the boy was done, and there was no use dwelling on a patch of bad luck in his otherwise exciting and happy life.

Forever an optimist, Dog focused on the fact that, setbacks aside, he knew himself to be a doer of good deeds. All he really wanted was to have fun, and whilst he didn't realise it at the time, it had something to do with why, years earlier, strange little blue beings from a small brown planet far away sent him off into space. Fun for Dog usually involved dropping a squeaky red rubber ball at someone or something's feet and seeing if they were not too busy to play. Most of the time, it went well, if even for just a few minutes. At other times, it did not. And in the light-years between seeing anyone at all, Dog rode upon passing waves of light, content to run in circles and captivated mostly by the simple pleasure of chasing his own tail.

The spread of bad blood towards Dog began the day he arrived in the land of Happysad and met a boy who had disobeyed his mother's orders. Having wandered off in a misguided sulk, the boy found himself too far from home and without any water. Following his hand-drawn map and scorched by the midday sun, the boy ventured across the deserts of Happysad in search of treasure. If he were correct, the treasure was hidden in a wooden box buried somewhere in the crust of a dried-up sea, as most treasure seemed to be. But because his map was upside down, the boy lost his way. By mid-afternoon, after hours under an unseasonably sizzling sun, the boy's mouth dried up, his eyesight clouded over, and he found himself blinded by shadows that swallowed the light.

Too young to know how to find water, the boy pushed forward in pursuit of his treasure. When his kidneys started to fail, his legs wobbled, and his muscles burned as though on fire. The dizziness of his rapidly approaching death spun his mind out of control. And at that moment, which he was convinced was the end, his confusion and mental fog cleared. A small doorway within his mind opened onto a vast sphere of silence and nothingness. And the boy, for the first time in his life, felt the contradiction of terror and bliss. A moment later, not too far away, he heard a popping sound, followed by a slurp. Something was breathing heavily and moving closer.

In the distance, Dog sat in the heart of a mirage, his sharp white fangs resting on his lower lip. After some quick nostril breathing and a half-sneeze to expel the dust, Dog opened his mouth, unfurled a long pink tongue, and started panting. He shifted his gaze and peered out into space. With his front paws placed neatly together, Dog sat with the patience of a lion watching a deer. His jet-black coat glistened from a diet of eggs and whatever other scraps he could find. And in the searing heat of the day, Dog half-closed his eyes and waited for whatever might happen next.

Through the shadows in his eyes, the boy saw the distant and distressing image of the panting dog. A commentary of desperate thoughts broke through the quiet of his mind.

Run! Get out of here; this is the end! What the hell am I going to do now?

Suddenly, a new voice entered his mind, telling him to find something sharp to protect himself from the likely outcome of the dog ripping him apart. At that moment, the boy was sure those thoughts were not his own—which meant the only other explanation was that the dog had somehow seized control of his mind.

With its teeth bared, the dog crept forward on its stomach across the burning sand. Between its paws was a red rubber ball, which it nudged forward with its nose. The boy kept his head down until the ball rolled between his feet. Looking up, he watched the dog inching closer, and when the world spun on its axis, the boy collapsed. He fell through the cracks of consciousness, and Dog, unsure what had happened, cocked his head to one side in an attempt to understand. And then, deciding there wasn't going to be any fun to be had at all, Dog retrieved his ball and went upon his way.

Sometime later, when the boy opened his eyes, he found himself in the arms of a woman. Her breasts, large and soft like pillows, heaved as she breathed, causing his head to roll to the side and back again. The boy managed to open his eyes just enough to see her smiling down at him while she pressed a wet rag against his lips. He sucked the cool water from the cloth, relieved as the water ran over his parched and swollen tongue. And when he tried to speak, he made no sound as his throat was filled with fire.

"Shhh," the woman silenced him. "Drink."

She rocked the boy back and forth, and he let his eyes close once more. Within seconds he was floating on a turbulent sea, then sinking like a stone into the dark waters of his muddled mind.

Scenes unfolded before him, revealing a thin veil of clouds spread across the burning sun. The black dog was there—sitting in the shadows with a red ball resting in front of its paws and with its head cocked to one side, panting through a shallow grin.

When the boy awoke, the vision was etched into his consciousness, and somehow—disturbingly—he could feel the dog inside his mind, whispering things the boy couldn't comprehend.

After what seemed like hours of drinking water scented with mint and sucking on the tender flesh of sweet melons, the boy felt strong enough to walk. The woman led him back to the village, and when he entered his home, clenched by the fist of fear, his mother slapped his face before squeezing him hard against her chest. Without words, they cried the silent tears of relief.

It was not long before the boy sensed the change. His parents looked at him with fear in their eyes. They watched him like a shopkeeper spies on a thief and not feeling quite himself; the boy watched back.

They know it. My mind is not entirely my own.

Awkwardly cheerful, his parents questioned why he started wearing a large-brimmed hat.

Clearly, it's protecting me from the sun.

But when the hat provided no relief from his anxious mind, the boy donned a veil instead and dressed in black from head to toe. Again, his parents questioned why.

Isn't it obvious? To protect myself from the virus of feelings sent by aliens on the rays of light from the great central sun.

In time, the tolerant smiles slipped from his parents' faces. The boy didn't care. For he had work to do.

Walking the streets of Happysad, the boy protested against the coded messages sent on the rays of the sun. At first, the villagers shunned the boy whose brain they believed were fried from exposure to the desert sun. But, undeterred, the boy knew exactly what he had to do.

It's up to me to protect the people from the confusion of feelings carried on the rays of the sun.

Slowly, and one by one, citizens of Happysad joined the boy as he marched through the streets. The lonely came first, then sad, closely followed by the curious folk who just didn't want to miss out on anything. The movement grew. It gathered strength.

Meetings were held in dark rooms where conspiracies were confirmed, and the facts made clear—all upon the word of the boy and his self-professed wisdom about messages sent from the great central sun. But not being completely mad, he kept to himself the visions of the black dog with the red rubber ball.

There's no need to tell them. No one really needs to know.

Instead, he blamed everything on the light of distant stars. According to the people of Happysad, the movement in itself was harmless. That was until the day they marched on the civic buildings of Happysad and demanded that the administrators take immediate action to protect their minds. Unfortunately, the administrators of the province confirmed they had better things to do than respond to the ramblings of a boy dressed in black. So they ignored him and went about their day.

Under the shade of black parasols, the crowd grew. The demonstrators marched fiercely through the streets, chanting about the conspiracy of beings from distant suns. People were injured, blood was shed, buildings were set on fire. And whilst the unrest was unfortunate, the boy didn't care. Because in his mind, it was all for the greater good.

19

When he was detained, the boy's followers refused orders to burn their black hats. According to them, the virus spread on the rays of the sun was a very real threat. Later, in the afternoon, backed by scientists and engineers, the boy called a meeting beneath the branches of a shady tree. After whispering between themselves for some time, the boy stood up and proclaimed himself their leader. And amidst a cacophony of chants and hoots, everyone raised their hands in the air and agreed—they would build Mentoria—a city protected from the virus of feelings on the far side of the River E.

2. THE BLINKING LIGHT

It was Tuesday in the magnificent city of Mentoria, and in a building towering above the skyline, there blinked a lone red light.

On. Off. On. Off.

Nestled within an enormous control panel that appeared more for show than functionality, the red light flashed on and off for some time before The Master's personal physician, Juaneeto, walked by. Startled to see the flashing light, he almost dropped the silver tray he was carrying upon which balanced a tall glass filled with green liquid. Juaneeto was unusually tall and thin, and his long, bony fingers gripped the tray as he steadied himself. With a quick glance back at the blinking light,

Juaneeto entered his master's room, where The Master, as he was known throughout Mentoria, lay on his back on the bed with his hands placed across his chest. With the stillness of The Master's sleep easily mistaken for death, Juaneeto hesitated—torn between doing his duty and wanting to let The Master sleep. For it was no secret—at least to those who worked closely with The Master—that sleep was often elusive, so turbulent was his mind. Juaneeto watched his boss, where he lay motionless in the middle of his triple king-sized bed. And whilst The Master was a small man by anyone's standards, the enormous bed engulfed him, making him look like a tiny child asleep on his parent's bed. The Master raised his hand and lifted the corner of his lavender-scented eye mask as he peered out beneath it. And Juaneeto couldn't help but think it looked slightly ridiculous on The Master's bulbous, bald head, but he'd never dare say a word.

"A long night, Master?" Juaneeto asked, approaching the bed and placing the tray on the bedside table. He straightened and shoved his hands into the pockets of his long, white lab coat.

"Only as long as the last," The Master replied, discarding the lavender mask as he sat up. He reached for the glass and took long, slow gulps. Juaneeto always felt intrusive watching his boss take his morning liquids, and instead, he let his eyes wander around the penthouse. Intentionally shaped like a pill, The Master's extravagant bedroom spanned at least half of the entire space. The décor was simple, with sterile white walls and lush white carpet, in stark contrast to the black satin sheets on The Master's bed. Juaneeto waited for the sound of the empty glass being placed back on the tray.

"Are you ready for the blinds?"

The Master nodded, and Juaneeto pressed a button on a panel beside the bed before standing aside and watching the black blinds draw upwards. The red lights of Mentoria shone below, and The Master swung his legs off the side of the bed and pulled his obsidian terry towelling robe around himself and joined Juaneeto. The window, shaped like an eye, was as unconventionally shaped as the penthouse itself, looking out across the whole of Mentoria. On a plaque above the window was the mandate of the city.

The Mind Matters Most

Juaneeto shot a discrete, sideways glance at the self-proclaimed, all-powerful ruler of Mentoria, waiting for him to speak. And as The Master scanned the city below, he nodded to himself. "Brilliant, is it not?" he murmured, looking across the city's skyscrapers.

"The mind boggles," Juaneeto replied.

Outside, just beneath the penthouse shaped like a pill, metal pods filled with fluorescent lights milled around the sky-like silver lilies.

"Anything to report?" The Master asked.

Juaneeto smiled to himself—as this was their morning ritual, their little game.

"Now that you mention it," Juaneeto said as he stepped back and pointed at the panel above their heads, "there is the matter of that flashing red light."

The Master glanced up, and his eyes widened, pushing his long, wiry eyebrows skywards. He rubbed his chin. "Hmm…"

"Is it bad?" Juaneeto drawled.

"Why didn't you tell me sooner?" The Master huffed.

Juaneeto opened his mouth to respond, but The Master continued. "Why wasn't there an alarm?"

"You turned it off," Juaneeto replied.

"I did?"

23

Juaneeto gave a slow, solemn nod, trying not to flinch under the sudden scrutiny of The Master's stare.

"Well, do *you* think it means something bad?" asked The Master, his voice dripping with sarcasm as the corner of his mouth turned upwards in a sneer.

Juaneeto felt a hot flush run up his neck and into his cheeks as he scanned the control panel, trying to understand what had triggered the alarm.

"I can't imagine a red flashing light could be good," The Master stated, leaning forward and pressing his ear to the window. "Can you hear it, Juaneeto?"

"What, Master?"

"That buzzing sound. Like a mosquito flying into a zapper. I can hear the 'zzztt' beneath the hum of the city…" the Master trailed off.

Juaneeto stood still and listened.

"We are under attack," The Master finally stated, slamming the heel of his bare foot onto the shiny white tiles, causing Juaneeto to jump. Peering down, he saw the twitching legs of a cockroach, and he smiled at the green liquid that oozed from its sides. And without a word, The Master climbed up onto his stool before the control panel and entered a sequence of numbers into the keypad.

With a hint of a smile, Juaneeto stepped back as he pondered the sequence of events that they repeated every day. Feeling fidgety in the surrounding silence, Juaneeto flicked his finger against The Master's empty glass. A bell-like *ting* echoed around the room, and Juaneeto turned on his heel and walked away.

Down in the Mentorian Guard, recruit Stanley Luka, somnambulist, and compulsive counter of things, found himself tangled in his sheets. He dreamed vividly of running down an icy slope, his legs freewheeling out of control as though he would lose his balance and fall into the abyss. The cold air pierced his lungs like dozens of tiny shards of glass, and a rumbling sound pursued him as he ran from the avalanche of ice and snow. Every time Stanley had the avalanche dream, he was convinced it was the last time and that it would bury him once and for all. Tiny white bullets of ice shot at his back and Stanley dodged to the side as he spotted a gap in the ice ahead. The black mouth of the crevice loomed, and with what little strength he could muster, Stanley leapt, his legs pedalling furiously through the air. It was only when he started his descent that he noticed the dog.

On the other side, the dog was large and black, only just visible from where it sat. Its front paws were together, and with a red rubber ball in its mouth, its shiny black nose was lifted to the wind as though awaiting a familiar scent. Suddenly the dog dropped the rubber ball, letting it roll towards the edge of the crevice as it watched on.

Stanley's eyes widened when he realised he wasn't going to make it to the other side. His arms and legs flailed, desperately trying to find something to stop his fall as he plummeted through the crack in the ice. Panic seized Stanley's chest, like a tight fist squeezing the air from his lungs. He couldn't breathe, and as he fell, a flurry of voices jostled for attention inside his head. Then there was a single voice, louder than the rest. It was the voice of a woman, soft and gentle, telling him to open his eyes.

Stanley gasped as his eyes flew open. His heart thundered against his chest as he lay motionless on his bed in the dark, dripping with sweat.

I'm okay. I'm okay. I'm okay. I'm okay. I'm okay. I'm okay. I'm okay.

Like each nightmare before, Stanley felt better when he repeated his mantra seven times. No more. No less. Stanley walked his fingers around the edge of his single bed, feeling for the certainty of the missing sheets that lay twisted on the floor. A familiar sense of panic churned within his stomach. At twenty-four years old, Stanley Luka was afraid of the dark and terrified by the increasing frequency of his dreams. He wondered how they'd gone unnoticed by the monitoring stations that scanned the city, looking for any sign of trouble.

Not superstitious at all, Stanley Luka did as he was told. He maintained what he'd convinced himself was a healthy fear of the stars and was grateful not to be part of the madness that lay beyond Mentoria. Yet despite every effort to stop the habit, Stanley Luka spent most of his days with his fingers crossed.

Beset with a sense that things were not quite right with the world, he fumbled on his bedside table for a bottle of pills marked with a letter "P." Following his prescription, Stanley popped six pills, plus one to make seven, in his mouth. He swallowed hard and lifted the small, silver, baguette-shaped device called a 'nummer' to his mouth.

About the size of a small gas cylinder, the nummer was the product of numerous clinical trials that, according to The Master, *"went well."* Designed to fit in a purpose-made backpack, the nummers were made from a lightweight alloy and were deliberately larger than they needed to be—to serve as a reminder to all that feelings were forbidden. Standard issue

26

nummer-packs were required to be worn, giving Mentorians an appearance that resembled scuba divers with small tanks of air on their backs. A long cord stretched from the top of the pack and extended over the wearer's shoulder. And at the end of the cord was a mouthpiece that was a cross between a mouthguard and a metal bit capable of administering serious but metered shocks of electricity that could last up to three days. Despite the fact that its inventor's disregard for the dangers of electricity saw him reduced to a smouldering pile of ash before he could revel in his success, the nummer did what he'd designed it to do. It made people numb. It made them feel nothing at all. And to minimise the chance of an outbreak of feelings, there were instructions on the side of every nummer which read:

1. *Bite down hard on the mouthpiece.*
2. *Suck the air in through your teeth until all feelings are gone.*
3. *Don't question the effectiveness of the nummer. Follow the instructions or suffer the consequences.*

As with everything, there were always consequences, both good and bad. Good was feeling nothing at all; bad included singe marks above the ears, possible rogue feelings, and the risk of developing resistance to the benefits of the nummer through overuse. When things went bad, as they often did, a small black truck with a revolving orange light would suddenly appear at the scene. "Dispatch," as the truck was called, was manned by two specially trained members of the Mentorian Guard. Their job was to strap the sick to a stretcher and take them away. "Away" happened to be a tall, unmarked building on the edge of the city. A couple of times each day, the two large steel doors of the facility opened, and two men wearing white protective suits and masks emerged through a thin wedge of light.

Without so much as a word, they took hold of the stretcher and carried it through the narrow opening and simply disappeared.

As the numbness took hold, Stanley considered that perhaps it wasn't his dream that had him feeling so disturbed on that Tuesday morning. There was something else, something in the recesses of his mind, like an old knot that was gradually working loose. But it was worse than that. To Stanley, it felt like something that was big, black, and shackled. It was twisting and stretching in the dark.

It was finally breaking free.

The thought sent a shiver up Stanley's spine. And feeling on edge, he wiggled each of his fingers and then crossed them again. He waited. And when the shiver left him, Stanley reassured himself.

I'm okay. I'm okay. I'm okay. I'm okay. I'm okay. I'm okay. I'm okay.

The metallic bitterness in Stanley's mouth was one of the many side effects caused by the small white pills marked with the letter "P." In the otherwise bleak history of Mentoria's pharmaceutical trials and despite the instant weight gain, dry mouth, constipation, dizziness, drowsiness, spasms, cramps, and a rapid reduction in white blood cell count, the drug was considered a resounding success. It was by accident that the exact combination of sedatives, antipsychotics, cannabis, and aldehydes was discovered in the stomach of the scientist whose heart exploded and left him spreadeagled with his face adhered to the floor of his lab. Tests on the chalky white liquid found oozing from his mouth confirmed that the pill marked with the letter "P"—minus an ingredient or two—was largely a step in the right direction. Even so, the important fact remained the same—It seemed to stop people from feeling anything…anything at all.

Without delay, the Council of Necessity (whose job it was to run the city and attend to things that needed to be done) sat around a large rectangular table and simultaneously popped pills marked with the letter "P" into their mouths. Convinced that their minds were clear, they ordered the distribution of compulsory doses to every Mentorian right away. And reportedly, the city had never felt less, and the benefits were clear.

Stanley bit hard on the mouthpiece of his nummer and closed his eyes. The machine buzzed and delivered a series of therapeutic shocks. At the same time, he imagined a circle, a triangle, and a square. He juggled the images in his mind as he always did but didn't know why. Stanley felt the shots of electricity start in his teeth before spreading throughout his body, leaving only the numbness in its wake. And then, taking a deep breath, Stanley opened his eyes.

He gazed around at his cramped apartment, which was little more than a couple of rooms hidden in the basement of a towering skyscraper of steel and glass. The dismal living quarters were standard for a security officer of the Mentorian Guard and directly reflected their usefulness to the city. Stanley stepped around the narrow troughs of water he placed around the bed as a precaution against his sleepwalking. He took a quick shower, brushed his hair to the left, and climbed into black overalls adorned with red trim, silver buttons, and engraved with the two letters, "MG." Stanley stood tall, suddenly a soldier. He looked in the mirror and read his surname from the white badge on his chest: "Luka – MG."

The lights on Stanley's e-reader—which was a small rubber wrist cuff with three lights and an alarm set within it—were green. This meant he wasn't feeling very much at all. But if he were, the problem would be rectified by the use of a nummer or a handful of pills marked with the letter "P." If that didn't work, the alarm would sound. A big computer that had other important things to do would stop and activate a loud horn. This would go on (keeping lots of people awake) until a member of the Mentorian Guard was dispatched.

Stanley made two pieces of toast without butter and bit into a genetically modified apple that was greener than nature ever intended it to be. The long rectangular window set high in Stanley's apartment let in a narrow beam of glowing red light. It shone across the only poster on Stanley's wall, which he admired as he chewed on his apple, his head tilted to the side. It was an image of a once-famous baseball player dressed in a black-and-white-striped jersey and matching cap. The pitcher was standing on one leg and throwing a white ball into the depths of space.

And without the ability to explain the poster's effect, Stanley stopped to study it every day. In the background hovered a constellation of stars that, according to The Master, were the tiny transmitters of evil feelings that disrupted the mind. In fact, it was the light from the stars that caused people to be either happy or sad, overwhelming them with feelings that would eventually drive them mad.

For Stanley, the pitcher was a hero, timeless and unafraid. And in those moments of admiration, it never occurred to him to consider the real fate of the baseball player, who, as it turned out, was no hero at all but merely the ambassador of a cigarette company forced to close its doors on account of its unhappy customers who filled their lungs with smoke and died.

3. SHINY SILVER TRAINS

On a good day, the mood of Mentoria was like an old man gazing pensively into the distance, scratching his temple, and straining to see something just out of sight. On a bad day, Mentoria was a city suffocating, a place spinning, exhausted, powerless, and gasping for air. The crutch on which Mentoria leaned was the absolute devotion of the people to the betterment of the mind. So, every year, on the eleventh day of the second month at exactly ten o'clock, The Separation divided the eligible youth into two groups. At nine o'clock, children older than thirteen but younger than fourteen were corralled into a single-storey, windowless grey building with a flat roof. Under the hum of white, fluorescent lights, they sat at a sea of tables and waited for a bell to ring. Then, with pens raised, their responses to the city's questions decided the rest of their lives. That afternoon, the candidates presented their left wrists and were branded with a small and scorching iron: "I" or "D" – intelligent or deficient.

It never occurred to Stanley that to be branded as "D" for deficient was no fault of his own. In a prestigious medical journal abandoned years before, it was hypothesised that the absence of breast milk was a likely retarding force on an infant mind. Stanley's mother, who sometimes appeared in the twilight of his dreams, was unable to breastfeed because he was born with sharp little teeth. Insatiable, he chewed on her nipples and made them bleed. And when the milk stopped flowing, Stanley cried. His mother cried too—first, for her hungry twins, and second, because she realised she could no longer live under the umbrella of her husband's oppressive rule. When Stanley's father fled to Mentoria, he took Stanley with him, having no use for a wife who couldn't feed her son and even less use for an infant daughter. In the last memory Stanley had of his mother, she was on her knees, with her daughter clutched to her chest. And with heavy, heartbroken-filled tears, she watched them disappear.

Ever since the day his father took him away, Stanley hung like a weak nut on the fragile branch of the tree of life. Sometimes he rubbed hard at the small tattoo of the "D" on his wrist, as if by doing so, something would change, or he could make it go away because the one thing that the letter "D" on his wrist meant for sure was that he would never be allowed to ride on one of the city's shiny silver trains.

Every hour of every day, one of Mentoria's silver trains slithered around the city like a silent metal snake. On a bed of magnets, it transported those branded with an "I" to the towers of magnificence—where the chosen Mentorians produced intelligent thoughts and did lots of smart things. But truth be told, they were really only there for one thing—to solve the enduring and unfortunate legacy of their forefathers who, long ago, marched into Mentoria, marvelled at their own magnificence, and patted themselves on the back without a single thought as to how to power Mindset, which protected them from the brainwashing barrage of the sun's harmful rays.

If Mentoria were a great ship heading into an inevitable and golden age, then the brilliant young minds of the youth were its captain, navigating the unchartered waters of the future. And in the absence of any bright ideas, it was The Master who decreed that the only way forward for Mentoria was under its own steam. The exercise tax was enforced the very next day, and Mentorians became the batteries of the city, running on cyclotrons and treadmills in the Great Hall of Power and generating enough electricity to provide Mentoria with adequate light.

The edict of the city was etched into a large concrete pillar that stood like a totem at the centre of the Plaza of Logical Thought. In large, bold font, the words read,

Think on it.

Then think on it some more.

Such was the constant activity of the citizen's minds that made it hard for them to sleep—because they thought about everything all the time.

Mostly, Mentorians shuffled through their days. Exhausted, their skin was pale with large black circles beneath their eyes. But it was their lack of energy that concerned the Council of Necessity most. The less people felt, the fatter they became. And despite dietary restrictions and increased exercise taxes, the obesity epidemic took hold. That was until a clever team of biochemists produced a sickly-sweet compound from fermented algae pumped from the River E. Bottled in small vials, the grey gel-like liquid provided just enough energy for the people to meet their exercise tax the following day. As decreed by law, The Booster, as it was called, was taken in the morning and sucked from a small squeezable tube originally designed for babies. And more addictive than fruit from the dumbnut tree, stockpiles of The Booster were kept under lock and key.

In the tangled pathways of their minds, Mentorians thought they knew more than they really did. It started with the forefathers of the city, who decided that solar beams were the harmful carriers of feelings sent by aliens from a distant and central sun. To them, this was the reason most of the inhabitants of Happysad were stark raving mad. And one thing was for sure—not even the strongest or brightest minds were immune.

Understanding the power of propaganda, The Master knew that a picture was worth a thousand words. Every morning at ten o'clock, a short video called 'The Story of Mentoria' was shown on screens scattered across the city. It aired three times a day. The opening scene was of The Master himself, dressed in the black cape of a hero and the flat square hat of a scholar. Standing at an angle of forty-five degrees, he stared into the distance whilst the first bars of a haunting melody played. The scene switched to one where ragged refugees from the old land of Happysad wandered aimlessly in circles on the far shores of the River E. In raptures of confusion, they both laughed and cried. They looked longingly into the distance, to Mentoria – hovering above the fog and illuminated in a halo of brilliant red light. Mesmerised, the refugees stared at the city skyline, at the spires that sat on buildings like hats and the golden domes that reflected the magnificence of Mindset—the city's protective shield of red laser light. Accompanied by a melody of strings, the city's gardens came into view. Concentric circles of manicured gardens with stone seats and spouting fountains filled the screens. The Master reappeared, standing on a small platform that jutted out of the penthouse shaped like a pill. Before him stood a large crowd, and he raised his arms to silence their applause.

"Fellow Mentorians," he bellowed. The crowd clapped loudly. Reiterating his brilliance, The Master spoke of the power of Mindset, without which, Mentoria would be ravaged by feelings transmitted from the great central sun.

When the focus turned from The Master, a spotlight zeroed on the image of a woman moving through the outer gardens of the city. She paced in circles, just beneath the concrete perimeter wall. Her e-reader flashed red as tears streamed down her cheeks, and she shouted behind her. But no one was there.

The woman ran, clutching at her chest with both hands. The distant sound of drumming grew louder as she tore at her clothes and yanked at her hair. Speaking into their radios, two guards crept along the base of the wall towards her. The woman turned, saw them, and laughed. Then she cried. The camera followed, as the woman, like an angry spider, scaled the city wall. Far below, fog spiralled across the waters of the River E. Balanced on the edge of the wall, the woman looked to the side. With her arms across her chest, she stepped out into the fog and fell like a broken branch from a tree.

According to The Master's calculations, anyone who presumed to jump from the walls of Mentoria had eight hundred and two metres to think about the impending consequences. Perched on a long, thick titanium spindle, Mentoria was a city above the uncertainty of weather—and just far enough away from the inhabitants of Happysad who endured eternal sunshine on the wrong side of the River E. If

Mentoria was a brilliant torch shining towards the future, then Happysad was a candle flickering in the winds of the past. In Mentoria, things were black, or they were white. In Happysad, life was a technicolour blur, like the intersecting hues of a rainbow after the rain.

4. BLACK BULLS AND BURSTING HEARTS

Stanley left his apartment two hours early. From the depths of his blue eyes, he looked out at the streets, and far above, arcs of electricity ripped across the sky. Mindset crackled, casting its thorny red halo of light as a living, breathing net. Pods of fluorescent lights hummed across the tops of skyscrapers. Running his hand over his hair to ensure it hadn't moved, Stanley looked left and right before locking the front door. He checked it twice while glancing over his shoulder to confirm he was alone. Stanley side-stepped the murky puddles on the pavement, for he was sure that stepping in puddles was the very thing that resulted in him having a bad day. He walked the streets of the city that were never home to stray cats and dogs on account of a law forbidding pets. Looking up, Stanley was about to cross the street, as he always did, when he saw a black dog sitting in the entryway of a dark and narrow alley. The dog appeared to be watching him, motionless and grasping a red rubber ball between its teeth. Stanley shook his head, trying to unsee the image of the dog, then, unnerved, he walked away. With his fingers crossed, Stanley quietly counted his steps as he walked. And when he got to seven, he stopped and started again. In the distance, he could hear the early morning train, and he looked up, his eyes wide as the train whizzed past in a flash of light. Like he'd done many times before, Stanley cursed the small tattoo of the letter "D" on his wrist, knowing it was the reason he would never amount to anything more than a security officer in the Mentorian Guard. His job was to monitor Mindset, which meant, every day, climbing the tall steel lattice towers that conducted electricity and reporting on the indicator lights if they changed from green to red.

At the top of each tower perched a large, crackling silver orb which had electrocuted many curious and careless guards. Beneath the orbs sat small black boxes, each with a big red button, waiting to be pushed when things went wrong. Once activated, a piercing alarm sounded from several important places, including the penthouse shaped like a pill.

Crossing the street, Stanley approached the base of the tallest inspection tower. It looked down upon the Ministry of Science, which was a skyscraper that protruded from Mentoria's skyline like a wayward tooth. The Ministry was constructed of steel and a particularly strong kind of glass that looked dirty, much to its inventor's incredulity even when it was clean. And nearby, in apartments far above the city streets, Mentorians wrestled with disturbing dreams and longed for a peaceful sleep.

Stanley stepped onto the platform of the inspection tower and pressed the button with the arrow that pointed up. The platform rose with a gentle hum, and he clicked his tongue while he looked out at the city lights that were dimmed to preserve power. Everything was as dark as it was supposed to be.

When he reached the top, Stanley peered over the platform and noticed a single light shining from the Ministry of Science below. A grey pigeon landed on the platform, diverting Stanley's attention. It blinked slowly as though studying him. And then, blinking again, the pigeon walked a tight circle on the rail and started to coo.

Watching the pigeon, Stanley wondered if there were any meaning to its walking in circles. He concluded the bird was simply nosey, and as he didn't like being watched, Stanley reached out and pushed the pigeon off the rail and out into the night. He watched the bird fall, gathering speed and then, with seconds to spare, spread its wings, banking hard to the left and disappearing into the shadows.

Stanley made an entry in his log,

Ministry of Science light on.

Gripping the metal rail, Stanley climbed up closer to the orb and walked out along the narrow arm of the inspection tower. Threading the ropes of his harness through a metal ring, he lowered himself towards the light cast from the window of the Ministry of Science. A gentle wind whipped around the building and rustled his hair. Instinctively, Stanley lifted his hand to smooth it back down. Beside him, a sudden *coo* sounded. Stanley jumped. The pigeon had returned and was perched on the metal rail, staring at him with its head tilted to the side. A shiver ran along Stanley's spine, and starting at the number 3467, he counted backwards and tried to forget about the bird.

Shifting in his harness, Stanley focussed on the lit window of the Ministry of Science. The rope started to swing. Inside the Ministry, a girl with short, white hair sticking up in all directions sat at a desk. She wore white gloves, her fingers flying across the keyboard while she stared at the computer screen. A bundle of coloured wires ran from her computer to a device that looked like a stubby, black, carbon cannon turned on its end. On its side was the inscription "I11" – which Stanley assumed was "I" was for invention, and the number eleven was the number eleven. Without thinking, Stanley shifted in his harness again to get a better view and swung closer to the crackling orb. Behind him, the pigeon hopped up and down, cooing louder than before. Stanley watched as the girl at the computer stopped typing, ran her hands through her hair, and leaned against the back of the chair. He felt a sudden surge of panic, fearing the girl would see him, but her eyes were closed. Stanley hesitated, uncertain whether to continue watching or return to the platform. Then, as though buoyed by a burst of inspiration, the girl whipped her head forward and furiously started to type. When she stopped, she looked expectantly at I11. Stanley watched too.

Nothing happened.

There was no movement. No lights. Nothing. The girl raised her hands above her head as though stretching before glancing at her watch. As if suddenly realising the time, she hurriedly stuffed a small computer into her bag. She stood up with the cord tangled around her foot and pulled I11 from the desk. It tumbled to the floor, cracked, rolled to the corner of the room, and broke into several useless pieces.

The girl shook her head, cursed at the computer, and tapped her e-reader to try to stop it from flashing red.

Is she crying?

41

Entranced by the girl, Stanley was unaware of how much the rope he was hanging on had started to swing.

Above, the pigeon cooed and flapped its wings. Arcs of electricity shot from the crackling orb, zigzagging too close to Stanley's face. There was a sudden surge, as though the orb had held its breath and then finally let go with a powerful bolt of lightning that struck Stanley just below the chin. The force flung him backwards, unravelling the supporting rope. And Stanley plummeted, twitching and unconscious, towards the street below.

Inside the Ministry of Science, the girl grabbed at the device on her wrist, turned off the light, and ran from the room.

When Stanley awoke, disorientated and dangling upside down, it was morning. Piecing together what had happened, it took a few moments to clear the fog from his mind. Reaching up, Stanley started to untangle himself from the charred rope which saved his life. Carefully lowering himself to the street, he tried to recall if he'd checked Mindset's status at the top of the tower. Unsure, Stanley had the unmistakable feeling that trouble wasn't far away. He decided not to make an entry in his log, and instead, he scurried through the streets, mouthing random numbers that spun in circles inside his head.

Stanley crossed the Plaza of Logical Thought, bordered by a row of cathedral-like buildings designed by an eccentric architect who had been dead for years. Ahead stood the Monument of the Mind—an oversized bronze sculpture of a brain perched on a twisted, tentacle-like spine. The black pillars of the Great Hall of Power loomed over the edge of the plaza, punching holes in the sky. Above the pillars, a large glass dome imposed its impossible symmetry, confirming the brilliance of its designer's sophisticated mind.

When he arrived at the Great Hall of Power, Stanley waved his e-reader at the sensor on the wall. It beeped and administered a small electric shock as a punishment for being late.

Inside, cyclotrons stood twelve feet high and were arranged in rows. Their design, which was borrowed from experimental equipment used on mice, optimised the extraction of energy to power the city's lights. Each cyclotron comprised a large hollow wheel mounted with steel arms on a thick rubber mat. One by one, the citizens entered the Great Hall and waved their e-readers across their chosen wheel. From each cyclotron, there extended thin copper wires which fed into the thicker copper wires running into the depths of the Great Hall of Power, where three huge batteries, two black, one red, hummed. Housed in a big bunker with a ceiling eighty feet tall, one black battery-powered Mindset, and the other black battery powered the city. The third red battery was taller and stood sixty feet high. On one side, a sign etched into the metal read: *Spare battery – keep charged.* Beneath the sign, a small three-pronged plug, like something from a toaster or a lamp, charged the red battery when the black batteries were full. It always worked, and because of that, no one ever entered the conspicuous and plain grey door at the back of the Great Hall of Power.

Not quite himself, Stanley walked down the aisles with his arms behind his back. He felt as though he was looking for someone but couldn't work out who. Distracted, Stanley missed the signs of imminent disaster as the obese Judge Elliott Spooner, compulsive ice cream eater, and pillar of Mentorian law, ran too fast and triggered his e-reader's alarm, which meant only one thing—his heart was about to burst.

At the front of the hall, a quiet procession of Mentoria's academic elite filed in. At the end of the line, a girl with white hair jutting out in all directions adjusted her headband and brushed the hair from her eyes. She stopped at the nearest cyclotron, waved her e-reader across the sensor, and the machine whirred to life. "Good morning, Delia," the machine said. "The city's counting on you."

The cyclotron clock started counting backwards. One hundred and eighty minutes was a long time.

Delia scrunched her eyes because she wanted to cry. For reasons unknown, her aversion to exercise or raising a sweat was not so much to do with matters of hygiene or fatigue. Instead, it had more to do with her heart that, for as long as she could remember, had refused to work any harder than it thought it should. From an early age, Delia had been commissioned to help solve the problem of the city's lack of power. But even though her exercise taxes were reduced, it seemed to make no difference at all.

Distracted, Stanley started vacantly across the rows of Mentorians in the Great Hall. When he spotted the girl with the crazy white hair, he remembered why he was there. Keeping his distance, he watched her running—lacklustre with her eyes closed. Deep down, a sense of recognition surged in Stanley.

44

I know you. But how?

Distracted, Stanley was oblivious in the moment Judge Elliott Spooner's heart burst, and legs failed, causing him to collapse in a tangled heap. The Cyclotron ejected him like a liberated seal, and in mid-flight, the Judge's face clipped the sharp edge of a black power box and was peeled back far enough to expose his brain. Blood spurted across the floor. Moreover, the Judge was dead before he hit the ground.

In less than an hour, cocooned in a sweaty plastic sheet, the Judge's body was taken away. A group of armed attendants formed a small circle, and all agreed it was best to blame one of the guards. So, Stanley, being the closest guard who missed the whole thing, was shot with a stun gun and left paralysed on the floor. Shortly after, two attendants dressed in black tracksuits with white stripes on either side took hold of Stanley's arms and dragged him away.

When Stanley opened his eyes, he blinked slowly. Trying to work out where he was, he realised he was handcuffed to a chair in a white, windowless and otherwise empty room.

Three bald men wearing matching glasses and white lab coats wheeled-in a monitor, a desk, and some chairs. They continued talking amongst themselves as if Stanley wasn't there. Feeling nervous, Stanley kept his head down and crossed the fingers on both of his hands—a gesture that was not so much for luck but because it somehow made him feel better—as though the simple act might somehow make everything okay. The men in white coats nodded in unison and stopped talking. They were inspecting a piece of paper on a clipboard, and Stanley found himself peering at them and wondering what it said. But whatever it was, it seemed their suspicions were confirmed.

"Well, the numbers don't lie—it's quite clear," stated the man on the right. The other two nodded before the left one continued. "There's certainly something not quite right with this officer's mind."

Stanley scowled and was about to protest when the fluorescent lights in the windowless room flickered as if the power were about to fail. The attendants looked up, shook their heads, formed a line, and shuffled from the room.

Exhausted from the events of the day, Stanley closed his eyes. Scenes from his childhood flashed across his mind and stuck like old food between teeth.

He remembered his father, Cain, standing in the doorway of their apartment, sleeves rolled up, shouting above the whir of a passing silver train.

"Listen to me, boy," Cain yelled, slamming his fist against the wall.

Stanley turned from the window to face his father; his eyes wide.

"Listen to me, boy," Cain said again, peering at him from somewhere behind glazed eyes. "You're a disgrace."

Saying nothing, Stanley, seven years old, swallowed his tears. He turned away, back to the window to watch the train.

His e-reader flashed red.

Cain's first punch floated through the air, catching Stanley beneath the eye. A bubble of blood leaked from his broken skin. The bruising began.

Cain's e-reader flashed red. "Look at me!" he screamed, drunk with rage. "It's your fault. Without you, I'd be happy. I should have left you with your mother and sister. All you ever did was cry."

Stanley swallowed thickly, his thoughts swirling around his head like a flock of crazed blackbirds stealing the light. And before he knew it, Stanley was running through midnight streets and hiding from the patrols of Mentorian Guards. It was dark when he finally returned home.

Cain was sitting at the table with his face in his hands. He didn't say a word.

The next day, Stanley waited for his father to come home from work. He was late, and when the lights of the city went out, Stanley sat alone in the dark. To stop himself from crying, Stanley bit down hard on his tongue — the pain distracting him from his fears. When he finally fell asleep, a woman with sad blue eyes and what seemed like half a smile came to him in dreams. She told him not to worry that one day everything would be okay.

When he woke, Stanley blinked nervously, pushing the memory to the back of his mind — where it belonged. In search of a distraction, he stared at the blank monitor the attendants left in the room. His thoughts flicked between confusion over the fate of Judge Elliott Spooner and the recurring and impossibly familiar image of the girl with the spikey blonde hair from the Ministry of Science. When the lights on his e-reader flashed red, Stanley called out for an attendant to bring him a nummer. And when no one came, he shouted out and started kicking at the walls. Exhausted and after what seemed like hours, Stanley stopped. With shaking hands and no way to make himself numb, a lifetime of buried anger awoke and rose in him — like lava.

At times, Stanley wondered whether the incident with his father all those years before was the root cause of his anger. Whenever he felt the emotion breaking through, it was always accompanied by a strange snorting sound that seemed to follow Stanley around. He finally made a connection when one night, while drifting off to sleep, the snorting sound started and was accompanied by the screech of a scraping hoof. As Stanley snoozed, he became aware that he was a small black bull with skinny legs, standing in the dirt of an arena, pulsating beneath the din of a screaming crowd. In front of him was a small man in a brightly jewelled purple jacket waving a red cape. The bullfighter's eyes, like his father's, were distant and full of fear. He stood with a defiant straightness of his spine and an arrogant jut of his chin. Stanley looked around and found himself backed against the edge of the arena. He snorted loudly and shook his head. With a golden ring in his nose, he could smell the blood, still wet, where it clung to his flanks. And he could feel the cold, sharp tips of the numerous spears embedded along his spine.

The bullfighter waved his cape; the crowd cheered. Stanley narrowed his eyes and scraped at the dirt with his front hoof. He dug a tiny hole, and the crowd laughed. When he kicked up a small cloud of dust, the bullfighter spat. Stanley charged. A grey film came down over his eyes, and he could no longer see the bullfighter's cape. Stanley only saw the man. He thrust his horns into the bullfighter's side and triumphantly flicked him in the air. The spectators gasped, and Stanley paused, splattered in blood. Dazed, he turned to the crowd and charged. Stanley leapt over the fence, trampled a spectator or two, and ran through an open gate. Suddenly free, he ignored the screams and followed the dusty road until it was dark. Then, exhausted, he lay down beneath the branches of an olive tree where he looked up at the stars and bellowed at the moon. It wasn't long before Stanley fell into a dreamless sleep, and at first light, he picked himself up, licked the dew from the leaves of the olive tree, and walked in the direction of the rising sun.

News of the raucous caused by the detained and angry guard reached The Master at the same time he learned of Judge Elliott Spooner's death. He slipped into his bed chamber and emerged wearing a dark three-piece suit and shiny black shoes. From behind, The Master's oversized bald head looked like a misshapen, upside-down egg. Standing before the window, The Master rocked on his heels, his hands clasped behind his back as he looked out across his magnificent city. Pods of fluorescent lights floated by.

Juaneeto appeared at The Master's side and waited in silence for him to speak. But when The Master said nothing, Juaneeto spoke first.

"What is it?"

"Judge Elliott Spooner is dead," The Master said.

"A great loss," Juaneeto replied, sliding his fingers across a computer screen and reading the report.

"Exactly how did it happen?" The Master asked.

"The guard," Juaneeto said. "He wasn't watching."

"Wasn't watching," The Master repeated slowly. Moving away from the window, he walked in a tight circle with his hands behind his back. Then he stopped, distracted by his reflection in the window. The Master closed his left eye and studied his right eye, which he considered rounder and perfect. Then, having lost his train of thought, The Master changed the subject altogether. "What of our preparations for the ceremony?"

"They're complete, master," Juaneeto said.

"And what of the scientists? The engineers? Tell me someone has invented something we can use." The Master said in a low and irritated tone.

"One of the scientists," Juaneeto said, "A girl. Some say she is closer than anyone before."

The Master squinted. "A girl?"

"Yes, master."

"Then bring her to me, and we shall see."

5.POWER? WHAT POWER?

The Master ignored the steady stream of scientists which came and went from the penthouse shaped like a pill. Instead, he sat in his high-backed white leather chair, which was low enough for his short legs to reach the floor. Adorned in his dark ceremonial robe, The Master distracted himself by running his fingertips over the sharp edges of the black crystal obelisk at his side. The largest of its kind and with what appeared to be a small circular door on one side, the big black crystal stood over five feet high.

Earlier that day, The Master sent Juaneeto to collect the girl whose invention might offer a solution to the city's problem with power. It wasn't until early afternoon when The Master heard the brass knocker, with its red-letter M, rap against the door.

"Enter!" The Master called out in his usual pompous tone.

The door opened, revealing a smug-looking Juaneeto and a young woman with blonde hair and wide, startled eyes.

"Come, come," The Master said, waving his hand impatiently. Juaneeto didn't need to be told twice. He strode in and stood to the side of the room, his arms rigid by his side like a soldier. The girl hovered at the threshold, her hands clasped in front of her as she shifted her weight between her feet.

With one hand still firmly pressed against the obelisk, The Master stood up from his chair. "Your name?"

"Delia," she said.

"De-l-ia." The Master sounded her name slowly, frowning slightly.

"Do you know what this is?" he asked, tapping his forefinger against the black crystal obelisk at his side.

"A transmitter?" Delia said with a slight shrug.

The Master laughed a little too loudly, mocking her. He stopped almost as quickly as he'd started and narrowed his eyes at the girl.

"I expected you to be smarter," he sneered. "But … after all, how could I expect you to recognise the greatest invention of our time if you've never seen it before?"

Delia nodded, seemingly confused.

"It's called The Sanitis-Or," The Master declared, gesturing with one hand in the air like a strange ringmaster, inviting applause.

Delia tilted her head to the side as she stared at the obelisk. "What does it do?"

"What does it do?" The Master mimicked her and rolled his eyes. He paused a moment, waiting until he saw the glint of anticipation in the girl's eyes before answering. "I take it, at school, you saw pictures of the forests of Happysad? And the golden sands on the shores of the River E, the palm trees, the clear waters brimming with coloured fish?"

"Yes, I've seen that in books," Delia replied, matter-of-factly.

"These were once places where the mind could run free," The Master said. "Free from feelings; the despicable, dirty, and deadly virus of feelings."

"A virus?" Delia asked, scrunching her face dubiously.

"Yes, a virus," The Master snapped. "Sent a long time ago from the Great Central Sun … it scrambles the mind and jumbles your thoughts. F-e-e-l-i-n-g-s." The Master spat each letter as though they, themselves, were poison. "They cloud your thoughts, confuse you, so in one moment you're happy, the next you're sad. It's relentless." The Master took a moment to catch his breath. He was pleased to see the girl gazing curiously at the Sanitis-Or as she took a few more steps into the room.

"So, what does it do?" she asked again.

The Master placed his index finger over his lips, assuming the girl was intelligent enough to appreciate the significance of what he was about to say. "It cleans," he said, stroking the obelisk. "It removes the filth and scum of feelings; it clears the fog of confusion from the mind."

"But how?" Delia asked as she moved closer still.

"You're asking the wrong question." The Master smirked. "What you should be asking is, where does it get its power? Which brings me to the reason why you are here."

Delia remained silent, but The Master could see a cloud of confusion drift across her eyes as though she was trying to connect the dots.

"Well?" prompted The Master. "How can you prove your usefulness to the city? How can we generate more power for Mentoria?"

Delia reached down for the satchel that hung by her waist and began shuffling awkwardly through the stash of papers in her bag. At the same time, she mumbled the energy requirements each Mentorian knew by heart.

"The city needs ten thousand man-hours of power every day."

The Master peered at her. "So?" His voice had taken on a dangerous tone.

Delia cleared her throat again. She shifted from one foot to the other. "The people are tired," she said.

"The people are tired," the Doctor repeated, mocking her. "The people, the people ..."

"I'm told you have been working late at night," The Master stated, changing the subject.

"Uh, Yes." Delia stared at him, her eyes wide as though taken aback by the new line of questioning. "I've been making adjustments to..."

"You've well exceeded your quota of power." The Master cut her off as his eyes narrowed further.

Delia was silent. She swallowed hard.

"I assume you're aware of the penalties?" The Master asked. He watched as the girl opened and closed her mouth like a fish out of water, gasping for air. The Master scowled at her, his frustration growing. "I'm told you have been working on something. A solution to our power problem?"

"Yes." Delia withdrew a sheet of paper from her satchel and held it towards him with a trembling hand.

The Master turned towards Juaneeto and nodded. Juaneeto strode towards the girl and snatched the paper from her hand before handing it to The Master.

Taking one look at the plans, The Master burst out laughing.

"It's the P4," Delia said defensively. "It could power Mentoria forever."

The Master's laughter fell away as he raised an eyebrow at her. "How would it work?"

Delia shook her head.

"Well?" The Master demanded.

"I can't say … not yet."

"Why not?"

"It needs power to produce power," Delia mumbled, avoiding The Master's increasingly hostile stare.

"So…I ask for a solution, and you give me a problem?" The Master roared. "You give me this … machine?"

"It's not useless! There is a way to make it work." Without thinking, Delia strode towards The Master and snatched the paper from his hand before slamming it on the low square glass table in the room.

Torn between his fury at her impertinence and his intrigue with the machine, he peered over her shoulder while she scribbled down images of a rotor, a curved plate, and a cloud of positive and negative symbols.

"It gathers energy from the air," she exclaimed as her pen scratched across the paper in a flurry of strokes.

"Impossible," The Master huffed as he returned to his chair and placed his arm around the obelisk. Then, in a slow, exaggerated tone, he asked, "How. Are. You. Going. To. Make. It. Work?"

"It needs something—a kick-start. A burst of energy," Delia explained. "If only we had something like that. A source of energy—a source of bright light?"

The Master turned away from her and stroked the obelisk. "There is nothing like that in Mentoria."

"Technically, no," Delia said. "That's why we must look beyond. We must look to the stars," Delia explained, grinning sheepishly.

"What?" The Master roared, jumping to his feet and waving his arms angrily above his head.

Delia stood still, her eyes wide as she looked from The Master to her drawing and back again.

"You are familiar with our laws forbidding contact with the stars?" he asked, his eyes two narrow slits of rage.

Delia nodded.

With his chest thrust forward, The Master turned and strode towards the window. Taking a moment, he composed himself before he spoke. "Well then, I assume you mean to tell me your grand idea has a plan B. Tell me that the future of Mentoria is not hanging on fanciful and blasphemous ideas about sunshine and stars."

Delia's gaze shot to her e-Reader as it flashed and flickered red.

"Tell me you have more!" The Master yelled as his patience ran out. He clicked his fingers, and Juaneeto hurried to his side and bowed slightly, awaiting orders.

"A vaccination will offer her some clarity."

"Yes, master," Juaneeto nodded.

"You have until tonight," The Master said to Delia.

"Tonight?" she gulped.

"Yes, tonight."

"That's impossible," Delia blurted, looking down at the drawing of her machine with its recent additions. "There's days, weeks of work in this."

"Then I suggest you get to work." The Master dismissed her, waving his hand for Juaneeto to take her from the room.

The ceremony for the Scientist of the Year was an important event—but not quite as important as The Master's birthday, which fell one week earlier, in June. Despite not liking celebrations, The Master decreed that on his birthday, exercise taxes would be halved. The parks of Mentoria were festooned with streamers and posters commemorating their short little leader, whose brilliance kept them safe from the viruses that indiscriminately shot through space. It was a day for The Master to look upon the alabaster effigies of himself that sat on Mentoria's manicured lawns. He sucked on a nummer for quite some time and decided it wouldn't hurt to take a couple of extra pills marked with the letter "P." So, ignoring the grave risks to his health, The Master spent his birthday feeling nummer than the day before. Which was precisely how he liked it—and exactly as it was meant to be.

As for the ceremony for the Scientist of the Year, the city waited with bated breath. They hoped one of the illustrious scientists had come up with a solution for the city's increasingly dire lack of power.

By late afternoon, The Master, sensing he was further from success than the year before, surrendered to a lingering bad mood. He took more pills marked with the letter "P" and fell asleep, only to be woken by the headache that had plagued him off and on for much of his life. The gravity of Mentoria's problems churned through his mind. And searching for distractions, his thoughts settled upon the guard whose negligence led to the death of Judge Elliott Spooner. In The Master's opinion—which was the only opinion that mattered—the death of one of the city's eminent lawmakers could only further fuel the city's air of growing discontent.

What we need is something to shock the citizens back into line.

Recalling how quickly discontent incited rebellion, The Master pondered the reports of provocative posters appearing on walls around the city with slogans like:

I Dreamed of Stars! and *Abolish the Exercise Tax!*

The people are forgetting their fear. A reminder is just what we need.

The Master smiled. Ever since boyhood, the ability to make others do as he wanted with a simple jolt of electricity or a cut with a sharp little knife had fascinated him. Whilst navigating the turbulent waters of his youth, he drew comfort from electrocuting, dismembering, and performing various other acts of cruelty on animals who could not fight back. Years passed, and his hobby became something of a science, and sometimes, even art. And it was when he progressed to humans that his abilities soared to new heights.

Years passed, and The Master's fascination with his techniques matured into a deep respect for the power he wielded to ensure people's attention was exactly where he needed it to be. His instrument of choice was a small, sharp wooden-handled knife. Toiling over subjects restrained by leather cuffs, The Master had found himself driven by a simple and insatiable curiosity, like that of a child. It was the small things that intrigued him, like, *I wonder what will happen if I make a little cut here?*

Or,

How will it look if I peel this bit back over there?

Sometimes—in his less than humble opinion—his subjects required surgery. In the name of science, The Master incised, extracted, and transplanted bits and pieces of their bodies. And because butchering had always been an imperfect art, things often went wrong. Blood was let ... people died. That was life.

As the idea of torture filled his mind, The Master's headache slithered away. He pulled an old leather wallet of knives from the drawer beneath his bed, and as he unwound the cord, his knives glinted in the light. The old cloak of excitement and adventure returned and rested comfortably upon The Master's skinny shoulders. And searching for inspiration, his mind spinning with thoughts, The Master walked to the window and stared out across the city.

The guards paid no attention to Stanley, who remained cuffed to a chair in a windowless, white room. Unbeknownst to him, it was early evening when the monitor in front of him crackled and buzzed, pulling him from sleep. An image of The Master's bulbous, bald head filled the screen.

"Luka-MG, I presume?" The Master asked.

Stanley didn't answer. Instead, he just stared, his mouth agape.

"Tonight is an important night." The Master continued.

Stanley diverted his gaze to the shiny concrete floor of his cell, twisting to find relief from the sudden throbbing ache in his neck.

"Well?" The Master prompted.

Stanley still didn't answer. He could hear The Master's irritated whispers, giving orders to someone off-screen. At the sudden sound of static, Stanley looked up to find the monitor fuzzy and The Master gone.

Moments later, a guard entered the windowless, white room and handed Stanley a plastic sheet with two holes, one for each of his arms.

"What's this?" Stanley asked.

"Put it on," the guard ordered as he left the room.

Stanley thought of the number 482. He crossed all his fingers. And he started counting backwards in multiples of 3.

Not far away, two men in white coats without stethoscopes around their necks dragged Delia, kicking and flailing, into a room. They sat her on a high-backed chair with a hole below the headrest and bound her wrists and ankles with leather straps. The chair hummed as it rose slowly in the air. Delia's heart thundered against her chest, her eyes bulging as one of the men in a white coat picked up an enormous syringe from the tray and moved closer. She bucked against the restraints and squeezed her eyes shut and clenching her hands into fists; she tried not to think about the contents of the needle. When the man in the white coat stabbed the syringe into the base of her skull, Delia's eyes bulged, and her mouth fell open in a soundless scream. Every muscle in her body seized, and white light flashed before her eyes. Excruciating pain flashed through her. Like fire.

Then it was gone.

Delia's muscles relaxed, and she gasped for air.

"Things a bit clearer now?" asked the doctor.

Whimpering, Delia struggled to form the words. "Yes. Yes, of course."

It was just before dark when preparations for the ceremony for the Scientist of The Year were complete. The Great Hall was filled with folding chairs draped in white cloths embroidered with a large golden *M*. Officials handed out doses of The Booster in small squeezable tubes, and when the procession of scientists wearing white coats shuffled onto the stage, the crowd hushed. The finalists for the title of Scientist of The Year

60

were handed small white pieces of paper, which meant they didn't win. On cue, polite applause filled the hall. One by one, the scientists moved out of the spotlight to the seats lining the side of the stage.

This left Delia, standing alone, centre stage in the burning light. Blinking rapidly, she tried to recall how she came to be there at all. Beneath her white scientist's coat, Delia could feel the zipper of her dress was fastened up to her neck, squeezing like a pair of invisible hands around her throat. A shiny film of tears spread across her eyes, and no matter how many times she blinked, they wouldn't clear.

"And now," a voice bellowed from a loudspeaker out across the hall, "I present to you, The Scientist of the Year."

Confused, Delia stepped forward to the microphone and stared out across a sea of expectant faces.

"Tell us your name," the voice said over the loudspeaker.

In a quiet voice, she answered, "Delia. My name is Delia."

A wave of applause rippled across the hall. Two guards in ceremonial black suits with silver buttons appeared from the wings, pushing a trolley with a black cloth draped over its cargo. A solemn recording of a drum roll started playing, and The Master's voice blared across the loudspeaker. "Tell the people about your invention, which has earned you such an honour." Delia frowned slightly, wondering if she imagined the slight, threatening tone to The Master's voice.

"It's a...well it can...umm...it's called P4," Delia stammered.

"Well, how about that?" The Master said. "She calls it P4."

The crowd clapped dutifully. One of the guards pulled at the black cloth, and from a distance, the audience couldn't see the wet glue struggling to hold the prototype together.

"Well? Tell us, what does it do?" The Master commanded.

Tears welled in Delia's eyes, obscuring her vision further. She bit down hard on her bottom lip; her e-reader blinked red from where it lay hidden beneath the coat.

"It produces power," she stated. The crowd erupted in cheers and applause until The Master cleared his throat.

"And how does it produce power?" he asked, his voice dripping with sarcasm.

"It's complicated," Delia said, fumbling and squinting in the bright light.

"Complicated? Or impossible?" said the Master.

Someone from the crowd raised their hand and called out. "Well? Show us how it works!"

"How does it work?" another voice cried.

A stony silence filled the hall as Delia just stared, consumed by the fierce pounding of her racing heart.

"Well?" The Master prompted, his voice agitated and curt.

The crowd started to stamp their feet, slow then fast. Delia wanted to run, to hide from the crowd's demanding eyes. She knew she was supposed to lie. Swallowing thickly, she set her shoulders and leaned into the microphone. "Light," she stated clearly. "It can be powered by light."

The crowd gasped in unison as the guards aimed their guns in her direction. Like a madman, The Master shrieked and laughed through the loudspeaker. The crowd jeered, and all around the hall, e-readers blinked red. It was then, overwhelmed by the heat of the spotlight and the noise of the crowd, that Delia fainted and was dragged away.

When the crowd's laughter subsided, a large white screen descended at the rear of the stage. An image of The Master, wearing a blue-and-white butcher's apron, appeared.

"Our greatest scientists have failed the city," The Master declared. "And because of that, tonight there will be no award." And as if the idea had just occurred to him, he added, "Exercise taxes are doubled and starting tomorrow, your personal electricity allowances are halved until someone thinks of a way to produce more power."

A murmur of discontent swept across the crowd, and the image on the screen changed as the camera panned out, revealing a man strapped against an upright table with a dome-like helmet, an Activat-Or, covering his head. One by one, the members of the audience momentarily forgot their anger as they focused on the screen.

"Before you is one of the city's guards," The Master announced. "Luka-MG. Though some of you may know him as Stupid Stanley!"

The crowd hooted, then clapped, their attention right where The Master wanted it to be.

"You are here in this great city to use your minds!" The Master said, his large head filling the screen in the Great Hall. "You are here to think, and any absent-mindedness is a crime. Any display of disobedience or distraction is a crime."

Silence fell across the hall as the crowd suddenly realised the seriousness of The Master's words. An image of Judge Elliott Spooner appeared on the screen, looking stern and majestic in his robes.

"You will recall the recent and tragic death of our Judge," The Master said, pausing to let his words sink in.

The Master turned to face Stanley. "So, Luka-MG, for the crime of absent-mindedness, for the crime of deciding to look the other way..."

All around the Great Hall, e-readers flashed red. Their eyes were on Stanley, his fists clenched by his sides, his body rigid and trembling, the opposite of numb.

The Master reached into the front pocket of his apron and withdrew a small device which he pointed towards the Activat-Or covering Stanley's head. A small blue light on the device blinked twice. Turning to face the crowd, his eyebrow raised, The Master pressed another button, and Stanley yelped as he twisted and tried to break free.

A stunned silence fell across the crowd.

"No need for alarm," The Master advised. "I assure you, Stanley here will feel no physical pain." He paused again, then circled Stanley and stopped at his other side.

"Stanley, tell the good people of Mentoria what you can see," The Master demanded.

"My Father!" Stanley screeched.

The Master smiled. The Activat-Or, another of his brilliant inventions, housed a small screen and two electrodes that probed into Stanley's brain for every thought and feeling he had buried, blocked, denied, and numbed his entire life. No longer numb, Stanley was avalanched with feelings, both good and bad.

A small puff of smoke shot from Stanley's e-reader.

"And there it is," The Master said. "All those numbed and buried feelings coming to light!" The Master roared and waved his arm in the air.

Aghast, the Ceremonial Hall crowd cheered, "Stupid Stanley, Stupid Stanley, Stupid Stanley!"

The more Stanley shook, the greater the fever of fear and anger in the hall. E-readers blinked red. Alarms sounded. And before he lost control, The Master turned the Activat-Or off. Stanley slumped against the cuffs on his ankles and wrists, his chest heaving as he mumbled to himself.

The Master looked into the camera with a triumphant grin. "Feelings are a crime. Focus on your mind!" And turning the camera off, The Master walked over to Stanley and listened for what he had to say. Intrigued and surprised, the Master stepped back when he realised Stanley was counting quickly in lots of nine.

"126, 117, 108…"

The Master raised his eyebrows as if he had been struck with a new idea. "I wonder," he said to himself. "I wonder."

When Stanley woke, the pounding in his head stopped him from opening his eyes. He could feel the tightly wrapped bandages around his head, and he frowned as he tried to recall the events of the night before. Stifled by the stiff infirmary sheets on the bed, he could hardly move. Cautiously, he opened his eyes, little by little, onto the ward filled with empty beds.

Across the hall of the infirmary was the ward reserved for criminals and the insane. A girl lay staring up at the ceiling and talking to herself. To Stanley, she looked familiar, but it was hard to say. And when she looked across at him, Stanley quickly looked away.

Distracted by a tapping sound, Stanley looked over through the glass window overlooking the ward, where a technician was staring back at him quizzically. The technician picked up a microphone, tapped it twice, and raised it to his lips.

Stanley jumped as the technician's voice crackled through the small speaker above his head. "Stanley Luka, you are assessed as no longer fit to be a member of the Mentorian Guard. You are now reassigned to the Great Hall of Power, where your job is to mop up the citizens' sweat." The technician's words floated across Stanley's mind like small clouds drifting on a windy day—and because he couldn't quite grasp them, he started to count.

"Why are you mumbling to yourself?" the girl asked from her bed across the room.

Stanley shrugged, then counted faster and louder, blinking rapidly to contain the tears in the corners of his eyes.

"You know he can't hear you, right?" the girl called out. Sitting up, she pointed to the technician behind the glass whose attention had reverted to shuffling papers into piles on his desk. "Stop counting!" she said, exasperated.

Stanley paused and looked at her.

"It'll be okay," she said.

Delia's words fell upon Stanley like soft rain. He stopped counting. "Who are you?"

She sighed. "My name is Delia. You're Stanley, right?"

"What are you doing here?" Stanley asked.

"I'm here because my invention doesn't work," Delia said, and thinking, she added, "Well, it could work. It just needs a source of power."

"Maybe I could help you with that," Stanley said in a hushed voice as his eyes darted around the ward.

"How so?" Delia asked, adjusting her glasses.

Stanley looked away, wondering if it was dangerous to confide in her.

"Well?" she said.

"There's the light that comes from the stars," Stanley whispered.

"Are you mad?" Delia gasped, her mouth open and her eyes wide. "And anyway, how would you know?"

"I can show you," Stanley said. "But you will have to meet me in the Great Hall of Power. Tomorrow night."

Discharged from the infirmary, Delia returned to the Ministry of Science. Her desk had been cleared, and P4 was left in pieces in the corner of the room. Feeling numb, she stared out the windows at the pods of fluorescent light meandering across the sky. Guards marched in pairs around the city that was supposed to be asleep.

Delia's father had said brilliant minds were not born but made. She never quite understood what he meant or the gravity of his words until the night when, as a girl, he found her dancing naked in her room. With tears and a faraway look in his eyes, Delia's father did what he had to do. He poured boiling water over her hands whilst reciting the mantra of the city, "The Mind Matters Most."

From that day, bearing the scars of her sins, Delia buried herself in books. She quickly understood the language of computers, making a name for herself with the invention of a brilliant vacuum cleaner that never lost suction and could make a cup of tea.

But somewhere in the deep shaft of Delia's mind, buried beneath piles of idle DNA, was the truth that she, despite her brilliance, was the direct descendant of a long line of erotic dancers – dancers who, centuries earlier, had performed naked before kings and been paid in gold. Renowned for the frenetic pulsing of their buttocks and hips and set to the hypnotic rhythm of flutes and drums, the dancers were exiled to Happysad long ago.

Hiding her hands in white gloves, Delia kept her scars from the world and, along with them, her dreams. She swallowed her desire and never danced again. And with her head buried in her father's books, Delia did what she had to do—all the while unaware of the small, black spider of denial that weaved its web of darkness across her shrinking heart.

The entrance to the Great Hall of Power was deserted when Delia arrived. As the red laser lights of Mindset flashed overhead, two hands reached out from the shadows and grabbed her. And before she could scream, a hand clamped firmly around Delia's mouth.

"Shh, It's okay! It's me, Stanley!" he hissed in her ear before releasing her.

Delia jabbed him in the ribs with her elbow before spinning around to face him. Stanley groaned, and she placed her hands on her hips and stared at him as he started mumbling under his breath. Looking up, Stanley pulled at a rope that was suspended from the ceiling and used by staff to clean the glass.

"Come," Stanley said, attaching a harness around Delia's waist.

"What's this?" she asked.

"Hold on tight, and you will see."

Delia closed her eyes as Stanley hoisted her up into the centre of the domed roof. When he tugged on the rope, Delia opened her eyes and stared out across the rooftops of the city.

"What am I supposed to see?" she hissed down to Stanley.

"Count to twelve," he said. "Then look up through the dome." Stanley tugged on the rope, and it began to swing. Delia started to count. Closing her eyes, she could feel the air brushing her face. She was flying. At the count of eleven, Delia opened her eyes and looked up. The rope reached the top of its arc. And on the count of twelve, she saw it—a flash of white. And struck by the cool light of a single star, Delia held her breath.

68

"No!" she gasped.

"Again," Stanley said, smiling as he swung the rope. "We have to be sure."

Delia counted again and once more saw the flash of light. A thousand thoughts flooded her mind, and without knowing why, she started to laugh.

"Shhh," Stanley called out.

Delia covered her mouth as Stanley carefully lowered her to the ground.

"This changes everything," she said as her feet touched down. And before Stanley could release her harness, she threw her arms around his neck and hugged him tightly.

Making no sense at all, it was then that the familiarity of Stanley struck her—like déjà vu.

Dismissing her thought, Delia left a bewildered Stanley in her wake as she turned and ran through the darkness of the Great Hall of Power. And when she reached the street, she turned and skipped her way home.

Later that morning, and excited to start the day, Delia woke before her alarm. She arrived at the Ministry of Science, and it was deserted except for the night janitor who was polishing the floor. Delia stepped into her office and locked the door. She reassembled her machine with a strange new logic, equivalent to shoving a square peg in a round hole.

After widening the hole to receive more light, Delia placed P4 on the floor. With the barrel facing up, she typed a new sequence of numbers into the keypad on her machine. The cursor flashed as if the machine were deciding whether it was going to work.

The answer—It was right there the whole time.

After a short pause, she reached forward, and with a coquettish smile, she tapped "enter" on the keyboard. The little light on the top of the machine turned on, and P4 jerked slightly to the right.

What we need is to turn the Mindset off long enough to capture the light.

It never really occurred to Delia that turning off Mindset was a bad idea. So, despite knowing people had disappeared from Mentoria for lesser crimes, Delia was resolute.

Surely the need for power far outweighs any possible complications a little ray of light?

The following morning, Stanley was dragging his mop around the Great Hall of Power when Delia arrived. She met his gaze, but neither of them said a word. Instead, Stanley flicked glances in her direction as he watched her mount a cyclotron and start to walk. Mopping and manoeuvring at the same time, Stanley stopped behind Delia's cyclotron.

"All we need is one ray of light," she whispered to Stanley over the hum of the machine.

Stanley looked around. "We?" he said.

"Yes, we," Delia replied.

Stanley lowered his head, keeping his eyes fixed firmly on the ground. And biting his tongue, he tried to hide his smile.

Outside and on the hour, a shiny silver train zoomed along Mentoria's tracks. Mindset cradled the city in its thorny halo of red laser light. And unbeknownst to Stanley or Delia, somewhere in Mentoria, an interested computer was watching—all of the time.

6. A FLASH AND A BANG

Delia's cyclotron slowed down. She reached out to Stanley with her gloved hand. Instinctively, Stanley stopped pretending to mop the floor and helped her down. Gripping his hand, a memory from Delia's youth popped into her head as she realised she knew Stanley from school. The memory unfolded with the children circling Stanley like sharks.

"Stupid Stanley, stupid Stanley!" They'd chanted, over and over. All except Delia.

"Stop," she shouted.

And the children listened.

The memory evaporated as a guard noticed Delia's cyclotron had stopped.

"Is there a problem?" His voice sounded metallic from beneath the helmet.

"No problem," Delia said, breathless as the guard approached, looking them both up and down. "He's wiping the floor."

The guard nodded, giving the cyclotron a quick once over before he turned away. He muttered into his radio, unaware as Delia swiftly reached out and lifted the guard's access card from his belt.

Watching Delia speak with the guard, Stanley's mind flashed back to when he was nine. He was standing in front of a class of his peers with his hands clenched fiercely behind his back.

"Well?" the teacher asked with a smirk. "Where's your homework? Your invention?"

Stanley fidgeted with nothing to show and did his best to come up with something on the spot. He rambled on about what it might be like to ride on one of Mentoria's shiny silver trains. But even before he was finished, the children laughed at him. The teacher hooted and encouraged the children's taunts. "Stupid Stanley." Humiliated, he felt the tears well in his eyes. It was then he remembered the small girl with blonde hair who yelled out from her seat at the back of the room, "Stop! Stop right now!" She stormed towards Stanley, grabbed him by the hand, and led him from the room. He recalled the softness of the white gloves she wore on her hands. She wiped his tears away. But when he asked the girl why she wore the gloves, she let go of his hand, returned to her desk without a word, and didn't look back.

It was then Stanley made the connection—the girl from his childhood wore gloves. Like Delia.

"Stanley? Stanley! Listen to me!" Delia said, giving him a quick shove and pulling his attention back to the Hall.

"I have an idea," she hissed.

"I know how to let in the light," he whispered, shaking his head, aware of what she was going to say.

"Yes," Delia grinned at him. "We'll stop Mindset. It's the only way."

"What about the virus? Everyone will be infected with feelings if they are exposed to the light."

"We have no choice," Delia said, adamant. "Besides, the risk is better than doing nothing. Look around. Everyone is already exhausted and sick. We have to try."

Delia reached out, clasped Stanley's free hand in both of hers, and pleaded. "Help me, Stanley. You have to help me."

In the depths of Delia's eyes, Stanley felt a familiarity beyond words.

"How long will Mindset be off?" he asked.

"Eleven seconds," Delia said. "It's all we need. It's nothing. No time at all.'

Stanley finished mopping the floor. He thought about the grey metal door at the back of the Great Hall of Power.

It must be hiding something because no one ever seems to notice that it's there.

After all the exercise taxes were paid for the day, the guards left. Dressed in his beige cleaner's uniform, one by one, Stanley removed the tiny pins that transferred the electricity from the cyclotrons to Mindset's batteries.

According to Delia, all he had to do was find the battery bunker, get inside without tripping the alarm, locate the black cord that connected the two big black batteries to a big red battery, unplug it, then run away. And of course, not get caught.

And if everything went as planned, Delia would be on the rooftop, waiting for Mindset to fail.

Certain he was alone in the Great Hall, Stanley wheeled his bucket to the side of the room and leaned the mop against the wall. He took a deep breath and strode towards the grey metal door at the back of the hall. Fighting the urge to look around, Stanley pulled the access card from his back pocket. As he swiped the card along the panel on the wall, there was a click, and the little red light flashed to green. Stanley heaved open the grey metal door, and straight ahead in the middle of the room, a spiral of steel stairs plunged into darkness.

I knew it!

A chill ran along his spine as he walked to the stairs. Focusing the beam of his torch, he shone it downwards. Below he saw three large cylinders—two black, one red. Exactly as Delia had said.

Stanley repeated the instructions inside his head,

Unplug the black plug, and Delia will do the rest. That's all I need to do.

Searching for a sense of calm, Stanley counted as he started down the stairs. But when the alarm in the bunker started to wail, he froze, his hands trembling as he turned off his torch. Stanley's heart thundered against his chest. He was sure he heard footsteps above, moving closer. Then they stopped. And knowing he had to move, Stanley crept forwards and hid beneath the stairs.

"We have a breach!" a loud metallic voice echoed from the top of the stairs.

The bright lights of the bunker snapped on, causing Stanley to throw his arm up over his eyes against the light. He could hear the pounding of the guards' boots as they filed in. Stanley lowered his arm and peered up through the gaps in the stairs.

"Who's there?" one of the guards demanded.

Stanley was silent—though he was certain he wouldn't be able to speak if he tried. He watched as the guard's torchlights crisscrossed through the darkness. The three big batteries hummed.

"False alarm," said one of the guards.

"You sure?" said another.

"Yes, let's go." The guards pulled back, their torchlights flashing across Stanley as he stood motionless in the dark. He listened intently to the sound of their boots as they walked back through the room above before closing the grey metal door. Then they were gone.

Stanley darted out from beneath the stairs. He crawled to the base of the first black battery, and searching for the black power plug, he ran his hands along the base of the wall. The darkness and the dust suffocated the light from his torch, and when he found a cluster of cords, he started counting under his breath. And with what amounted to something as precise as "eenie, meenie, miney, mo," Stanley yanked the middle cord. The humming sound that filled the bunker stopped, and a small red light on the other side of the big red battery flashed. Stanley grinned to himself before he got to his feet and scampered up the spiral stairs, turning his torch off as he went. Terrified of the thick, inky dark, he slowly opened the grey metal door, quickly scanning the rows of cyclotrons to make sure he was alone. Then he ran as fast as his legs would go, away from the Great Hall of Power.

It was quiet in Mentoria. For hours, its citizens had sat opposite each other, eating their meals as usual, in silence.

Guards patrolled the alleyways and parks, pointing their little lasers and following fugitive shadows across skyscrapers' walls. When the big red battery beneath the Great Hall of Power gave its last surge, it shuddered and ran flat. Far above Mentoria's streets, Mindset flickered, then stopped. Darkness descended upon the city. Alarms sounded. Everywhere.

Stanley climbed up to the roof of the Great Hall and sat across from where Delia inspected her machine. Saying nothing, he wondered if he had disconnected the correct black plug after all. Raising his head, Stanley looked up at the canopy of stars. Delia stood up and aligned the front of her machine with what looked to be the brightest star.

It was Friday night when the random, blazing bolt of light shot from the Great Central Sun and slammed into Mentoria, turning night into day. Already in bed and wearing his eye-pillow scented with rosemary and mint, The Master was preoccupied with a black nose-hair that tickled his nose when he breathed.

"What was that?" The Master called to Juaneeto.

"A light," Juaneeto said from where he sat at the control panel of the penthouse shaped like a pill. There was a loud bang.

"There's a fire in Sector Three," Juaneeto reported.

"Flick the fire switch," The Master ordered.

"Which one?"

"The big one with the red handle," The Master barked, realising he would have to get up out of bed. "What started the fire?"

"The light," Juaneeto replied.

"What light?"

"The one that stopped Mindset."

The Master gasped, sitting upright as he wrenched the mask from his face. "Impossible!"

A small fire smouldered on the rooftop of the Great Hall of Power. Plumes of wispy smoke billowed. Sparks flew. When Delia opened her eyes, her sleeves were on fire. She spluttered on the smoke as she patted at the flames. There was a burning in her throat, and she felt different as if a part of her had splintered away. Confused, she laughed. Then she cried.

When Delia heard the strange squeaking sound, it sounded at first like it was far away but moving closer.

"Who's there? Stanley? Is that you?" she called out.

There was no reply.

Far below, platoons of black boots marched through the Great Hall of Power. Like angry ants, they scurried in through the small grey door to the bunker of batteries.

"Over here," said one metallic voice to another.

"Report?"

"Battery's flat," the voice replied. "Somebody pulled the plug."

Delia stood still in the dark and waited for the surrounding flames to extinguish. "Stanley?" she called out.

It was then that a bouncy, red, saliva-soaked rubber ball rolled out from the thinning smoke. With great precision, it stopped at Delia's feet. Behind the ball, wrapped in a blanket of haze, something panted. It paused now and then to produce what sounded like the smacking of lips. Delia stood still as the smoke thinned further, revealing two large, sharp, white teeth nestled in blood-red gums. Through the smoke, the teeth appeared to hover in mid-space, and as the darkness shimmered, two eyes, slightly bloodshot, opened wide. Delia swallowed hard. The beast tilted its head to one side as if it were calculating and preparing for whatever would happen next.

"A dog?" Delia asked unwittingly.

But, not understanding her words, the dog, which went by the name "Dog," continued his panting. Then, distracted by what was both a habit and a small joy, the dog cocked one of its hind legs and licked its balls.

I'm losing my mind!

Delia remembered something she had read years before—that a dog is only one meal away from being a bloodthirsty wolf.

Is it hungry?

The dog looked up as though sensing her thoughts, and then, baring its teeth, it lunged.

Delia screamed.

Far below in the bunker of batteries, a guard inserted the black plug back into the wall. The light on the big red battery flickered "*On*," and with a crackle and a hum, the web of red lasers that was Mindset spread across the Mentorian sky once more.

When Stanley heard Delia's scream, he ran towards the sound of her voice and grabbed her from behind.

"Are you okay? What happened?" He stared at her, wondering why her arms were wrapped protectively around her head.

"There's a dog!" Delia screeched.

"What dog?" Stanley asked, peering through what was left of the smoke.

"A big black dog with a red rubber ball," she said.

Stanley scanned the rooftop, but it was already too late. Both the dog and the red rubber ball were gone. He turned back to Delia as she lowered her arms, sweat dripping from her brow.

"What about your machine?" Stanley asked. "Did it work?"

Delia looked at him with wide eyes, her mouth open, as though she wanted to answer—and then she fainted. Stanley scooped Delia up in his arms and, keeping to the shadows, carried her away.

Below, on the far side of the Great Hall, heavy boots were already pounding up the steel stairs. In the streets, other guards, confused by what had happened, kept their fingers on the triggers of their guns and walked in circles, unsure of exactly what they were meant to do.

The Council of Necessity, better known as the CON, called an emergency meeting. Seated around a large black table in a small white room, the members were not paying much attention to the unfolding events as they tried thinking of something smart and important to say. Images of lines forming outside vaccination clinics across the city flashed across a screen.

Within the hour, demand for pills marked with the letter "P" tripled. Then tripled again. Reports poured in of citizens looting the city's stockpiles of The Booster. Additional regiments of guards were dispatched to keep the peace, and the people were told to quarantine in their homes. New, reassuring messages flashed across the sides of buildings, confirming an unprecedented surge of power as the source of the random flash of light. Then, everything returned to normal. Everything was under control. There was no need for concern. It was a false alarm.

One hour before dawn, Stanley, exhausted and blackened with soot, entered one of the clinics in the city. In his arms, Delia wept, clutching at her chest. The attendant, who was half asleep, asked for the patient's name.

"Delia," Stanley said.

But when Delia started gibbering and murmuring about a black dog with a red rubber ball, the attendant rubbed his hands nervously together and ran from the room.

When Juaneeto received the clinic's disturbing news, he scanned the console in The penthouse shaped like a pill and pushed the red *"Alarm"* button right away. Lights brightened. The city's sirens wailed. Citizens were yanked from their beds and ordered to sit and stare at the sides of buildings where a brief video message, titled an *"Important Safety Message,"* was screened.

A younger version of The Master appeared in a white coat and wearing a medical mask across his mouth. Before him was a steel table upon which lay a young girl. Her wrists and ankles were bound to the table by steel shackles, and she appeared to be distraught and overcome with fear as she shrieked obscenities at the blank walls.

"Behold," declared The Master in a theatrical tone. "The advanced and rancid effects of feelings." He pointed a long plastic wand towards the girl, demonstrating the need to keep a safe distance away as an assistant unlocked the shackles around her hands.

"Note the patient's suffering!"

As though on cue, the girl placed her hands over her ears, closed her eyes, and shook her head from side to side, screaming in pain.

The Master continued, waving his long plastic wand towards the patient's head as he spoke.

"The pain of her feelings continues to increase as the pressure mounts within her skull." The Master whipped the wand through the air and struck the girl on the top of her head, causing her to hiss and spit. Unaffected, The Master nodded to his assistant, who shackled her hands once more.

"At this point, nothing can be done—there is no stopping the rising force of her feelings." The Master said.

The girl's eyes rolled back in her head, and she moaned before choking on the foam that spilled from her mouth. After a quick convulsion and a loud popping sound, she fell limp against the table.

"And there we have it," The Master said, a hint of triumph in his voice. "She is dead."

A dramatic surge of violins erupted from the speakers attached to the pods of fluorescent light that circled the city.

"This is the agony of feelings," The Master said dramatically, waving his hand through the air. And when the image of The Master disappeared, the citizens were ordered to return to their beds.

"Stay indoors—Go back to sleep!" was the message repeatedly broadcast across loudspeakers until dawn.

It was daylight when The Master slipped into his enormous bed. He tossed and turned, bothered by the idea that Mindset might have failed. His thoughts flashed to the forests of Happysad, when once, as a boy, he was chased by a swarm of blood-sucking mosquitos. Bitten mercilessly, he was beaten by his father for disturbing the insects that were known to be carriers of the disease. That night he remembered scratching until he bled. And it was then that the silent vendetta against mosquitos lodged itself in the small chamber of his heart.

Years later, the scales were balanced once more when The Master was inspired to harness the buzzing sound of the angry insects. He trapped swarms of mosquitos in a collection of different-sized glass jars, and his invention, the mosquitorium, was born. The Master clicked his fingers, and carrying a buzzing glass jar, Juaneeto appeared at his side.

"Your mosquitorium, master," he said.

"Over there," The Master instructed, pointing to the table beside his bed. He fell asleep, drawing solace from the sound of the little suicide bombers buzzing and crashing into the glass, but when he awoke later in the day, he was uncertain whether he'd really slept at all.

Even after swallowing a handful of pills marked with the letter "P," it was impossible for The Master not to think about the different kind of headache that was spreading in painful waves across his skull. Juaneeto, whose reputation for masking pain was confirmed by the tinctures he prepared, knew exactly what to do. After examining The Master from head to toe, he announced The Master's symptoms were caused by the overuse of his larger than usual brain. Juaneeto rummaged through his leather bag and withdrew a vial of clear fluid. "Drink this, then go back to bed," he said to the Master.

"Block out the light, and the pain will go away."

Stanley arrived at Delia's apartment, swiped her entry pass, and locked the door behind him. He placed a pillow on the floor with the intention of lying beside Delia whilst she slept. He noticed her speaking softly, though her eyes were closed, and tears streamed down her cheeks. Delia's e-reader blinked red. Then, as though sensing his presence, she opened her eyes.

"What?" she said. "You look worried?"

"I think you were dreaming," Stanley said.

"Was I?"

"We can't stay here," said Stanley.

"Where will we go?"

"I'm not sure," Stanley admitted with a sigh.

"It's okay," Delia smiled at him. "Everything is clearer now. We're going to be alright."

"Alright?" Stanley asked, pointing to Delia's e-reader. "It's just a matter of time before the guards are at the door."

Delia's laugh started small. It gathered momentum, like a boulder rolling down a hill. Then she began to howl. Sweat streamed from her brow, and Stanley covered her mouth to muffle the sound.

"Shh! You'll get us both killed!" Stanley said as he stared into Delia's eyes, trying to make her understand. Her laughter fell away as she stared back at him, her mouth agape.

"I know you!" she whispered.

"Of course, you know me!" Stanley hissed, lowering his hands.

"No, I mean, I know you from before." Delia grabbed him by the shirt, her eyes wide. "Can't you feel it? A connection?"

Stanley pulled back. "You're not making sense. We need to go. Now." But before he could get up, Delia clapped her hands to either side of his head and pulled him close, so their foreheads touched. Staring into her eyes, he felt pulled into a whirlpool of blackness. Then he heard the sound—two heartbeats.

I'm in a womb.

Yes, Delia's voice whispered within his mind, *We're in the womb. Together.*

Stanley pulled back, intuitively aware that what Delia was saying was true. Before he could speak, he noticed a shift in his sister's expression. He was suddenly afraid, as if something

85

was there, just behind her eyes, dangerous and dark and swimming slowly, flicking its tail and stealing the light.

Somewhere in Mentoria, a message flashed across a screen. The guard who happened to be paying attention at the time pushed a button. Other guards responded, grabbing guns from glass cabinets and assembling in lines in the streets.

The Mentorian Guards formed neat rows before the Monument of the Mind. Standing stiff, they wore the black and red uniform of war. Helmets hid their eyes.

In the penthouse shaped like a pill, a small door opened, and The Master, adorned in black pants and a red military-style jacket with shiny gold buttons and deep pockets, stepped onto a small platform.

"Soldiers of Mentoria," he began before hesitating, as though he was unable to think of anything inspiring to say. "Mentoria is under threat."

The guards looked straight ahead. The Master raised his chin to the night, then paused.

Images of Delia flashed in blue light across the buildings of the city.

Then clearing his throat, The Master continued. "Guards. Your orders are clear. Find the girl. Now go!"

The guards broke from their lines and scoured the city streets in pairs. They were ready for anything. Well, almost anything…

Disobeying orders, Mentorians flooded the streets. News of the girl infected with the Virus Called Dog spread. Temporary medical posts were erected and manned by members of the

Mentorian Guard. Women, hugging their children close, ran through the streets. Spontaneous rounds of gunfire pealed across the city. In a dark alley, a woman who laughed out loud was gagged and then silenced by a blow to the back of the head.

The gentle sound of Delia's voice woke Stanley from a short sleep. He sat up and frowned.

"Who are you talking to?"

"It's okay," Delia replied.

"No, who are you talking to?"

"Dog," Delia said, turning and glancing at him over her shoulder. "He was on the rooftop of the Great Hall of Power when you—oh, it doesn't matter. He's not at all what I thought. He just wants to play ball."

"Play ball?" Stanley said.

Delia looked away.

"Stop being silly. What are we going to do?" he asked.

"Well," Delia said. "Dog has all the answers. He's quite the traveller and seems to know lots of things. He told me about Brightspark—a crystal I can use to power my invention."

"Huh?" Stanley asked, confused. "Brightspark? There is no dog," he said, scanning what appeared to him as an empty room.

Delia smiled and giggled into the empty space.

Stanley watched her and frowned. *What is going on? Has she lost her mind? What happened to her on the roof?*

Delia's laughter stopped as quickly as it started. She bent over and began to groan.

"What is it?" Stanley asked.

"It's getting worse."

"What's getting worse?" Stanley asked.

"The pain," she said. "It's all my old feelings, and my chest feels like it's going to burst. You have to go to Happysad."

"Happysad?"

"According to Dog the—"

"There is no dog!" Stanley snapped. "You're sick."

"You must find Brightspark. It's in Happysad. It's both a healing oracle and a source of light."

"What?"

"Dog says it can cure the virus," Delia pleaded.

"If I go to Happysad, I'll catch the virus and go mad."

"Please," Delia begged as she started to choke. "The guards are coming, and I don't want to die."

Delia yanked her gloves, tossing them across the floor and covering her face with her scarred hands.

Stanley spun around, startled as three loud bangs sounded at the door.

"Find Brightspark. I can't breathe, and my chest feels like it's going to burst. The exercise taxes will kill us all," Delia hissed.

"Open up!" a loud metallic voice ordered from outside the door. Stanley's e-reader pulsed red and started to beep.

"Run, Stanley. You must run," Delia whispered.

There was another loud bang at the door. "We're coming in," shouted a guard.

For a moment, Stanley held Delia's scarred hands. Then he was gone.

When the Mentorian Guards burst through the door, they found Delia sitting alone on the floor with her hands over her face, heaving in a pool of sweat. Looking through her fingers, everything went dark when the guard slid a black bag over her head. She heard the clicking sound of the window closing in the next room. Delia sensed Dog sitting tall by her side.

Dog panted, his mouth dripping with saliva, probably wondering if perhaps the guards were willing to play ball.

Delia smiled.

Stanley watched from a rooftop across the street as four guards carried Delia away. He hid in the shadows, uncertain of what to do. He didn't have to wait long before The Master's oversized and bulbous head appeared on the sides of buildings as a special broadcast. In a monotone voice, The Master began his address.

"People of Mentoria," he said. "The virus is contained."

An image of Delia was projected onto the sides of buildings. She was sedated and strapped to a metallic bed with a battery of wires attached to each side of her head. Unexpectedly, Delia opened her eyes. Trying to sit up, she shouted at the camera, "It's a lie. The dog is loose in the city. Run Stanley, run!"

The screen went blank.

The Master cursed and looked out the window of The penthouse shaped like a pill. Without the citizen's belief in his virus propaganda, it wouldn't be long before he lost control. Rubbing his chin, The Master called for the commander of the Mentorian Guard. His orders were clear. "Find stupid Stanley—alive." He paused. "Or dead. Either will do."

In Stanley's mind, the best place to hide was the first place he could be found. The Great Hall of Power was deserted. Outside, regiments of guards marched by. But when one particular platoon in white helmets stormed through the steel doors of the Great Hall, Stanley ran, avoiding the searchlights that flashed across the walls.

Unbeknownst to most Mentorians, the only means of escaping the city was through two long cylindrical drains that expelled waste and other useless things from the city. Mounted on the walls at the edge of the Mentoria, the drains were powered by two large air-driven pumps and a master timing device. Every seven minutes, the flap on the drains whooshed open. Waste, which happened to include the odd dead body, was crushed, sucked out, and spat into the River E, far below.

Stanley slipped through the shadows created by a line of tall trees until he reached the city's perimeter wall. He scaled the wall, slowing as he neared the whooshing sound of one of the drains. It had not occurred to him what he would do when he reached the top. The guards, who had followed him from the top of the wall, approached. Stanley moved closer and saw the metallic mouth of the drain open and close. He started to count inside his head. On the wall beside the drain was a glass case with a sign *In Case of Emergency, Break Glass.* Ignoring the approaching sound of marching boots, Stanley smashed the glass and took the four nummers from inside the case.

"Stop!" a guard ordered from behind.

The mouth of the drain opened. Gunfire ricocheted off the blades of the vent, and Stanley leaped with two pocketsful of pills marked with the letter "P," four nummers, and a heart full of fear. With his eyes squeezed shut, Stanley slid down the dark and smelly tunnel littered with waste. Then suddenly weightless, he fell through a thin layer of cloud. Above, shots rang out, and alarms sounded.

The cold, whistling wind whipped Stanley's face, and after what seemed to be the longest time, he splashed into the icy waters of the River E. It was likely that without the nummers, Stanley Luka might have floated to the surface. Instead, unwilling to let go, he sank. And when his lungs started screaming, he thought of Delia, back to the time when they were children, siblings unknown to each other, as she grabbed his hand and led him away from the bullies so no one would see him cry.

PART TWO

HAPPYSAD

7. AN ENCOUNTER WITH A BOG

Sinking slowly, Stanley wondered how long it would take to reach the moment of his death. He sank through the murky depths of the River E, holding his breath while suffocating slowly. Pain ripped through his chest as he swallowed his last mouthful of stale air. Hugging the nummers, Stanley opened his mouth and watched as his last bubble of air rose rapidly towards the surface. Then closing his eyes, he surrendered to the cold waters of the River E.

Not far away, a formation of dark shadows glided stealthily through the water, moving closer. Despite being half the size of more impressive whales, Heinrich was the leader of the pod. A majestic old mammal with sad, blue, barnacled eyes, he meandered the depths of the River E with his mouth gaping in the hope of snagging something better to eat than plankton or krill. Ever since the rise of Mentoria, he had seen the River E become contaminated with the toxic waste that dripped from its drains.

The pod of itinerant whales was mostly vegetarian, except for the rebellious calves who snacked on fugitive fish and exposed themselves when they shat blue-green bile that muddied the waters even more.

Seconds from death, Stanley was sucked into Heinrich's mouth. He landed with a thud, popping a bubble of putrid gas that had troubled Heinrich for quite some time. Relieved but suddenly concerned about the footsteps marching up and down inside his gut, Heinrich sensed that something was wrong.

Despite his sad blue eyes, Heinrich was an optimist. In recent years, he had learned to filter out a number of the different voices that had battled for attention inside his larger than normal brain. Nevertheless, he was certain this was a new voice that called out to him.

"Hello? Am I dead? What is this place?"

Thinking it only polite to reply, and through a unique mode of communication (possible in only more evolved whales, even ones of small stature), Heinrich spoke to his accidental meal.

"Obviously, you are not dead," he said, indignant. "You are in my stomach, so I would very much appreciate it if you stopped banging around in there. You're giving me quite the stomach cramp. And by the way, it may help you to know; I am a whale."

Stanley tripped on a pile of putrefying debris in Heinrich's gut, cutting his foot on the razor-sharp bones of a rotten fish.

"Shish," he said, pressing his foot to stop the blood.

"What are you doing?" Heinrich asked, lurching to the left and causing Stanley to fall backwards into the soft and spongey lining of his stomach.

Stanley stood up, gagging at the smell. "It stinks in here. It's disgusting!"

"Well, what did you expect the inside of a stomach to smell like?" Heinrich exclaimed, most offended.

Stanley muttered to himself as he regained his balance. "Who are you, anyway? Do you always swallow your meals whole?"

"Heinrich's my name. Heinrich, the third," the whale said in a pompous tone. "And for your information, you're in *my* territory. It's not my business or my fault if a silly human decides to drown themselves in the river E."

"Well, I didn't intend to drown..." Stanley grumbled, but the whale ignored him.

"Anyway, we are on our way to the distant and deep blue sea and out of this wretched river. Now tell me, what made you think you could just invite yourself into my stomach?"

"You tell me," Stanley said. "You were the one with your mouth open. I was all but dead."

"Hmmm," Heinrich said, as though he was pondering the fact. A deep vibration coursed throughout his body, causing Stanley to wobble as he tried to stay on his feet.

"I suppose you're right." The whale conceded. "So, the least you could do is tell me your name.".

"Stanley Luka," the voice inside his stomach said.

Heinrich rolled to the other side, pitched upwards, and groaned, trying to loosen another bubble of gas.

"What are you doing?" Stanley screeched as he toppled over, gagging at the stench.

"Rolling," Heinrich replied. "It helps...sometimes."

As Heinrich fishtailed through the upper layers of the River E, Stanley moved himself towards the centre of the whale's stomach. Hoping he'd have better luck staying on his feet, Stanley braced himself as a rumbling of acidic gas encircled him before rushing out of the whale's stomach, followed by the near-deafening rumble as Heinrich burped.

"Ah…that's better," Heinrich said. "Much better indeed."

Stanley felt the whale start to accelerate, and he grabbed at the nearest thing, which happened to be a didgeridoo. Stanley imagined it was once played by a musician who had sunk into eternal despair after years of searching for meaning in the instrument's otherworldly sounds and drowned himself in the River E.

Stanley felt the rumble as another bubble of trapped air burst. And despite his grip on the didgeridoo, the force of the air hurtled him forward, back through the whale's body, and pinning both him and the didgeridoo to the roof of Heinrich's mouth. The vacuum tore other small and shining gas bubbles from the gut of the whale, shooting a putrid wind across the surface of the River E.

"That's better," Heinrich said.

"You've got a real problem with gas," Stanley grumbled.

"Yes," Heinrich said, resigned.

"I have an idea," Stanley said, picking himself up from the back of Heinrich's mouth. He placed a fishbone with a small umbrella of cartilage into the didgeridoo. And, pointing at another shiny bubble of gas, he blew. The dart shot through the darkness, popped the bubble, and sent a ripple of relief around Heinrich's gut.

"Again, do it again," Heinrich demanded.

"Yes," Stanley said. "Then all you have to do is open your mouth."

And seizing the opportunity to end the conversation with the colicky whale, Stanley aimed the didgeridoo at the biggest and shiniest bubble of gas that he could see. The dart flew upwards into the dark night of Heinrich's gut and disappeared. A second later, there was a loud popping sound. Heinrich opened his mouth, wiggled his jaw, made a few other visceral adjustments, and let out a deep burp.

The vortex of putrid air sucked Stanley past the bristles in Heinrich's mouth. And clinging to his nummers, he shot up and out of the water and landed on the hard and sandy shores of the River E.

Stanley rubbed his gritty, sand-filled eyes and watched Heinrich moan with relief as he rolled and disappeared back into the depths of the River E. Clearing the last of the sand from his eyes, Stanley paused as he caught sight of a different, larger eye on top of a slightly sideways yellow front tooth, blinking from the bushes that lined the shores of the River. Stanley bit down hard on the mouthpiece of a nummer. Exhausted, he clenched his teeth for as long as he could, revelling in the relief from the shot of electricity to his brain. Then, overwhelmed and surrendering to his fatigue, Stanley closed his eyes.

The sun shone all afternoon, and hours later, it was a slimy tongue licking Stanley's mouth that pulled him from his sleep. Before he could open his eyes, Stanley gagged on the lingering stench of foul breath. When he opened them, he found two yellow eyes staring at him, blinking slowly. The animal's sizeable front tooth hung down over its bottom lip, and when its mouth opened, Stanley saw the other rows of teeth, yellow and jagged. The creature let out a cry that was somewhere between a bark and a squeal before standing on two hind legs and bobbing up and down before it ran in circles in the sand.

Stanley waved his hand at the beast, who promptly stopped and cocked its head to one side.

"Ha!" the beast said, as though delighted to have the stranger's attention.

"What are you doing?" Stanley asked. But when it occurred to him he was trying to communicate with another animal, Stanley started counting. Inadvertently, he turned his face upwards to the sun with an awareness that he was probably already going mad.

"Nothing. What are you doing?" asked the beast.

"666, 667, 668," Stanley counted, ignoring it.

"Why are you counting?" the animal asked.

Stanley sighed, conceding that, crazy or not, he would answer. "It doesn't matter," he said. "Who are you?"

"My name is Blabbermouth. I am a citizen of Happysad. And I'm a bog."

"A what?" asked Stanley.

"Yes, a rarity," Blabbermouth replied. "A bog. Part beaver, part dog."

Stanley shook his head and continued with his counting. "669, 670, 671."

"This is so exciting," Blabbermouth said, "It's been a while since I've spoken to anyone because I've been away, but now that I'm back, there is lots to do. Though that doesn't mean there isn't time to make new friends. Do you want to be my friend? Do you?"

Stanley looked at the bog and kept counting.

I'm losing my mind. How else could I be talking to a bog?

"You're still counting," Blabbermouth said.

"What?" Stanley squirmed as he flicked his gaze from the bog to the river and back again. He reached over his shoulder for a nummer and groaned as he realised they'd disappeared. Stanley got to his feet and scanned the shores of the River E.

The nummers are gone. All gone. I can't go on without them. What if...

"Looking for these?" Blabbermouth asked, holding up the last three metal cylinders.

"Give them back," Stanley growled as he lurched forward, his hand outstretched.

"Tell me what you're doing in Happysad," Blabbermouth said. "Because no one just appears out of nowhere on a sunny day for no good reason at all."

"I'm looking for something," said Stanley. "Now give me back my nummers."

"Your nummers? It's an adventure, isn't it? You're going on an adventure, and you need your nummers. I love adventures. I can come with you, and we can adventure together because I happen to be a bit of an adventurer myself," Blabbermouth blurted.

Stanley rubbed his eyes. "Give me the nummers," he demanded.

"What's a nummer? What does it do? Tell me why you're here," Blabbermouth said.

"What? No. It's none of your business," said Stanley.

"Then I can't help you," Blabbermouth said, sulking. He bit on his bottom lip with his single front tooth and made a squelching, sucking sound.

"Well, I'll be off then," he said. "Lots of other things to do, and soon it will be dark. I don't like the dark because of all the things you cannot see."

Blabbermouth paused for a moment and then added for good measure, "And watch out for the lizards."

"What lizards?"

"Oh, the large ones," Blabbermouth said. "They're flesh-eaters, with big claws and enormous teeth. They only come out at night. They're always hungry, and they always attack from

100

behind—I suppose that's because they don't like to look their food in the eye. Can't say I blame them, really."

"Flesh-eaters?" Stanley asked.

"Yes, they're not fussy, but mostly they like two-legged flesh because it's cleaner and less gamey than other meat. Not that I need to worry, of course. Lizards don't eat bogs."

"Well, what keeps someone safe from them?" Stanley asked.

"Ah," Blabbermouth mused, "What does your nummer do?"

"I'll tell you, but first I need my nummers and for you to tell me more about the lizards."

"Fine," Blabbermouth said. "But if I were you, I would be more worried about the owls."

Stanley groaned, and Blabbermouth appeared to take that as a sign to go on.

"You see, just like the lizards, the owls of Happysad only come out at night. They're a band of ruthless birds—they frighten people with their ability to turn their heads all the way around. It's not natural! They also have oversized, large yellow eyes that never seem to blink. If you ask me, the owls are evil liars and are always prickly on account of their difficult diet of hedgehogs. Mostly, the owls live in the Woods of Eternal Calamity and Darkness and sell their allegiance to the payer of the highest price. But being purveyors of information, they also travel far and wide and don't care about anyone except themselves. Their only saving grace is that they frighten the lizards, which is probably on account of their non-blinking, but you'd have to ask a lizard to be sure."

"Is there a point to any of this?" Stanley asked.

"Of course, there is. Aren't you listening? I just told you, and quite clearly, I might add, that wherever there are owls, there are no lizards. I've also explained why the lizards, despite the size of their claws, never climb trees." Blabbermouth finished his tale by offering Stanley two of the nummers.

101

"All of them," Stanley said firmly.

"Nope," Blabbermouth said. "First, I need to know about your adventure."

"I'm looking for Brightspark," Stanley said, his feet shifting beneath him as he gripped the nummers.

"Brightspark?" Blabbermouth swallowed hard. The bog's eyes widened as they darted from side to side. "Umm, yes, Brightspark. Hmm, no one talks about that anymore. Yes, Brightspark. Hmm. I think I best be off now. It's getting late, and soon it will be dark," Blabbermouth's voice quietened with every word until it was barely a whisper.

"What?" Stanley said.

"Well, now that you mention Brightspark," Blabbermouth whispered, "I wouldn't be too worried about the lizards or the owls. Because now there's the problem of the witch."

"What are you talking about? What witch?"

"Her name is Evil Eva."

"Evil Eva?" repeated Stanley.

"The witch. Yes, she's beautiful and dangerous, and everyone is scared of her because she casts evil spells and does terrible things to children. Brightspark is cursed because of her," Blabbermouth hissed.

"Look, I'm sure there's some point to this story, but as you said, it will be dark soon and…"

"You'd be a fool to think you can get to Brightspark without knowing about the witch—but that's up to you." The Bog tilted his head at Stanley as though considering the possibility.

"I don't understand," Stanley stammered.

"Well," said Blabbermouth. "The story of Evil Eva riding side-saddle on a broomstick across a moonlit sky has been the most effective way to get the children of Happysad to go to sleep for years." With this, the bog seemed to forget all about whispering as he regaled another story for his newfound friend.

"Her reign of terror began many, many years ago, after Evil Eva fled, apparently invisible, from the largest asylum in Happysad. Then, in the dead of night, newborns started disappearing from the Fields of Crying Babies. It was said Evil Eva stole them for experiments; she tore the babies limb from limb and bottled their screams to make potions to rid herself of her own inconsolable sadness."

Blabbermouth paused and started swallowing rapidly as though his mouth had suddenly run dry. He wrapped his tongue around his single front tooth and then nervously licked it, up and down.

"What are you doing with your tongue?" asked Stanley, his lip raised in distaste.

"Cleaning," Blabbermouth said, changing the subject. "I don't want to lose this one too. The other tooth fell out—rotten, you know? I should have flossed, but no one likes flossing, and now that I only have one tooth. I'm not quite as attractive as I used to be." And as if to punctuate his statement, Blabbermouth stood up on his skinny hind legs that seemed to buckle slightly under the weight of his large, round stomach. His orange, shaggy fur was filthy and looked long overdue for a bath. He pulled a pair of glassless, black-rimmed frames from somewhere within the fur of his back and perched them on his nose. His eyes darted left and right as if the empty frames might somehow help him to see things differently.

Stanley sighed. "What are they for?"

"For protection," Blabbermouth said.

"Let me guess, from the witch?"

103

"No, the lizards," Blabbermouth sounded exasperated. "Have you been listening at all? Lizards don't like glasses because they think they're eyes. And they won't eat anything with eyes larger than their own."

Speechless, Stanley shook his head slowly from side to side.

Blabbermouth started backing away. "I can't help you," he said, trembling.

"Then tell me one thing. What is Brightspark anyway?" Stanley asked.

"All I can tell you is it fell from the skies long ago. Somehow it generates light. Some say it's a healing oracle and can answer questions. Others say it will send you mad."

"Send you mad?" asked Stanley.

The bog nodded. "Evil Eva found it in the woods, and it made her madder than she was before…it told her something terrible, and her mind cracked in two. But that's enough about that. It's late, and I'm hungry," Blabbermouth said as he turned and walked away.

"If I don't find Brightspark, Delia will die," Stanley blurted out.

"Die? Who will die?" Blabbermouth spun around quickly, dislodging his glasses, so they sat lopsided on his face. "That's terrible…it's tragic when someone dies, and I have never liked funerals because there are lots of tears and everyone feels bad, and no one knows what to say, and who is Delia anyway?"

"She's my sister and a scientist," Stanley said, taking the tube from the nummer and clenching the mouthpiece between his teeth. "And she's sick."

"Does that thing stop you from getting sick too?" Blabbermouth asked about the nummer.

"In a way. It makes feelings go away," Stanley said.

Blabbermouth's eyes widened. "Does it hurt?"

"Sometimes," Stanley said. "It's electric."

"Can I try it? Please can I try it? I feel bad about the owls and lizards and the witch, and now that I'm hungry, I feel even worse. I could do with some electricity…please."

"So…" Stanley said, "you take me to Brightspark, and I'll let you use my nummer. How about that?"

Blabbermouth tapped his paw nervously on the sand.

"Ahh," Stanley moaned, exaggerating the relief from his nummer. He checked the lights on the side of the device and confirmed they were green. But when he started sneezing, he was suddenly reminded of the symptoms of madness caused by the sun. "I have to get out of the light," Stanley declared, not waiting for Blabbermouth to respond as he rubbed his nose anxiously and scurried to the nearest tree.

A sneeze is just a sneeze. It's nothing. I'm okay. I'm okay. I'm okay. I'm okay. I'm okay. I'm okay. I'm okay.

The relief only lasted until Stanley sneezed again, sending him into a spiral of counting inside his head.

"Well?" asked Blabbermouth.

"What?" said Stanley, distracted.

"Give me the nummer, and then we can go."

Stanley bit down hard on the mouthpiece of his nummer and sucked the air in through his teeth, closing his eyes as he held it out towards Blabbermouth. He felt his feelings sink back into the shadows, and when Stanley opened his eyes again, he watched Blabbermouth manoeuvre his yellow front tooth around the mouthpiece of the nummer. The bog bit down hard, and when his eyes bulged, it was clear that the electricity had shot its way to Blabbermouth's small, walnut-shaped brain. Stanley smiled to himself as he watched the glaze spread across the bog's eyes, and a vacant smile stretch across his face. Then, as though no longer fearful of any thoughts of lizards or owls or witches, Blabbermouth stood tall.

"I'll take you as far as the woods," Blabbermouth declared as he picked up a crooked stick and walked away from the shores of the River E. And without a word, Stanley followed him through the trees.

After what seemed the longest time, Blabbermouth called over his shoulder. "What do you know of Happysad?"

Stanley fumbled in the pocket of his pants and pulled out a small wet book. He started to read.

The villages of Happysad stretch from the Eternal Snow-Capped Mountains to the River E. It's home to shore dwellers who live by the banks of the river and who have, in recent times—and owing to a slur of evolution—started to grow scales. In the deserts, the nomads sleep under cover of tiny tents and spend their days searching for water beneath scorching skies. The plantations form a canopy of tangled vines, coconut palms, and trees with colossal green leaves.

"Interesting, but I've never been to the desert," Blabbermouth interrupted.

Stanley continued, paraphrasing the text. "There are also the families who fossicked for food and accidentally cultivated a peculiar yellow moss that is used in the asylums as a balm for sadness, bad temper, and the laughter that infects everyone."

"In Happysad, the sun affects everything," Blabbermouth said. "We have madmen, martyrs, sages, and saints. Here, we feel everything all the time. And it rains a lot."

"Clearly, you are mad," Stanley frowned. The sheer thought of emotions flying around unchecked was enough to cause him to bite down fiercely on his nummer.

"Pfff," Blabbermouth huffed, then continued.

"We do have our problems. You see, everyone says exactly what they feel. Most people have at least two conversations

106

with the voices inside their heads, and because of this, they get confused about how they really feel at all."

"Exactly my point," Stanley gasped, feeling short of breath.

"Oh, that's not even the half of it," the bog declared. "It was only after the tragedy of the six-year-old girl that the Brothers of Perpetual Denial decided something must be done. The girl, who had minded her own business all her life, happened to listen to the bad advice of one of the voices inside her head which, identifying itself as a bee, instructed her to jump from the nearest bridge to find out whether she too, could fly."

"What happened?" Stanley asked.

"Well, what do you think happened?" Blabbermouth said.

Stanley paused.   "Who are the Brothers of Perpetual Denial?"

"The administrators of Happysad," Blabbermouth replied. "We see them sometimes, drunk and speaking from small wooden podiums to anyone that will listen. When the girl died, the Brothers ordered the construction of asylums in the forests—places where people could stop and feel their feelings and hopefully find some sort of peace. They built them in the shape of the letter "U," with two separate wards: One for the happy, one for the sad. The inmates wear flowing white gowns and mostly stare at the walls or across the courtyard at each other. I don't know why, but each asylum seems to be built around a single lemon tree that is always bulging with fruit." Blabbermouth looked intensely at Stanley. "And another thing, it's quite possible that our ancestors were the survivors of a stray comet, you know?"

Bemused, Stanley shook his head, "Really?

"Some say it's true," Blabbermouth said. Then he turned and walked in silence into the approaching night.

Despite the fluctuating mood of Happysad, the Brothers of Perpetual Denial kept the peace. Their practical approach to administration was assisted by the consumption of whisky, which they brewed in the cellars of the asylums and sold from rickety carts that they dragged through the streets. According to themselves, The Brothers were closer than anyone else to the God of whom they spoke. And so, unchallenged and through bloodshot eyes, The Brothers managed the asylums and everything else. And they were especially mindful of the Parzens, who, ever since The Brothers took control, tried to meddle in their affairs.

Not civically-minded at all and indifferent to both the future and the past, the Parzens were an aloof community of ascetics who wandered around Happysad with their red faces turned towards the sun. Naked, except for the small white cloths covering their groins, the Parzens trod lightly on the earth. They sang strange songs, walked with knotted brown staffs, and smiled the sentient smile of a people who knew something others did not. And despite the fact that they had somehow mastered the art of levitation, it was their smile that threatened The Brothers most. For The Brothers were convinced the Parzens were hiding something — like the important piece of the puzzle of life that everybody else had overlooked, somewhere along the way.

In the face of The Brother's concerns, the Parzens were no real threat at all. The focus of the Parzen's life was a one-time pilgrimage to the Villa of the Stony Crag that began on any given day in May. The pilgrimage, it was said, offered the chance of miracles for the afflicted and the mad. Nevertheless, few Parzens ever made it because of all the distractions along the way. And of the handful that ever returned, one or two maintained The Villa of the Stony Crag was home to a labyrinth of secret chambers and that it housed Brightspark—the fabled egg-shaped crystal that apparently fell off the side of a comet, many years before.

Blabbermouth pulled up short. "We will stop here for the night." he declared, gathering wood for the evening fire. Without words, Stanley lay beside the fire and fell asleep, only to be woken two hours later by the sound of flapping wings. Sitting bolt upright, Stanley struggled to see in the inky night. A squadron of squawking birds passed overhead.

"Nothing to fear," Blabbermouth said quietly. "It's not the owls. They're the albatrosses of Happysad."

"What are they doing in the middle of the night?" Stanley asked.

"Catching babies," Blabbermouth said.

"What babies?"

"The unwanted babies from Mentoria," Blabbermouth answered.

"Where do they take them?" Stanley asked, bewildered.

"To the Fields of Crying Babies," Blabbermouth said, his voice sounding choked up in the darkness. "We'd best be on our way."

"But it's the middle of the night?"

"We can't be late," Blabbermouth said. "We have to get to the village before first light."

"Why?" Stanley asked.

"Because I'm starving, and my brother will be roasting meat."

Blabbermouth dipped a large branch into the fire. And when it caught alight, he threw dirt over the campfire and led Stanley further into the woods.

After walking for some time, Blabbermouth stopped. It was mostly dark, but as he peered over the top of the bog, Stanley could see the glowing torchlights that marked the edge of the village, hidden beneath a tangle of vines.

Blabbermouth whistled and appeared to be waiting for a response.

"Why are you whistling?" Stanley asked.

"For my brother," Blabbermouth said. "He is an inmate of the asylum. And he speaks the language of the birds."

Even before first light, the asylum in the village hummed with excitement. Hearing the whistle, Blabbermouth's brother, who preferred to sleep on the floor, got up and shuffled to the door of his cell. Whereas most of his life had been spent raging along the corridors of the asylum and cursing at the moon, in recent times, he had been frequented by an unexpected and enduring happy mood. Despite his blindness and inability to understand the language of his peers, nothing would ever prevent him from responding to his brother's call.

Earlier that evening, he was visited by the premonition of Blabbermouth's arrival. And as part of his preparations, he had returned from the asylum grounds just after midnight and roasted the carcass of a lizard for them both to eat.

Once a year, Blabbermouth joined his brother in the celebration of the Procession of Miracles. Just after dawn and dressed in white loincloths, the Parzens pushed the lunatics and

110

the lame into a line in readiness for when the ringleader sounded his horn.

Blabbermouth's brother felt his way to the square where the crowd gathered. He turned his face to the tops of the trees and whistled to the birds. Other inmates hooted and cheered and wandered in circles. Dawn cracked, and the rusty metal bell in the middle of the square tolled three times. Claps rang out, and the excitement grew as a young man stepped up onto a makeshift wooden stage. The able pilgrims whistled and clapped and then jumped up and down in anticipation of a miracle.

The young man cleared his throat. "Welcome," he said. "I give you Constance Flabert."

Constance, short and plump, climbed the three steps of the stage. Dressed in a red velvet jacket with gold brocade and a top hat, he had the appearance of a lion tamer. He raised his arms to the sky to soak up the applause. At the appropriate time, he nodded to the younger man, who lit the fireworks that burst into the sky. Amidst the cracks and flashes, the birds, who had sat watching from the tops of the trees, took flight. The acrid smell of smoke filled the sky, and an aura of festivity embraced the crowd.

Blabbermouth followed the scent of roasted meat and jumped from the bushes at the edge of the square. Stanley followed Blabbermouth as he pushed his way through the crowd.

When the fireworks stopped, the spectators cheered. Ushered by some drunken officials from the Brothers of Perpetual Denial, the pilgrims formed a jagged line. Behind them, Blabbermouth's brother scratched in the dirt looking for the roasted meat that he'd dropped following an unfortunate collision with a tree. Sensing his brother was near, he turned around. The two bogs embraced in a shaggy hug about the same size, and with an exchange of whistles and the clicking of his tongue, Blabbermouth explained what he was about to do.

"What was all that?" Stanley asked.

"I told him about our adventure."

"Our adventure?"

"Well, it's your adventure, but I'm sharing it because I'm showing you the way, and without me, it would not be nearly as exciting, and you would get lost," Blabbermouth said.

When Stanley went to speak, Blabbermouth's brother tilted his head back and whistled at the sky.

"Why's he whistling?" Stanley asked, covering his ears.

"Because we'd best be on our way," Blabbermouth said.

When Constance Flabert blew his wooden horn for the first time, a black chariot drawn by seven white donkeys appeared beside the stage. Etched into the front of the chariot was a large brass eagle with its wings spread to the wind. The crowd hushed. And then they cheered.

Constance, who always thought of himself as a kind of gladiator, blew his horn for the second time. One by one, the white donkeys dropped obediently to their knees. Constance climbed onto the chariot, and when he shook the reins, the donkeys stood and lurched forward. The crowd hooted, and the procession started on its way.

Sensing Blabbermouth was about to leave with the Procession of Miracles, his brother handed him four gold coins, a roasted lizard limb, and kissed him on the cheek. Fighting

112

back the tears, Blabbermouth whispered in his brother's ear, patted his shoulder, and walked away. Stanley followed, watching as Blabbermouth's brother bit into his lip, looked up at the sky, and then wandered in circles, looking for the birds.

To distract himself from feeling anything at all, Stanley turned his attention to the end of the procession, where a young boy was running in circles and stirring up a cloud of dust. One of the asylum's youngest inmates, the boy, was on all fours and screeching like a monkey. His thin lips were peeled back over tight gums, revealing morsels of old food trapped between yellow, razor-sharp teeth. His appearance caused a shiver to run along Stanley's spine, and he quickly looked away.

Later, and after walking for hours, Constance blew his horn. Covered in donkey spit and dust, the chariot with the big brass eagle, came to a halt at the side of the road. Constance wiped the sweat from his face and ordered the donkeys to be watered in the nearby stream. In the absence of a morning miracle, a number of pilgrims had already given up hope. They sat, weeping dirty tears by the side of the road. Helpers handed bread and offered quiet words of inspiration, reassuring the pilgrims that the journey had only just begun.

Just after lunch, Constance blew into his wooden horn. The donkeys heaved the chariot with the big brass eagle back onto the road. The pilgrims struggled to their feet. Constance raised his arm and, with a well-rehearsed, slightly prophetic tone, issued his orders. "Quiet from here," he said. "For only in silence can you be healed."

At the front of the line, the Parzens, who had not uttered a word all day, nodded and faced the afternoon sun.

"Keep your eyes on the road," Constance called out. "Don't look the mourning mothers in the eye, for their sadness is infectious and greater than your own."

"What's he talking about?" Stanley asked Blabbermouth, who was already taking deep breaths in anticipation of what was to come.

"The Fields of Crying Babies," he said.

"You mean it's real?"

"Wait, and you will see," Blabbermouth replied.

8. THE FIELDS OF CRYING BABIES

T he road narrowed. Stanley kept his distance from the small boy at the end of the line, who appeared to be agitated by the silence. For the first time since they began, the boy stopped running in circles like a monkey on all fours. Instead, he started chewing the ends of his fingers that had no nails.

When the procession reached the top of the hill, a huddle of cloaked figures lined the edge of the road. They might have been mistaken for small dark pointed trees from a distance — but they were rocking slowly, back and forth, and wearing veils. Their lament, which was mostly boos and hoos, filled the air beneath the grey clouds that hung like thick blankets, low across the hills. It started to rain, and as the Procession of Miracles moved closer to the plain, the small sucking sounds of sleeping babies grew louder.

Constance pulled at the reins of the chariot, and the procession slowed.

"Keep your eyes down and keep walking. Then we will pass right through," he said, placing a finger across his lips.

"What happens if they wake?" Stanley asked Blabbermouth.

"Their cries will drive you mad," Blabbermouth whispered. "Their sadness is like poison. It suffocates the heart."

"Who are the women?" Stanley asked.

"They watch over the babies, and they carry knives," Blabbermouth replied.

"Knives?" Stanley asked.

"Yes, to stop anyone sent by Evil Eva from coming and taking their babies away."

Stanley looked straight ahead and started counting to distract himself from the growing heaviness in his chest. He frowned to himself as he tried to make sense of the unfamiliar clenching ache, and slowly he recognised the seeds of sadness that were sown in his heart the day his father wrenched him from his mother. From that moment, Stanley spent his life anaesthetised by the pills marked with the letter "P," and he'd all but forgotten his mother, except in his dreams.

Surrounded by sadness, Stanley ran his gaze over the rows of wooden cribs that stretched as far as the eye could see. The mourning women fell silent and, with their faces to the ground, glided in circles like ducks on a pond. Occasionally, they paused to look up at the sky as though hoping to find some relief. Once, they too had walked in the Procession of Miracles, but upon seeing the orphaned babies in the fields, they had given in to their despair. And drowning in the sadness of their swollen hearts, the women lost their way, carrying out their remaining days in sadness in the fields with the crying babies.

By the time the chariot with the big brass eagle passed the first line of cribs, some pilgrims, intoxicated by the sadness of the place, had already wandered off. Immediately, the mood of the mourning women switched from grief to rage.

"Don't look them in the eye!" Blabbermouth whispered loudly to Stanley. A line of mourning women started closing in and a lump formed in Stanley's throat. Unable to swallow, he found himself overwhelmed with the tragedy in the air, feeling as if the seeds of sadness planted deep inside his heart had suddenly become a tree. Unfamiliar with the pain, Stanley cried out as the clenching sensation within his chest tightened. Fumbling with the mouthpiece of his nummer, Stanley shoved it in his mouth and bit down hard. Suddenly disorientated, he walked in a circle, clutching at his chest. The monkey boy, who had watched Stanley the whole time, let out a hysterical shriek. And overcome with a longing for his mother that he buried long ago, Stanley did the only thing he could. He ran.

With his face turned to the sky, Stanley tripped on the rope that tethered the monkey boy to an old man who was tall and wide and the size of a small tree. Flung forwards, Stanley smashed into a wooden crib, knocking it on its side. The baby startled, disturbed from rubbing its nose with the end of its sheet, grimaced, then started crying in an ear-piercing bleat. Seeing what had happened, the mourning women snarled and turned their eyes to Stanley. One by one, across the fields, the gentle sucking sounds of sleeping babies stopped. Alarmed by the rage in the mourning women's eyes, the pilgrims scattered, and Constance blew his whistle harder than ever before. The sound startled the donkeys, causing them to lurch forward, pulling the chariot with the big brass eagle up on one side.

Blabbermouth cupped one hand across his ear and fumbled with the mouthpiece of his nummer as he shoved it past his single front tooth. Surrendering to the commotion and not knowing what else he could do, Blabbermouth sat down on the ground and closed his eyes.

All around, red-faced babies with clenched white knuckles spat the rubber pacifiers from their mouths.

Demented with rage, the mourning women gripped the sickles they used for harvesting grain, and unable to console the crying babies, they slashed at the pilgrims who ran haphazardly towards them. Blood splattered the fields, and when somebody's arm flew through the air and smacked him in the face, Blabbermouth jumped to his feet and ran. Since frightened bogs always ran faster than anybody else, Blabbermouth passed Stanley within seconds. He reached the chariot with the big brass eagle, which, moments later, slammed into a line of sickle-wielding women. Constance ducked below the blade swinging towards him to avoid losing his head, and the chariot with the big brass eagle surged forward, clearing a path in its wake. Just behind, Blabbermouth, the monkey boy, and others were running free as the donkeys ran for their lives, heaving the chariot with the big brass eagle along the stony path.

When the squadron of large black birds appeared, they traced a circle in the sky. The women saw them and stopped their attack. Then, heeding the omen of Evil Eva, they waved their sickles in the air. With their backs to the pilgrims and their eyes cast down, the women mumbled and spat on the ground and returned to the fields. One by one, they gathered the sobbing bundles and held the babies to their breasts. When finally, the babies went to sleep, the women surrendered to their tears. And as if nothing had happened, they closed their eyes and rocked the small wooden cribs with their blood-stained feet.

9. EVIL EVA

Whether it was true that Evil Eva came in the night to steal children away was of little consequence. For in the people's minds, she was guilty. Beset with seductions greater than any man could bear, Evil Eva had fled many years earlier and taken up residence in a faraway amethyst cave. She surrounded herself with candles and only slept on nights windy enough to distract her from the memories of her past. A beauty like no other, Eva was tall with long hair that cascaded down her back in ebony waves. She had voluptuous breasts, slender limbs, and in her youth, she had worn a red flower in her hair. In her ears, she wore two large golden rings. And adept in the healing arts, Eva was the envy of all women who took great joy in hurling accusations of her dabbling in witchcraft and communicating with the dead. Convinced she was a conjurer; Eva was two things: evil and a witch in the women's minds.

The real trouble began the day Eva administered an herb poultice to the ankles of a desperate and barren woman who sought her help. Eight months later, the woman gave birth to triplets with skin unlike their father, who, being a prominent public figure, was both angered and shamed.

So it was, that men had always come and gone from Eva's life—like the day that Salieri, a strong, handsome black stallion of a man, entered the village and saw Eva bathing, naked, waist-deep in the river. For years, Salieri had gone from village to village selling tinctures and capturing the hearts of many women in fleeting affairs but never had such beauty enamoured him so. He dropped the small brown bottles that were attached by short lengths of string to his staff at the side of the road and leapt from the bridge that crossed the river. Sunlight flicked across the water, giving the illusion that the unknown woman was bathing in liquid gold. From a safe distance, Salieri held his breath and watched her, mesmerized by the water as it trickled down the curve of her spine.

When she was finished, Eva glided up the banks like a goddess reborn and covered her shoulders with a thin red robe before disappearing through the trees.

The following afternoon, Salieri watched the woman picking flowers from her garden—so engrossed in the task at hand that she seemed to have no idea of his presence until he stood behind her and cupped her full breasts in his hands. She'd gasped, and as she moved to turn her head, he whispered in her ear.

"I must know who you are."

"My name is Eva."

"There's something I need you to see."

She'd turned and looked him straight in the eye, and for reasons unknown, agreed to follow him in silence to the shores of the River E. There, they lay on the sandy banks as dark and ominous clouds billowed overhead. Lightning flashed, and Salieri, unable to contain his desire, kissed her hands before tearing at her dress. There was no protest as he rolled on top of her. Eva lifted herself up and gripped his shoulders, letting her head fall back as she closed her eyes. When the rain started, Salieri was all but oblivious to the grape-sized raindrops that pounded his naked buttocks. As the last shudders of pleasure rippled through them both, a bolt of lightning tore through the sky and struck Eva on the shoulder, illuminating her with an unearthly light. Moments later, and refusing death, Eva opened her eyes. But she was not the same — it was as if her mind was half there in the present, and at the same time, far away. Eva pushed Salieri aside, ignoring his bewildered expression as she stood up like nothing had happened. Then, covering her breasts with what she could salvage of the torn fragments of her dress, Eva walked off quietly through the rain.

Salieri could only presume that the lightning had opened Eva's eyes to a strange new world. Because it was only after being struck by lightning that Eva started to sing. Beautiful melodies cascaded from her lips as she ran through the streets of Happysad, proclaiming her allegiance to the light. "Miracles," she said would happen, to which she added, "mostly at night."

Months later, the inmates of the asylums were inspired to meet with Eva at night in the village square. Supervised by the asylum staff and dressed in their white Sunday robes, the inmates carried candles through the streets, some chanting, others hooting like owls. They sang through the night, mesmerized by the patterns of the stars. And despite the growing burden of carrying twins, Eva paraded in front of her followers on a makeshift stage and refused to rest. Her voice floated on the breeze like a delicate ribbon. Wrapped in Eva's spell, the inmates of the asylums spoke in the forgotten language of their souls. A lame woman walked. A mute man spoke. And when the full moon broke free from a bank of clouds, the healing frenzy began. Waves of euphoria surged across the crowd whose hands were waving like tentacles in the air.

When it was over, Eva, exhausted and dripping with sweat, collapsed upon the stage. Silence swept over the crowd as they stood as still as statues in the cold night air. Unwittingly, Eva soaked up what remained of their secret sorrows and fears and fed it umbilically to her helpless, unborn sons.

Completely unaware, Eva slept for the next six days, and Salieri, with his hand on her growing stomach, refused to leave her side. When she finally woke, the crowd—who'd congregated outside her home, patiently waiting for her news—jumped to their feet and cheered. Stories of miracles travelled fast, and Eva's power soared.

When Eva's twins arrived early, it was just past midnight, as she danced and sang before a tireless crowd, unaware that a stream of bloody fluid ran down her legs. Oblivious to her condition and overwhelmed by the potency of her powers, Eva sang on. But when her first boy fell from her womb and lay, naked and bloody in the rain, she stopped, staring at his odd, bulbous-shaped head. The second son arrived eleven minutes later with a thud. The crowd erupted in cheers, and Eva, not quite herself, groaned at the realisation she would have to stop her song. Under black skies and torrential rain, the boys reached up for their mother's hand. But troubled by the feeling that her heart was going to burst, Eva immediately turned away. In the horror of it all, Salieri swooped down and picked up both his sons. He spat at the earth and cursed Eva, who, even before the last large and tattered placenta dropped to the ground, staggered and spun around the stage in a chaotic rapture that only meant one thing—the beautiful woman had lost her mind.

Later, when she regained at least some of her senses, Eva refused to feed her sons for fear of hurting them further. Instead, she sat on the hard floorboards in the dark corner of her hut, rocking back and forth with her knees pulled to her chest while murmuring strange incantations and whispering at the moon.

On the fourth day, seven Parzens arrived and escorted Eva away. Desperate and alone, Salieri fed his sons a tincture of water infused with orange and handed them to a neighbour whose breasts had benevolently fed the village children for years.

Upon news of Eva's arrival, the asylum's cook—a large woman covered in warts—wrung the necks of two geese she had intuitively kept for a special day. Eva arrived in the dark and was taken to a cell with walls lined with the jagged shadows of a dead tree. Shackled to a large, rusted ring on the old stone wall, Eva sat quietly in the corner, accepting her fate without a care. Later, when the door opened, the cook appeared, holding two cooked geese on a silver plate. The scent of oranges filled the cell. Eva looked up and studied her from the shadows.

"Your face?"

"I'm cursed," the cook said, holding up her hand and hiding her eyes. She leaned forward. "For you," she said, presenting the geese.

Eva reached out and touched the cook's hand.

"You have a kind heart." she said, touching the cooks' warts, "And I can help with these."

"I have no money to pay you," the cook said.

Eva looked around the room, the ghost of a smile dancing across her mouth.

"You don't have to pay me," she said. "Freedom is worth more than gold."

Eva took the cook's hands and started to sing. Tears streamed down the cook's face as Eva's words healed her.

At that moment, the cook felt as though the sadness that had clung to her all her life lifted like steam. The cook touched her face and gasped as Eva's song fell away. The warts were gone.

Later that night, when the alarm was raised, the guard unlocked the door to Eva's cell and found her lying motionless on the floor. An evening wind rippled across the nearby lake. The blow to the unsuspecting guard's head came from the shadows behind the door. And whilst Eva never intended for him to die, the cook's strength caught them both by surprise. Eva crept from her cell like a cat on a fence in the night. She left through an open door and hurried towards the village. But when she arrived at her home carrying fresh bunches of flowers and herbs, Salieri and her two baby boys were gone.

The heavy boulder of despair sank in the dark waters of Eva's heart. She broke into her hut and wrapped a chunk of old cheese in a cloth before leaving the village and following the river. When she was stopped by an idle but excitable bunch of girls, they decided to chase her with a stick. Devastated and disarmed, Eva stood still as the girls chanted in time, "The witch is out! The witch is out!"

Within minutes, a crowd gathered, armed with machetes and necklaces of garlic to protect them from Eva's evil spells. When her instincts kicked in, Eva fled, only to find herself pursued hours later by a pack of wild dogs that appeared to be mildly interested in her small chunk of cheese.

Some people said that Eva ran for two whole days before collapsing in the Forest of Calamity and Eternal Darkness. They said she survived on berries and herbs and sampled the fruit of the dumbnut tree. Others claimed she died. Tales of the evil and beautiful spectre of the witch in the woods billowed into legend. Some claimed her voice danced across the treetops frightening the black birds into flight. That was until the day she rode triumphantly from the woods on a sleigh pulled by a pack of demented and cheese-loving dogs. Rumour had it she took refuge in the mountains where, beneath the light of a full moon, she cast evil spells and spread an eternal sadness across the land.

10. THE VALLEY OF THE MARTYRS

Haphazard and much smaller than before, the remaining Procession of Miracles stopped at a drinks stall. The attendant, a monk, and Brother of the Order of Perpetual Denial were fast asleep and snoring softly. One of the donkeys, unable to hold on any longer, snorted and urinated on the brown robes of the sleeping monk, startling him awake as it ran down into his sandals.

"My pilgrims need to drink!" Constance demanded, disregarding his donkey.

"Then they will drink," the monk said, wiping the drool from his face and blinking rapidly.

Pitchers of diluted whisky passed from mouth to mouth, and it was not long before the pilgrims were either drunk or asleep.

With a strange sense of ease and his walls down, images of Stanley's mother crept into his mind, like the pieces of a broken dream trying to become whole. Stanley rubbed at the swelling pains in his chest and repeatedly bit on the mouthpiece of his nummer. Exhausted, he finally closed his eyes and counted his breath.

In long sentences and speaking to anyone who would listen, Blabbermouth sat down and recounted the drama of his life. In particular, his bravery in an incident involving a lizard and the sighting of a witch, which it turned out was no witch-sighting at all, but the shadow of a particularly creepy-looking tree. And he spoke of his partiality to whisky and how, despite moments of overwhelming pain and temptation, he had remained sober for years.

Worse for wear, the Procession of Miracles continued for two days under the relentless heat of the sun. Stanley walked behind Blabbermouth, sufficiently numbed from the repeated overuse of his nummer. He counted his steps one at a time in an attempt to distract himself from the possible onset of madness caused by the rays of the burning sun.

Ahead, night fell upon the Valley of the Martyrs. Stanley, who had lit his torch hours before dark, looked down the dusty road into the valley. Small rolling hills were speckled with wooden crosses. A constellation of small fires flickered and filled the air with the scent of burning cypress.

The procession stopped at the stone gates to the Valley of the Martyrs. A small boy stepped from behind one of the stone pillars. Young and small for his age, he placed his hands on his hips, grimaced, rubbed his eyes, and cried.

Constance, not wanting any trouble, asked him what was wrong. His reply was simple—he was hungry and craving something sweet. Constance turned to the pilgrims, his eyes pleading for one of them to offer up some honey or a date. But the best they could muster up was a stale crust of bread and a half-eaten carrot that Blabbermouth had licked for hours.

"Sweet ice. I want sweet ice!" the boy screeched, clasping his forehead with his hands before throwing himself on the ground.

Moments later, a centurion, wearing a shiny metal helmet with a white feather and dressed in a heavy red cloak despite the heat, arrived at the top of the hill carrying a spear. It was clear to Constance the centurion intended to cause them alarm, and in a pompous tone, the centurion rocked on his heels and looked down his nose as he spoke.

"And why is this boy crying?"

"He wants something sweet," Constance said.

"Hmm," the centurion replied.

He looked at the boy who by this time was lying face-down in a lather of dust and tears, his small fists beating against the earth. The boy stopped crying as though realising there was no sweet ice to be had. He looked up at the centurion. "It's your fault too," he declared before poking out his tongue and taking off down the hill and out of view.

Stanley looked at the centurion; the centurion looked at Blabbermouth and then turned to face Constance. He tightened his grip on his spear. "Well then," he said, "by the looks of things, you had better come with me."

The Valley of the Martyrs was bathed in a mix of purple shadows and orange light. All was quiet except for the sound of guilty snores and stories of regret whispered around campfires whose fragrant smoke prevented most spectators from falling asleep.

Despite being an arduous pursuit, the business of being a martyr was booming. Mostly, the martyrs lived as long as anybody else, as it was considered bad practice for any of them to use nails. Of itself, the lack of nails had never raised questions with the hordes of spectators who travelled from far and wide to watch the martyrs bind themselves with rubber rings and hang on home-made crosses in the sun.

By the time the Procession of Miracles reached the foothills of the valley, the martyrs were packing up for the day. Mostly in foul moods, sunburned and resentful about what their lives had become, the crucified untied themselves and, aided by an elaborate system of pulleys and ropes, lowered themselves to the ground. The martyrs gathered the dead flowers and crusts of stale bread left at their feet and complained because, as usual, most of them were intolerant to gluten and were facing another night of hunger and broken sleep. Driven by pains in their bellies, the martyrs strode into the village in the valley, searching for something better to eat.   Behind them, the landscape of empty crosses faded into the night.

Salieri, the quiet and self-proclaimed Captain of the Martyrs, was, after a long day in the sun, seated at his desk and rubbing a balm of beeswax and camphor into his wounds. He cursed at the dancing and flickering of the candle flame as though it intentionally made it hard for him to see. Outside the Captain's tent, a centurion, who had watched over him patiently for years, waited for something—anything—to happen. And when it did, he cleared his throat to get his master's attention.

"What now?" Salieri asked, not looking up.

"Travellers, sir," the centurion replied.

Preoccupied with the cracks on his bleeding heels, Salieri raised one eyebrow and kept searching for the best angle to apply the healing balm. "Take down their names and stop bothering me," he replied.

"It's the Procession of Miracles," the centurion stated.

Salieri slammed the small wooden tub of balm on the desk and looked up.

"How many this year?"

"Less than last year, sir," the centurion replied.

"A number, Centurion?" Salieri asked.

"Not sure, sir."

Salieri sighed. "Well, count them, feed them, water the donkeys, and arrange somewhere for them to sleep." He paused, sensing an opportunity, then added, "And charge them double because it's dark, and they are late."

The centurion nodded and walked backwards out of the tent.

Outside, Constance was busy picking fleas from behind one of his donkey's ears as the centurion approached.

"It'll cost double," he declared.

"Double?" Constance growled.

"It's dark. You know the rules," the centurion replied.

Annoyed, Constance mused that if it weren't for the monkey boy, then the procession would not be late. The blood rushed to his face, and he considered that he wanted nothing more than to bathe in the cool waters of the brook that cut the Valley of the Martyrs in two. Constance moved from behind the donkeys and counted nineteen pilgrims plus the monkey boy.

In the beginning, there were thirty thought as he handed the centurion four gold pieces.

Then, with a wave of his hand, the centurion looked into the distance as if issuing orders to an army. All right then," he said, "Come this way."

He led the procession down a narrow alley filled with puddles from night-time rain. When they arrived at the small city of tents, the monkey boy took to pulling at the ropes of the flimsy shelters as he passed them by. The residents of the valley cursed as their canopies collapsed. And it was hours before the remaining lunatics in the procession stopped pulling at the ropes to which they had been tied—and in the end, they gave up, stopped their struggle, looked up, and howled at the moon.

When the pilgrims retired to their tents, Blabbermouth stayed outside. Alone beside the fire, he couldn't sleep. No matter how much he tried to think about other things, the guilt from the valley seeped in. It lassoed his mind, and he realised that the pain felt by the martyrs who tied themselves to pieces of wood in the burning sun was all his fault.

Stanley, overwhelmed with a wave of guilt he'd never felt before, started scratching nervously at his neck. The image of his father popped into his mind—there he was, standing in the doorway and shaking his fist, reminding Stanley how everything that went wrong was all his fault. Stanley tried to shake it off, and when that didn't work, he threw his empty nummer out across the tops of the tents. In the distance, someone shrieked. Itching and agitated, Stanley marched to Constance's tent. He pulled back the curtain and demanded that the procession continues on its way.

But Constance, who was far too drunk to make sense of anything at all, replied, "I can assure you, that's one miracle we won't see today."

For years, Salieri managed the commerce of the valley by renting out tents and selling small, glass, pyramid-shaped pendants. Over time, it occurred to those who visited the valley and never left that the pendants, while precious, were impractical because the hole in the middle was only big enough to hold a single tear. The idea for the pendant had occurred to Salieri on the last day of happiness in his life. Nursing two crying sons and stroking Eva's feverish brow, he watched as her tears slipped down his wrists and into an old metal bucket that cocky male cats used as a convenient place to pee. Inspired, he decided to collect Eva's tears. And later that day, he confirmed their magical qualities when he rubbed the teardrops into his sons' cheeks, and they instantly fell asleep.

After Eva fled, Salieri stayed in Happysad with his sons. He sold small glass pendants that seemed to change colour according to the state of the wearer's heart. Joy turned the pendants pink, sadness turned them blue, and it was not long before news of the pendants spread across the land, and their power grew. The pendants became talismans of fortune and luck and were bestsellers, almost overnight.

In the season of guilt, which was most of the time, the faithful flocked to the Valley of the Martyrs. They stood in lines, holding their pendants in the hope of bottling one of the martyr's single, sad, and precious tears. At night, the pilgrims sat around the campfires with their pendants around their necks, feeling guilty and worse than ever before.

But the die of Salieri's destiny was cast the day he watched the children with their sticks chase his beloved Eva away. Forcing the memory from his mind, he swallowed hard and looked the other way. In his heart, he wanted to follow Eva up into the hills. But as he held his crying sons to his chest, he discarded his desire and surrendered to the weight of responsibility. He vowed never again to think of Eva bathing naked in the lake or the comfort of her whisper in his ear when he couldn't sleep. Salieri kissed his sons' bald heads, knowing this was where he would have to stay.

The final straw for Salieri's wounded heart came years later when his older son took to wandering off into the desert for days. Searching for something better to occupy his mind, his son grew obsessed and constantly muttered about visions of a black dog with a red rubber ball.

Then one morning, Salieri woke to find him gone, and doing the only thing he could think of at the time, he tied a thick rope around the neck of his other son. He led him from the village like a dog, along the winding road, blinded by the strange light of the dying day. Almost a week later, they arrived, dusty and dispirited, at the Valley of the Martyrs. And staring into a campfire of broken dreams, Salieri declared, for better or worse, that this was where they both would stay.

Every day, before first light, the martyrs dragged themselves from sleep. Their faces to the ground and with the slow gait of the sick, they shuffled to their personal wooden cross, where all being well, they would hang for the day.

The crowd, who mostly never slept, already lined the sides of the road. They reached out to touch the naked, nicely tanned, and skinny body of their chosen saint, only to receive a poke from the spears of the cranky centurions.

When the first rays of light shot across the valley, a cock crowed. The martyr whose turn it was to be the first to perform that day happened to be a small man on a small cross. Wearing a crown of flowers, he started to moan, opened his eyes, and looked across the crowd with a vacant stare. But despite having rehearsed his look for years, sometimes it worked, and sometimes it did not.

The crowd moaned.

On the inside, the martyr smiled. Buoyed by his apparent success, the martyr spoke to the crowd. "It's okay. It's not your fault. Don't worry about me. You go off and have a nice breakfast. I'll just be here, waiting in the hot sun...without water." On cue, he let the tears roll down his cheeks before turning his head to one side. "Can anybody spare me a sponge?"

A young woman raced to the base of the small cross and sponged his feet with cool water from a bucket hanging from the crook of her arm.

"Thank you," he said, "but the pain is unbearable. Help me. Please. Can anyone help me?"

The crowd was silent—all except for the woman at the base of the cross, who wept tears of guilt because she didn't know what to do.

"It's our fault," a young man called out from the crowd.

"No," the martyr said. "The fault is mine. I suffer for you. Go. Live your lives. Be happy. Be free."

The crowd sobbed beneath the gravity of the martyr's words.

"Let us help you," someone shouted.

"There is nothing for me now," the martyr said, "only death."

Many of the women, who made up at least half of the crowd, dropped to their knees and spoke, "We will do anything."

The martyr opened one eye and peered at the crowd that seemed to heave with sadness and guilt. "Anything?" he whispered through cracked lips.

"Anything," chorused the crowd.

"Well, if you must do something, I wouldn't mind a cup of tea. And maybe some sausage. I really wouldn't mind a piece of sausage," he whimpered pathetically.

There was a flurry of activity as a small group of women left, mortified for having not considered the martyr's needs sooner. The others remained.

Just after midday, their attention was diverted by the tragedy of another martyr struggling up a nearby hill. Bruno, an ox of a man, was dragging a large, heavy oak cross that had been dipped in burning tar for effect.

Three years earlier, Bruno had embarked on the Procession of Miracles, hoping to reclaim his memory, erased by one too many beatings from his father. After three long years in the Valley of the Martyrs, he received the title of "Martyr of the Month." With bleeding feet from stepping on sharp stones and broken glass, he kept his eyes downcast. Dragging himself along the rocky road, Bruno slowly climbed the mount where he hoisted himself up onto his black cross and bound his arms with rubber rings.

Wanting to feel worse, the crowd left the smaller martyr to watch Bruno, who, after some slight adjustments, hung in the right place. A hush swept over the crowd, and even the feral dogs that fought over a dead bird stopped to hear the massive man speak.

"Don't worry about me," he said. "I am not worthy of your pity."

"Oh, you are perfect," a young woman shouted from the crowd. "It is we who are not fit to see you suffer."

"If only I were good enough," Bruno continued. "Then you could love me. No. Strike that. I will never be worthy of your love."

The crowd heaved. For effect, Bruno added, "I am nothing."

He looked up and embraced the crowd with his puppy-like brown eyes. "My struggle will soon be over," he said.

"No," Blabbermouth called out, captivated by the martyr's control.

Stanley, agitated by the display, elbowed Blabbermouth's side and itched at the red scaly rash that had spread to his neck.

"Shhh," someone in the crowd called out.

"No, speak. Speak," Bruno said, through cracked lips and a dry mouth.

Salieri, whose job it was to maximise the profits of the valley, stood on a small wooden box with folded arms at the back of the crowd. He raised his left hand slowly in the air and gestured a thumb of approval. Bruno saw Salieri from the corner of his eye.

Invigorated, Bruno went on, "Your children are hungry. Look after them. Go, be safe and forget about me up here in the burning sun."

Mesmerised by the martyr's words, the crowd started to leave the mount. One by one, they walked to the base of the cross and placed silver coins and morsels of food in the martyr's wooden bowl. Bruno stopped talking. He let his head droop slightly to one side.

When the crowd was mostly dispersed, and Bruno was too thirsty to speak, his mood changed. He pressed his fingers into his arm, and, realising he was sunburnt once again, he cursed. He swore at the centurion who helped himself to a tip from the martyr's bowl. And he cursed at the fact that, other than his name, he still couldn't remember very much at all.

Bruno raised his head to the sky. It started to rain.

Later, Stanley stood beside Blabbermouth, who was shaking his nummer in the dark street. People passed by, pretending not to notice the strange animal with the strange device.

"It's stopped working," Blabbermouth said.

"It's probably empty," Stanley replied.

"Well, then I'll need another because, without it, I won't survive this place."

Stanley looked at his reflection in the side of the empty nummer. His rash had spread.

"There's only one nummer left," he yelled at Blabbermouth.

"Then give it to me," Blabbermouth said as he started to cry.

Stanley's frustration rocketed into a rage. "Stop crying," he shouted at Blabbermouth. "You are useless, and I have to go."

"Well, you don't know where to go, and you will get lost, and your nummer will run out, and you will have to feel everything everybody feels, so how about that!" Blabbermouth blubbered.

Stanley felt a lifetime of trapped rage bubbling beneath the surface. Like lava, it started rising, threatening to erupt. The taste of bitter almonds filled his mouth, and his body started shaking. He sneezed and, not knowing what else to do, pulled on the cord from his last nummer and placed the mouthpiece in his mouth.

That was when One-Eyed Jack, who'd witnessed everything, stepped from the shadows. Whilst no one knew the exact reason for his missing eye, some said he had poked it out with a stick to make other people feel bad; others said it didn't matter because the clairvoyant abilities inherited from his mother produced visions far more valuable than sight. Wearing the long brown waterproof coat of a thief, One-Eyed Jack survived by eavesdropping on visitors and doing dirty deals in dark alleys. He drew hard on an aromatic cigarette and stared through a ribbon of smoke.

"Is there a problem?" he asked, releasing a puff of smoke through stained yellow teeth.

Shocked by the idea of everything he imagined to be lurking in the dark, Stanley stepped back.

"Ah, nothing, we are fine…best be off…getting dark. We don't really like the dark, and there's lots to do," Blabbermouth said.

One-Eyed Jack moved closer, squinting at Blabbermouth.

138

"Well, what do you know?" he said. "I haven't seen a bog in years."

Stanley watched as Blabbermouth seemed to tremble with fear as he tried to put Stanley between himself and the stranger.

"Interesting," One-Eyed Jack said. "Bog's teeth used to fetch a pretty price."

"Yes, well, we best be off," Blabbermouth said, letting out a nervous hiss as he bared his single front tooth.

"And what about you?" One-Eyed Jack said, turning to Stanley.

"Me?" Stanley said, spitting out the mouthpiece of the nummer.

"Yes, you. I might have only one eye, but I can see further than any man, and your eyes speak of trouble. Yes, it's clearer now. You're looking for something."

Stanley swallowed hard.

"Well, now that you mention it," Blabbermouth interrupted, "we could do with some directions."

"Shhh," Stanley said, but it was too late.

"Ah, directions," mumbled One-Eyed Jack. "Especially if you are running out of time."

"How do you know?" Stanley asked.

"How do I know?" One-Eyed Jack said.

Excited, Blabbermouth cut in, "We're having an adventure, and we are going to save someone's life when we find what we need to find."

Stanley looked around. They were standing on an empty street with nowhere to hide.

One-Eyed Jack placed one hand on his hip, and Stanley saw the glint of his larger than necessary knife. "Safety is the most important thing," One-Eyed Jack said with a menacing smile. His glass eye, which was made from a misshapen old piece of green glass, rolled to one side.

Blabbermouth shuddered.

"Quick, we'd better go," he whispered to Stanley. "He can't be trusted, and I don't like his green eye."

"Do you think you will make it out of here alive?" asked One-Eyed Jack.

"What do you want?" Stanley asked.

One-Eyed Jack reached behind his large shiny knife and into a small brown leather pouch.

"Well," he said. "For the payment of three gold coins, you can have one of these and be safely on your way."

One-Eyed Jack held up a pyramid-shaped glass pendant.

"Give him the gold coins," Stanley ordered Blabbermouth.

"No," Blabbermouth protested. "They're from my brother."

Stanley lunged forward and ripped the coins from Blabbermouth's hand and pushed him to the ground.

"Here," Stanley said, handing One-Eyed Jack the three gold coins.

"It's the best way," said One-Eyed Jack, closing his coat and hiding his knife.

"I suggest you fill it with a martyr's tear," he said handing the pendant to Stanley.

"What for?"

"For luck," said One-Eyed Jack. "And then, of course, there's the lizards and the owls..."

In the early hours of the morning and when it was still dark, a commotion started when the monkey boy began squealing and yanking on his rope. Ordinarily, the disruption from his sleep would make Constance irritated—but he was in the midst of a particular dream that seemed only to visit him when he ate too much cheese. In the dream, he was reclining on a bed of cushions as a beautiful black woman fed him sweet purple grapes. For reasons unknown to him, the dream always left

Constance feeling calm, and he dragged himself from his tent and slapped the monkey boy, who was hopping and pointing at Stanley and Blabbermouth as they walked away in the dark. Annoyed but curious, Constance followed the pilgrims out of the village, dragging the monkey boy behind him with the rope tied around his neck.

Having never taken the procession beyond the Valley of the Martyrs, it occurred to Constance that the pilgrims must be lost. But as he walked, he was aware of a feeling of dread spiralling in his gut as he had never really given much thought to what lay beyond the camp. Constance yanked hard on his rope and kept the monkey boy close. The path narrowed. The morning air seemed to thicken, making it harder to breathe.

In the distance and far from the other martyrs, a single cross stood on a smaller hill. A sense of sadness unfurled along the overgrown path, like a tongue. Already agitated, Blabbermouth squeezed his fingers in knots and muttered a string of curses at Stanley under his breath.

"Hey," Constance called out to the pilgrims ahead. "Where are you going? And why is that martyr out in the night?" He couldn't tell if the pilgrims heard him or even if they answered, as he called out again. "It's against the rules, you know!"

Ahead, the sinewy shadow of the lone martyr cut across the side of the hill. Constance coughed nervously, dragging the monkey boy a little closer.

As they neared, they heard a whimpering sound, and the monkey-boy stopped pulling against the rope. When Constance caught up to the pilgrims, he stood just behind Stanley, who had stopped beside Blabbermouth at the foot of the cross. Above, the martyr hung by his wrists. In the place of the martyr's usual rubber rings was a tangle of rusty nails.

141

Stanley stared at the martyr's feet that were crossed at the ankles and black with the stains of old blood. The monkey boy squawked, baring his teeth and running in circles until the rope tightened around his neck, and he turned blue.

Eight feet up, the lone martyr flinched at the sound. The first ray of morning light cut across his face. Up until then, he had drifted in and out of sleep and was quite unaware of his first visitors in years. He lifted his head slightly and muttered something through cracked and swollen lips. Slowly, his lifeless and bloodshot eyes opened wide. One was green, the other brown.

When Stanley looked up, the voice of reason—that kept everything in his mind exactly where it was supposed to be—detached. It faded away, replaced by a sudden silence, and as Stanley saw the emptiness in the martyr's eyes, he recognised it as his own. One by one, his bottled feelings welled within him. They attached to his thoughts and started shaping stories about everything his numbness was supposed to hide. Stanley sneezed. His mind started spinning. And when his e-reader blinked red, he smashed his wrist against the ground. Mesmerised by the martyr's eyes, Stanley felt himself falling into the black hole of despair, and as his mind spun and tumbled, his thoughts gathered speed, and his numbness peeled away. Stanley coughed. Then he started to choke.

Kissing the silver pendant of an eagle that hung around his neck, Constance stepped forward and slapped Stanley on the back. Blabbermouth howled in horror. The monkey boy, gasping for air, opened his mouth in the shape of a big and silent "O." Certain that they had looked into the eyes of the angel of death, the party of four scampered down the hill. But

142

it was no use because whenever they blinked, the image of the lone martyr was etched into their minds—looking out with his two-toned eyes and poisoning them with his despair.

Finally safe in the village of the tents, Constance tried to replace the image of the martyr with the memory of the black woman in his dream. But when that didn't work, he filled himself with nuts and dates, took a deep breath, and blew into his horn. The remaining pilgrims who had waited for him since before dawn formed a jagged line. Flustered, Constance yanked on the donkey's reins and cursed with words they didn't understand. When he cracked his whip, the chariot with the big brass eagle rolled forward, leading the pilgrims along the narrow road that led upwards and out of the valley. Morning sunlight settled on the hills, and in the distance, the mountain peaks were frozen and covered with snow.

Constance loosened the rope around the monkey boy's neck and then, not wanting to be alone, lifted him into the chariot with the big brass eagle. Confused, the monkey boy sat in silence and watched the wheels as they turned and bumped along the rocky road.

It was not long before the few remaining pilgrims fell out of line. Further back, Blabbermouth cursed Stanley to distract himself from the memory of the martyr's eyes.

In the event Constance ever delivered a pilgrim to the Villa of the Stony Crag, his bonus would equal his following year's fees. Closer to success than ever before, Constance held the donkey's reins tight. And as the chariot with the big brass eagle gathered speed, Constance was quietly overcome with a shallow wave of optimism.

Could this be the year?

He imagined what he would do if it were—how he would never stop searching for the black woman who visited him in his dream and whom he was convinced was real.

The donkeys trotted at a merry pace. When they reached the base of the mountains, the road narrowed and veered to the right. Centuries-old, the path to the Stony Crag was paved with moss-covered, slippery black stones. The donkeys sniffed the air, and with a dark determination in their eyes, took off up the winding path. Unnerved, Constance pulled hard on the reins, but it was no use. The chariot sped up the hill, tilting and bumping and sliding across the stones. The road narrowed further still.

At first, Stanley chased the chariot but was quickly left behind. Further back, Blabbermouth walked with his legs slightly crossed, trying not to think about how much he needed to pee. As the chariot with the big brass eagle skidded across the stones, the wheels started to crack. Intoxicated by the speed, the monkey boy jumped up and down, screeching and screaming and pulling at Constance's hair. Instinctively, Constance let go of the reins and slapped the monkey boy's face. Suddenly free, the donkeys darted to the side, lifting the chariot up on one wheel and out of control. It was a small, sharp stone that caused the left wheel of the chariot to break free. The other wheel wobbled, came loose, and hurtled through the air. Then, the chariot skidded across the icy road, causing the monkey boy to scream louder, excited at the thrill in his stomach that somehow felt like falling.

The chariot with the big brass eagle broke apart. The donkeys hee-hawed, panicked, and pulled to get away, and losing their grip, they slid sideways off the mountain. Almost flying, the donkeys pedalled in time, dragging the broken

144

chariot with the big brass eagle through the air. The monkey boy's eyes opened wide, while Constance closed his, as it occurred to him, he would never meet the black woman of his dreams. Moments later, a splinter of wood from the shattered axle of the chariot shot up and stabbed Constance through the heart. Shocked, the monkey boy screeched louder. That was until his skull struck the hard ground, and his neck snapped like a tiny twig.

From a distance, Stanley saw it all. He itched at the red rash on his neck and started counting. Gripped by the fist of horror unlike anything he'd felt before, he careened over and vomited across the icy road.

Blabbermouth, who had stopped to pee, caught up, covered his mouth, and started heaving at the smell.

"Ugh, if I smell vomit, then I'll be sick. That's disgusting. Stop it, Stanley," he said.

And unable to say a word, Stanley continued counting inside his head… "781, 782, 783…"

11. BRIGHTSPARK

Despite all the exciting stories, in the end, most agreed that Brightspark was, in fact, the piece of a passing comet that had broken off and tumbled into the Woods of Calamity and Eternal Darkness. The Master, after considering all the information gathered by the owls, had decided that Brightspark was:

1. Not magical in any way.
2. The perfect source of power for his invention–The Sanitis-Or.

Getting a hold of Brightspark was another thing. For as long as anyone could remember, the Parzens at the Villa of the Stony Crag had dutifully guarded Brightspark. The Master—who had always found the Parzens unnerving with their mysterious ways—had never tried to steal Brightspark himself, just in case the superstitions surrounding the crystal were true.

Yet that didn't stop him from pondering what would happen if he did — for secretly, The Master had always wanted to return to the land that he loved as a little boy.

Powered by Brightspark, the Sanitis-Or would whir to life and send its broad and exceptionally harmful laser net across the whole of Happysad. In an instant, everyone would be protected from the harmful rays of the sun and feel the blissful numbness that came from feeling nothing at all.

Triumphant, The Master would then walk along Happysad's silent streets. He would sit on a plastic chair beneath the shade of the plantations and look out across the River E., and he would feel nothing. Nothing at all.

High in the mountains and far from the shores of the River E, the Villa of the Stony Crag was mostly hidden by mist and the sticky humidity of the intermittent rain. The villa itself was in ruins, partly destroyed by hailstones the size of boulders. However, on a rare and sunny day, the outline of the Stony Crag looked like it was etched onto the horizon, like something drawn by a shaky hand. The rest of the time it was invisible, hidden in the lingering fog. Six thousand feet above the sea, the air was thin and caused light-headedness in anyone who dared to travel so far. Known as the spiritual home of the Parzens, the Villa was a place where pilgrims came to learn the ancient art of levitation — and as if this wasn't enough, they were seekers of a peaceful state that placed them somewhere between feeling happy and sad. Seekers of the middle path, the Parzens, kept mostly to themselves. Yet if anyone were ever to ask, they would willingly discuss the euphoria they achieved through starvation, exposure to the cold, and a lack of sleep.

At the age of seven, and not having eaten for weeks, initiates were blindfolded and spun in circles. Completely disorientated and incapable of a single logical thought, they were taken deep into the heart of the Villa of the Stony Crag and sat before a small white crystal that was kept in the centre of a circle of truth—a circle which happened to be drawn on the ground with white chalk. Mounted on a black marble plinth, Brightspark's brilliant light burst from the small windows of the chamber. At night, it shot illuminated silver beams of light deep into space, and in the language of the stars, which was mostly misunderstood and misinterpreted, Brightspark's message was clear.

Help!

When they reached the summit, Stanley and Blabbermouth stood motionless as waves of fog rolled across the Stony Crag. Blabbermouth jumped and elbowed Stanley, causing him to startle. And when Stanley glanced back at him, he could have sworn Blabbermouth was staring at something through the fog. "What? What can you see?" Stanley asked.

Blabbermouth didn't move his gaze from the fog as he answered. "There's something small and grey with horns. First, it was there; now it's gone."

Stanley frowned as he watched Blabbermouth's tongue flick back and forward over his single front tooth. "See that?" Blabbermouth said.

"What?"

"The goat."

"What goat?"

"Right there," Blabbermouth said, pointing into the mist.

"There's no goat," Stanley said, yet he could feel his heart racing, as though his senses knew something his mind refused to accept.

"I can't breathe," Blabbermouth said, his voice shaking with terror as he stepped behind Stanley. He closed his eyes and bit down hard on the mouthpiece of his nummer. Moving slowly forwards, Stanley thought he heard what sounded like a door creaking on a rusty hinge. After a few steps, he glimpsed an old wooden door opening onto a dimly lit, rectangular room. Despite Blabbermouth clutching at the leg of his pants, Stanley moved forward, through the door, and inside towards the middle of the room. It was then they both saw the skinny and mostly naked man sitting with his legs crossed and his eyes closed. He appeared to hover a few feet above the ground.

"Hello?" Stanley called out.

There was no answer.

"What are you doing in there?" asked Stanley.

The skinny man lifted his hands from where they rested on his knees and raised them over his head. "A-a-almost levitating," he stuttered.

"What do you mean, almost?" Stanley asked.

"M-m-magnets," he replied. "I've always had a thing for m-m-magnets. C-c-come closer, and you will see," he said, pointing to the large iron plate strapped to his buttocks. "The m-m-mountain is full of magnets. Get the polarity right, and it works a t-t-treat. I don't need a cushion, and it's g-g-great for haemorrhoids. I've discovered it's b-b-better to be floating—it a-a-alters the brainwaves and h-helps me f-f-forget about the cold." The man lowered his hands, leaving them resting loosely in his lap as he spoke.

"Y-you are here to see B-B-Brightspark?" he stuttered.

"How do you know?" asked Stanley, guarded.

"Why else would you c-c-climb the Stony C-C-Crag? And by the way, it's m-m-much easier on the w-way down."

Hearing movement behind him, Stanley glanced back to see Blabbermouth shuffle closer. Sheepishly and wide-eyed, Blabbermouth's eyes fixed on the floating man in the middle of the room. As though unable to understand how the man happened not to be sitting on the ground, he asked, "Any chance of something to eat—an apple or a carrot, perhaps? I'm famished. I see you have a goat. So maybe you have some cheese?"

"You saw the g-g-goat?" said the floating man. "It's b-b-been missing in the f-f-fog for years." The floating man raised his right hand and clicked his fingers, and a small arched door opened in the wall.

A boy dressed in a thin brown robe tied at the hip with a frayed rope entered. "Yes, teacher?"

There was a pause as the floating man stared off into space, as though his thoughts were elsewhere before the boy cleared his throat.

"My apologies. I was m-m-momentarily distracted by a passing thought about cheese. He settled his hands in a position of prayer in front of his chest. "How rude of me. Let me i-introduce myself. My name is F-F-Freeman, and I am the keeper of B-B-Brightspark."

Blabbermouth bowed, whispering under his breath, "Please, no witches; let there not be witches."

Stanley gave him a quick tap with his foot, sending Blabbermouth upright again. "What is wrong with your voice?" Blabbermouth asked the floating man. "It sounds weird, and you're hard to understand. Might you want to see someone about that? In fact, I know someone in the plantations. It's amazing what they can do..."

150

"T-t-take the bog and give him food," Freeman said to the boy, ignoring the bog's remark. "And s-s-see if you can find the g-g-goat."

The boy nodded, bowed, and beckoned Blabbermouth to join him across the room before leading him through the arched door without so much as a look back.

"A-as for you," Freeman said to Stanley, "B-B-Brightspark is through the Other D-d-door."

In the far corner of the room was a larger door that seemed to materialise out of nowhere. Above it was a sign that read "Other Door."

"Just like that?" Stanley asked.

"A-a-almost," said Freeman. "Y-you've travelled this far. D-d-do you have a question?"

"Yes," said Stanley.

"B-b-b-best to be sure," Freeman said, "otherwise your m-m-message w-won't make sense. All you will g-g-get is more c-c-confusion and despair. E-e-everything will seem w-worse than it was b-b-before." Freeman paused, tilting his head to the side as he peered at Stanley. "S-s-so, what do you w-want to know?"

"I'm not telling you," Stanley said.

"O-only trying to h-help," said Freeman. "Because y-you must ask the right q-q-question." Still hovering above the ground, Freeman looked around the room. He started bobbing up and down like a cork on the sea. "W-well, that's th-th-that then," he said.

Stanley thanked the floating man, picked up the bag he had placed on the floor, and walked towards the Other Door made from wood and unremarkable in any way.

Inside the middle chamber, it looked to Stanley as if there was no way out. Lined with a seamless, shiny metal sheet, the walls were smooth and stretched upwards as far as the eye could see. A pillar of light shot downwards from a hole in the top of the chamber. In the centre of the room was a white marble staircase that spiralled around an enormous, black, five-sided plinth.

I suppose Brightspark's up there?

Bolted to the wall beside the first step was a wooden box with a small hole in the top. On the front was a small sign with an arrow pointing up the stairs that read,

This way to the crystal. Donations welcome.

Stanley cautiously climbed up the stairs as light danced across the metal walls of the chamber. Feeling dizzy as he ascended the spiral, Stanley counted his steps and tried to ignore the awkward, heavy sensation inside his chest.

Below, Stanley heard a door close, followed by what sounded like footsteps climbing after him. With one hand on his chest and the other braced against the wall, he continued circling the plinth until, finally, he found himself blinded by a dazzling light and a gentle humming sound.

Brightspark.

Balanced on the razor-sharp point of the black plinth and shaped like an egg, the crystal was not much larger than a fist. The funnel of light streaming from the top of the chamber seemed to be the cause of the hum. Brightspark balanced on the point of the plinth like a sleeping bird standing on one leg. Beside the crystal was a stone bench with a red cushion and just in front of that was a small console with a black button. Inscribed on the bench were the words,

Only ask the question if you're ready for the answer.

Stanley sat on the cushion and caught his breath. He eyed off the small black button before reaching out and pushing it. Far above him, the canopy of the chamber slid closed. Everything went black, and Brightspark started pulsing with a brilliant blue light. The pompous-sounding voice of a middle-aged woman filled the chamber.

"Welcome traveller. All you need to do is ask your question. Focus on Brightspark, and you will receive your answer. We apologise for any delays caused by sunspot activity or other interstellar interruptions. Be patient, remain calm, and keep quiet. Please be advised we take no responsibility for the answer, and be sure to leave some money in the box on your way out because nothing is free."

There was a slight pause, then the voice continued. "In the end, you will have exactly seven minutes to exit the chamber — that is, if you can find the door. Thank you for visiting Brightspark and have a pleasant day."

Without any further thought, Stanley asked his question, "How can I save Delia from the Virus? The Virus Called Dog?"

He stared at Brightspark, focusing his attention on it with everything he had. When nothing happened, he looked around the room and started counting. On the count of four, Brightspark started humming. It spun on its axis, shining a kaleidoscope of speckled light around the room.

A man's voice replaced the woman's. "Hoh, hoh, hoh, hoh, hoh," he laughed, haughtily, sounding like someone who knew a lot about many things but on this particular subject, knew nothing at all.

"Well?" Stanley asked.

"Ssssshhhhhhh!" hissed the voice.

Moments later, an impressive show of lights filled the chamber. Overhead, the canopy slid open and filled the room with the single white light that was there at the start. A bell chimed, and Stanley looked up. A small, white, rectangular piece of paper floated down towards him, sweeping from side to side like a feather. Stanley reached up and plucked it from the air and noticed that it was folded in the shape of a duck. When he opened it, the words were scrawled across the paper, looking like the handwriting of a small child.

Only Delia can save herself. Right now, she is the least of your concerns.

Stanley read the words again and called to the top of the chamber. "What? That makes no sense!"

The man's voice, now sounding irritated and not like a recording at all, replied, "No loud noises. Shh! Be quiet."

"Huh?" said Stanley. "Delia's losing her mind. I have to save her!"

It was then that the recording of the woman's voice returned. "Thank you for stopping by. We trust you're satisfied with your answer. Have a nice day—and don't forget to leave some money in the box on your way out!"

Unable to stop his frustration, Stanley screamed. Stabbing pains seized his joints, and he doubled over.

"Master?" a voice called from behind.

Blabbermouth, in a lather of saliva and sweat, was sitting on the marble stairs.

"I feel much better now because I had something to eat— they have vintage goat's cheese marinated in secret herbs—and they said you had gone up the stairs and even though I'm finding it hard to breathe, I am here, and I heard noises. And by the way, apparently, the boy found the goat in the fog...Anyway, did you get your answer? Tell me what Brightspark said."

"Shut up!" Stanley screamed at the bog, his voice maniacal and loud.

Blabbermouth stepped back, his mouth slack and his eyes wide.

Stanley picked up his backpack with the sudden urge to hurl it at Blabbermouth when his intentions were disrupted by a clinking, followed by what sounded like the sharpening of knives coming from the walls. Long sword-like blades started extending across the stairs.

The woman's voice returned, counting down. "Four minutes," she said politely.

"Run!" Stanley yelled.

"Yes, good idea," said Blabbermouth. "Run."

Feeling cheated, Stanley pulled Brightspark from the tip of the plinth. He started down the stairs, jumping and dodging the tips of the swords.

"Wait, master, that's stealing. It's not a good idea," Blabbermouth declared as he bounded down the stairs after him. "Wait for me!"

The chamber filled with flashing red lights. Alarms sounded. Sirens wailed.

A burst of mustard-coloured gas invaded the stale air. Stanley and Blabbermouth took a deep breath as the woman's voice continued counting down. And as the fugitives neared the bottom of the spiral stairs, her tone changed. She now sounded more like a child whose lollipop has been taken away. "Bother. No. Wait. You seem to have made a terrible mistake. Stop! Put it back. *Put Brightspark back!*"

Aided by magnets and floating far above worldly concern, if there was one thing that could upset Freeman, it was the theft of Brightspark. Mostly for practical reasons, any such disruption could not be tolerated. At the precise moment Stanley pulled Brightspark from the black plinth, the lights of the villa went out. The current of electricity that had boosted

155

the polarity of Freeman's magnets stopped, and he crashed to the stony ground with a thud. For twenty years, three months, and eleven days, Freeman had spent most of his time with his eyes closed, but when he struck the cold floor, he was forced to face the outside world again. He tried to pick himself up off the ground, but his legs were weak, and he fell back down. After a couple of deep breaths, Freeman lay on his side and recited something similar to "Om." But it was no good. The harder he strived for calm, the more agitated he became, cursing his stupidity at not being more prepared for the likelihood of thieves.

A collection of old memories flooded Freeman's mind. In the days before his success with magnets, Freeman was a technician with a good brain and a promising future. A colleague of The Master was Freeman, who helped design the plans for Mentoria. But on the day the construction of the great city began, the reality of the project was too much for Freeman to bear. Convinced it would never really work due to a lack of power, Freeman stepped aside. The following morning, naked as the day he was born, Freeman left the plantations of Happysad for good. He set course for the mountains on a pilgrim's diet of water, berries, air, and leaves. But never good with directions, he got hopelessly lost and stumbled, starving and delirious into the Woods of Eternal Calamity and Darkness.

That night, freezing and close to death, Freeman stopped beneath the trunk of a large tree that grew beside a lake in the centre of the woods. No one heard him scream when he opened his eyes and was confronted by the inquisitive face of a luminous alien with large beady eyes and a big, bald head. The alien who communicated in the language of thought asked quite politely if Freeman knew how to fix spaceships. But before

Freeman could answer, the alien continued to share its story of what it considered to be a stroke of bad luck when, years earlier, whilst searching for the most absurd thing in the universe, its spaceship crashed. Astonished and not knowing what else to say, Freeman shook his head from side to side.

With the sudden courage of someone who thinks they're about to die, Freeman blurted that he was quite good with electricity. The alien replied that electricity was of no use because its spaceship had sunk to the bottom of the lake. What it needed was someone more mechanically minded, someone more practised at pulling things out of deep water. Then seizing the opportunity and sensing the skinny man was no help at all, the alien reached out its luminous hand and touched Freeman on the chest. Stealing the last crumbs of peace and quiet from Freeman's heart and feeling better than before, the alien strutted off quietly into the woods.

The following morning, not quite dead, Freeman opened his eyes and found a small posy of white flowers sitting on his chest. A woman of exquisite beauty with long black hair the colour of coal was cradling his head in her hands. She spoke softly and stroked her finger across his lips. The woman hummed an ethereal tune, and Freeman closed his eyes, assuming that she was the angel of death despite her beauty. His mind drifted on the calm waters of her song. "Somewhere in the woods," he heard her sing, "there is a crystal egg called Brightspark that shines like a light. It can open the doorway to your heart so your dreams can take flight."

Two days later, and unsure exactly how long the woman had sat nursing his head, Freeman opened his eyes. He sat upon a mattress of bark in the perpetual darkness of the woods. Alone and inspired by the message of his dream, Freeman wandered the Woods of Calamity and Eternal Darkness for a year, indifferent to the strange and beady eyes of the luminous being that kept its distance and hid behind trees. Then, one day and completely by mistake, while looking for a particular berry that was red and sweeter than honey, Freeman stubbed his toe on something hard and covered in mud on the side of a path. When he wiped off the dirt, Freeman recognised Brightspark right away. He held it to the sky and asked the question of his life, which was something like, "What's the meaning of it all?"

Satisfied with his answer, which happened to be a burst of silence, Freeman was inspired to join the Parzens of Happysad. Immediately, he travelled to the Villa of the Stony Crag, where he discovered the magic of magnets, took the weight off his feet, and never looked back.

Alarms sounded deep inside the Villa of the Stony Crag. Sirens wailed. A flurry of initiates shuffled hurriedly through the small door to the outer chamber.

"F-F-Find Brightspark," Freeman ordered, as they assembled, hand in hand, by his side.

"Is it too late?" one of them asked.

Frustrated for the first time in years, Freeman rubbed the spot where his bony buttocks had hit the ground.

"Just g-g-go," he stammered.

The initiates bowed and walked backwards, each collecting a staff from a cabinet attached to the wall as they passed. When they found the handle of the "Other Door," they pulled hard and went inside.

Two by two, they climbed the stairs, each spinning their staff in a figure of eight. The rumble of something heavy bouncing down the stairs muffled the sound of sirens. The villa's second line of defence was a basketful of stone balls designed to crush everything in their way.

When they saw the line of spinning staffs, Stanley and Blabbermouth stopped. Desperate and brave, Blabbermouth grabbed Stanley's arm and charged. Some of the spinning staffs snapped. Others bounced off Blabbermouth's arms. The fugitives plummeted down the stairs, narrowly missing the blades protruding from the metal walls. Through the outer chamber, they raced into the dark.   Outside it was snowing.

Running as fast as he could go, Blabbermouth dragged Stanley close behind. Blinded by fear and unaware of the extra bony hand clinging to his fur, Blabbermouth slipped on a sheet of ice. He skated to the edge of the path before catapulting down the side of the Stony Crag, dragging Stanley and Freeman's bony body behind. When the limb of the tree he grabbed snapped, the party of three dropped like small shooting stars into the wintry valley below. Snow filled the air, and the wind howled as the three bodies slammed into the turbulent waters of an estuary of the River E. Blabbermouth snapped at the water, clicking his teeth in the hope of snagging a fish. Stanley choked on a lump of weed, and Freeman, who had talked non-stop during his descent, considered the possibility that he had overcome his fear of death.

It was not long before the current washed Stanley and Blabbermouth upon the stony shore. From there, they gasped and panted. They watched as Freeman drifted closer, talking to himself while clutching a log.

"W-What have you done?" was the first thing Freeman asked.

"Your stupid crystal didn't work," Stanley said.

"R-R-Remember what I t-t-told you," Freeman said. "Now g-g-give it back."

"No," Stanley said, adamant. "I need a proper answer." And with a show of solidarity, Blabbermouth barked.

Stanley pulled Brightspark from the pocket in his nummer-pack. It was glowing blue.

"What if you ask a different question, master? Maybe it will tell you what you want to hear." Blabbermouth asked.

"That w-won't work," Freeman said. "One question p-p-per person. That's how it w-works."

"Works?" Stanley said.

Freeman leaned back against the log that had saved his life. "There is one other th-th-thing you can do," he said.

"And what's that?" Stanley asked.

"There's only one p-p-person who can give that k-k-kind of advice," Freeman said.

"And why would we trust you?" asked Stanley.

"Yes, why?" added Blabbermouth.

"Because she s-s-saved my life, and she knows the w-ways of magic. B-b-besides, it just so happens she's c-c-clever and happens to be a w-witch."

Blabbermouth gasped and swallowed hard. He sat up, puffed out his chest, and eyed Stanley's last nummer. Like a cup, his mind filled with thoughts of everything bad about witches.

Was it true that they could fly? Did they have skinny fingers and bony knuckles and wear black pointed hats? Did they steal children away in the dead of night? It must be true because that's how the stories go. Witches were to blame for the strange goings-on in the Woods of Calamity and Eternal Darkness.

Then, distracted by the fact that Freeman had lost his loincloth in the river, Blabbermouth asked, "Where are your clothes?"

Freeman shrugged.

"Anyway," Blabbermouth continued, "All this talk about witches is ridiculous. Witches. Ha! No one believes in witches."

Freeman looked at the bog and started laughing.

"What's so funny?" Stanley asked.

Freeman pointed at Blabbermouth and laughed even harder.

"W-What witches?" he said, mimicking Blabbermouth. "Of course, there's w-witches. It's just that b-b-bogs are terrified of witches."

"No, we're not," Blabbermouth said.

Freeman stood up, raised his arms above his head, and wiggled his fingers at Blabbermouth. "Ooooooo, w-itches," he said.

Blabbermouth's tail curled between his legs. "Okay, okay." He looked around. "I'm afraid of witches. There. Happy? Nobody likes witches."

Ignoring Blabbermouth, Stanley turned to Freeman. "How can this witch help me?" he asked.

"She's a h-healer," Freeman said. "If it w-wasn't for her, I w-wouldn't be alive."

Ever since the day Eva was chased from Happysad by children with sticks, she was blamed when something — anything went wrong. And that included the weather. Children lying on their backs in fields and making shapes from passing clouds often saw witches with white cats drifting across the sky. But this was nothing compared to the storms when angry black clouds twisted into mouths with jagged teeth and lightning cracked the sky. It was Eva. Always Eva.

For who else could be blamed for the things people couldn't explain? Even Blabbermouth, who—despite his efforts to forget about witches once and for all—knew that the sadness that shaped his brother's life had to be the work of a witch.

He stood beside Stanley, compulsively licking his putrid coat.

News of Brightspark's theft travelled fast. Even Eva, cloistered in the amethyst cave in the mountains far away, received word from an overweight owl who flew through the night and crashed into the side of the amethyst cave.

"Stolen?" Eva asked the owl.

The fat bird nodded. Eva's attention shifted slightly from the air of sadness that had followed her for years. She stared into the flames of her cooking-fire where she slowly roasted a rabbit. Throwing caution to the wind, the fat owl stared across at Eva through the flames. It completely forgot about Eva's black dogs, one of which crept up behind and more for fun than hunger, ripped the fat owl apart. Feathers flew around the cave, and Eva sat still, watching as if she were suspended in the middle of a disquieting dream.

A breeze slipped in through the mouth of the amethyst cave, and the candles flickered, casting a crowd of shadows across the wall.

I wonder?

12. ESMERELDA AND THE DUMBNUT TREE

The young girl, who believed herself older than she was, stood before a leafy thicket at the entrance to the Woods. With blonde plaited hair and bright white teeth, she wore a cream-coloured bell-shaped dress that stopped just below her knees. She stared into the distance with her feet turned in, and her hands crossed neatly in front of her dress. With a sense of urgency, the girl was trying to remember something which had slipped her mind, and she couldn't shake the sensation that something was going to happen, and soon.

It was then that Stanley walked into view, followed reluctantly by a hairy creature and a skinny, naked man. As the strangers drew closer, the girl fidgeted, twisting her fingers around each other as if she were trying to tie them in a knot.

Sensing the intensity of her stare, Stanley looked up and jumped. "Who are you?" he asked.

"Esmerelda," she replied. "But that's about all that I remember."

"What?" Stanley said.

"Some things I remember," she said. "And some things I don't. But it's okay because I'm good at remembering secrets."

"Secrets?" Blabbermouth said, excited.

"Yes, secrets," she said, "And I can share one with you now if you like."

Unknown to Esmerelda, the problem with her memory stemmed from the fact that her brain stopped growing at the precise moment it reached the size of a pea. Esmerelda's memory was quickly overloaded with its limited capacity, especially when performing simple tasks like breathing and thinking about what she was going to eat. For this reason, Esmerelda struggled to remember anything beyond her name, and sometimes, the whereabouts of the fabled dumbnut tree.

"Why would you tell us a secret?" Stanley asked.

Esmerelda bowed her head as tears welled in her eyes. "Well, because everyone seems to like a good secret, and it's a good way to make friends. Only no one comes this way, she explained. "People fear the woods because it's always dark, and it gets very noisy at night."

"Noisy? At night?" Blabbermouth asked, his voice suddenly raspy and breathless.

"Yes," Esmerelda said, raising her head and closing her eyes. "It's noisy at night." Then, changing the subject, she added, "Have you heard of the dumbnut tree?"

Blabbermouth licked his lips.

"Well, I happen to know exactly where it is," Esmerelda said confidently.

"The dumbnut tree?" asked Stanley as he looked from the stranger to Blabbermouth and then to Freeman, awaiting further explanation.

"Once upon a t-t-time," Freeman said, "Dumbnuts were w-worth more than g-g-gold."

"Really?" Stanley asked, "How come I've never heard of them?"

"Conversations about dumbnuts stopped years ago," Esmerelda said sadly.

"Why?" Stanley asked.

"Firstly, because no one dares enter the Woods of Calamity and Eternal Darkness, and second because people think the last-known dumbnut tree shrivelled up and died," Esmerelda said.

"Th-th-they're not unlike a b-b-black coffee bean in appearance," Freeman added. "Only d-d-dumbnuts are addictive, h-hallucinogenic, and fatal when eaten in n-n-numbers greater than three," he continued.

What Esmerelda didn't tell them, mostly because she couldn't remember, was that the name of the nut derived from the fact that after days of hallucinations, a user's thoughts slowed to the point where their mind broke free. The downside was that people often went off and did dumb things like crying and hugging trees. Others lay in grassy fields, staring in wonderment at the sky as the clouds drifted by. And then there were those who waded into the deep waters of the River E and floated away on the current, never to be seen again.

"Dumbnuts could be the answer to my fear of witches!" Blabbermouth exclaimed and slapped Stanley on the back.

"What are you looking for in the woods?" Esmerelda asked.

"We're g-g-going to the amethyst c-c-caves," Freeman said. "We're l-l-looking for a sorceress who p-p-passed this way."

"The river runs from the lake and out of the woods," Esmerelda said. "It follows the valley to the mountains on its way to the River E."

"The g-g-girl is right," Freeman said.

"How does she know if she can't remember?" Stanley asked.

Freeman looked to Esmerelda.

"That's easy," Esmerelda said, offended. "I follow the path of white flowers all the way to the dumbnut tree. It must be near the river because when I'm there, the sound of water makes me want to pee."

Stanley pulled Brightspark from his nummer-pack and gripped it in his hands.

"Exactly how dark are the woods?" he asked Esmerelda.

"Black as night," she said.

"Then there must be another way."

"Don't worry," Blabbermouth interrupted. "I will protect you, master. What's a little darkness when we have Brightspark, and we can eat dumbnuts from the dumbnut tree?"

Esmerelda's eyes lit up as she gazed upon Brightspark, as though she'd seen nothing like it before. Brightspark glowed in the darkness that stretched its bony black fingers from the edge of the woods.

"What's that?" Esmerelda asked, pointing at Stanley's hands.

Freeman interrupted. "It's B-B-Brightspark."

"It's beautiful," Esmerelda said. "What does it do?"

"It glows and h-helps with levitation. It c-c-can tell you what you n-n-need to know," Freeman said.

Esmerelda thought for a moment. "Well, how about this?" she said, "If you let me hold it and ask a question, I will take you to the dumbnut tree. Then you will find the river."

"No," Stanley snapped, looking at Freeman.

"Well, we can't s-s-stop because you're a-afraid of the d-d-dark," Freeman said.

Stanley's face went red. "Me?" he said, embarrassed.

166

"I won't drop it," Esmerelda said. "I promise."

"Why should I believe you?" Stanley asked.

Esmerelda's mouth fell open. "Why would I tell you a lie?"

"Please… please, mister, can I hold it?" asked Esmerelda.

Stanley looked up over the thicket into the dark woods. A shiver rippled down his spine.

"Fine then," Stanley said, begrudgingly. "If you hold Brightspark, I'll walk just behind."

"Yes, yes," Esmerelda said excitedly.

"I'll take it when we get to the river," Stanley said.

"Yes!" Esmerelda replied.

"How far do we have to go?"

"Just to the dumbnut tree," Esmerelda said, stretching out her hands to take hold of Brightspark.

"The dumbnut tree," Stanley said, handing Brightspark to Esmerelda.

Brightspark glowed blue in her hands. "What do I have to do?" she asked.

"Th-Th-Think of your question," Freeman said.

Esmerelda frowned, and her eyes narrowed as though she was trying to grasp a single thought from her pea-shaped mind. Holding Brightspark up in the air, she whispered to herself and closed her eyes. The crystal pulsed blue light.

Nothing happened until slowly, a smile stretched across Esmerelda's face. She opened her eyes and seemed somehow different… as though intoxicated. Then she looked around and said, "Come. Follow me to the dumbnut tree."

Suddenly clear, Esmerelda skipped off into the woods as though Brightspark had removed the confusing fog from her tiny mind. Old memories surfaced, like driftwood washed-up on an empty shore—things long forgotten returned. But one memory stood above all others, of the day everything went

167

wrong for Esmerelda—the day a spaceship from a distant star fell out of the sky. Thin and shaped like an after-dinner mint, the barely three-dimensional craft had a large piece missing from the front. It crashed into the lake in the centre of the woods, sank into the dark waters, and was never seen again. On that day, Esmerelda was sitting at the edge of the lake picking small white flowers for her mother whilst keeping her eye on a nearby swarm of bees.

So, when the wayward ship slammed into the lake, the bees, who startled easily, stopped what they were doing and stung Esmerelda repeatedly on the arm. The poison raced through her veins and stopped her heart. With her eyes closed and on the brink of death, she was saved by a sudden rocking motion that made her want to vomit. As the pale, skinny alien, with its oversized head and big, black, beady eyes held Esmerelda in its lap, it muttered something in the language of thought.

When Esmerelda opened her eyes, the alien was looking the other way, and one of its hands—which incidentally had six fingers—was hovering above her heart. Esmerelda screamed, and the alien opened its small mouth in the shape of an "O."

Frightened by loud noises, the alien dropped the girl and ran into the woods. From that point, things quickly rearranged themselves in Esmerelda's mind. She filed the image of the alien and its big bald head in the "That didn't happen" and "What alien?" compartments in her mind. But unfortunately for Esmerelda, the gravity of what she saw also stole other important parts of her memory away. At that moment, she forgot who she was, what she was doing beside the lake, and the purpose of the small chain of white flowers that were resting on her lap.

From that day, the hand of sadness touched Esmerelda's life. Convinced that the alien took something away, her small mind was scrambled. That night, late and exhausted from wandering around in circles in the dark, Esmerelda accidentally found her way home. A woman she vaguely recognized as her mother scolded her for telling stories and sent her to bed. But Esmerelda couldn't sleep for feeling she was forgetting something and that suddenly everything in her life was not quite right.

Years later, one rainy afternoon, a drunk woodchopper strode into the woods, tripped on a log, and planted the head of his axe in his thigh. Not in his right mind, the woodchopper later reported sighting something scary and white with an enormous head watching him from behind a tree. The story travelled fast, and it soon became official that:

1) the woods were dark,
2) they were scary, and
3) it was a place of strange goings-on.

As for Esmerelda, her memory was gone for good. And she spent her days wandering in circles in the woods.

Stanley followed Esmerelda along the path into the woods, constantly checking to see that Blabbermouth was just behind.

His heart punched like a fist in his chest in the growing darkness. Remembering fragments of an old song, Esmerelda sang to herself as she skipped between the trees, seemingly elated that she could now recall the lyrics. Trailing behind, Blabbermouth chattered to himself about dumbnuts and tried to distract himself from the idea of witches. When the dampness of the woods filled Stanley's nose, he started sneezing, which was a distraction in itself until he saw an eyeball staring up at him from a pile of dung on the side of the trail. Stanley pulled up short and screamed, startling Freeman, who was far behind on account of his resolution not to walk any faster than he should. The eyeball, which seemed to be interested in everything, kept looking from side to side.

Esmerelda stopped and turned around, and when she saw what made Stanley scream, she chuckled. "Oh, don't worry about that," she said. "The alien leaves them lying around. If you stay still, the eye will lose interest and look the other way." And with that, Esmerelda continued following the trail of white flowers, singing the only verse of the only song she could remember.

Stanley stood still. He swallowed thickly, and it wasn't long before the eyeball stopped moving and stared straight ahead.

"The alien?" Stanley finally asked as he regained his senses.

"Yes, the alien," Esmerelda called back. "It drops the eyeballs into its dung. I suppose to see if it really is alone."

"B-B-Brilliant," Freeman remarked as he caught up with Stanley.

"What?" asked Stanley, unnerved.

"A t-t-telepathic surveillance eyeball."

"A what?"

"G-G-Genius. That's what it is," Freeman said, captivated by the eyeball that seemed to be just as interested in him.

But what neither Freeman nor Stanley saw was the footprint of the army boot in the dung that had been left the day before— a footprint that, had it not been partially covered in alien dung, would have revealed the letters "MG."

As for the alien, things would have gone much better if long ago it had not fallen asleep at the controls of its spaceship at the worst possible time. Flitting between the stars, the spaceship veered off track, clipped the corner of an asteroid, and crashed into a lake in the woods on an insignificant planet stuck in a fragile orbit around a dying sun.

Not wanting to drown and putting personal misfortune aside, the alien broke free from the craft and swam up through the dark waters. Once dry, the alien stood at the edge of the lake in the middle of the woods and decided things couldn't possibly be worse. So, when it found itself suddenly distracted by the screaming and wailing girl poisoned by a swarm of angry bees and left to die, it came as something of a surprise. Capable of restoring life, the alien placed its hand across her chest. Immediately, the girl's heart jumped back to life.

Perhaps it wasn't going to be such a bad day after all?

And thinking it only fair, the alien took something in return. It closed its big, black eyes and pulled the last crumbs of happiness and joy from the young girl's fragile heart.

Not mechanically inclined at all and overwhelmed by the need to find food, the next problem for the alien was that it could not figure out how to pull its ship from the bottom of the lake. The idea of failure and a recurring bout of diarrhoea had placed it in an enduring bad mood. Cranky, the alien moped in the shadows of the woods, surviving on a diet of bugs and small yellow flowers with orange leaves. As time went by, any relief from the misery of being marooned came from following Esmerelda through the woods. And so, it was that the alien quickly memorised the inconsequential acts of the girl whose life it had saved and who, as far as it could tell, repeated everything she ever did.

Unbeknownst to Esmerelda, there were others who were interested in the antics of the alien. Commander Aachoo of the warring fleet of Quadrant Delta Three had always kept a keen green eye on the comings and goings of unusual traffic through the corridors of space. When he saw an after-dinner mint moving erratically between the stars, his interest piqued. And having failed to impress his girlfriend at the time, Aachoo was adamant to prove to her he was not so mean after all. He announced his plans to reopen a tiny space portal that was, for reasons unknown to himself, closed for works. So, when the alien—in his spaceship shaped like an after-dinner mint— nearly crashed into one of Aachoo's ships, the commander resolved to spare its life. In return for his generosity, he sent the alien off to find out why the space portal had closed.

According to Aachoo, his was a brilliant plan. He would pass through the small space portal and show his girlfriend the four million, six hundred and forty-seven thousandth wonder of the universe, which was a small and unremarkable-looking orange seahorse.

Close to the bottom on *The Galactic List of Interesting Things to See*, the orange seahorse swam around a small pool of brown water on a radioactive and otherwise uninhabited planet. Somehow it had survived for ten years without a single meal, and for this reason alone, it was something mildly interesting to see. For Aachoo, everything was going well until the day the alien disappeared. And not one to ever let anything go, the commander immediately ordered his fleet of starships to change course.

"Head for the small space portal in sector nine," he ordered the captain of his ship, "And prepare to blow something up, even if it is the middle of the night."

From the moment she held Brightspark in her hands, Esmerelda remembered certain things. She recalled having never been partial to the fruit of the dumbnut tree. She also remembered signing an agreement with the owls. And there was something about an illuminated egg-shaped stone that was very important, and she didn't know why. As far as she could tell, it had something to do with her agreement to report anything suspicious to the owls.

"I remember," Esmerelda said unexpectedly, out loud.

The further Stanley travelled into the woods, the darker it got. His heart raced, reeling from the idea that things were lurking and waiting in the night.

Perhaps everything isn't going to be okay. What about Delia? Soon the Virus will steal her mind, and not long after that, she will die.

The hairs pricked on the back of Stanley's neck. He looked around, his eyes darting nervously.

What are the chances of something jumping out from behind a tree?

Terrified, he looked up to see Esmerelda's shadow as it bobbed along the path of white flowers. And counting inside his head, he ran after her.

173

13. THE LITTLE BLUE BEINGS ON A SMALL BROWN PLANET FAR AWAY...

Meanwhile, on a small brown planet far away from the Woods of Calamity and Eternal Darkness, a band of little blue beings became more animated than before. They spoke amongst themselves in a dialect of star-talk that they barely understood themselves. Watching Stanley through a holographic bubble of blue light, their excitement intensified when they saw the girl. She wore a cream dress and carried something delicately in her hands as though it was something precious. As they peered in for a closer look, they noticed the object appeared to be a glowing crystal egg. She clutched it to her as she skipped through the woods, all the while singing a happy song.

14. WHAT'S IN THE WOODS

When the trail of white flowers ended, Esmerelda stopped. She gazed up at the short and bulbous dumbnut tree with its widespread branches. With the appearance of a gigantic gourd, the tree was home to a swarm of intoxicated bees and a bubble of fireflies, which gave it an eerie glow.

Stanley stopped beside Esmeralda and inspected the tree, frowning and feeling increasingly unsettled. He wondered if perhaps it was the tree's strange slippery orange bark before he suddenly felt sick and started sneezing for no good reason at all. Then he burped.

"What is it, master?" asked Blabbermouth. "Isn't this exciting? It's the dumbnut tree. We can collect our dumbnuts and be on our way, and everything will be okay because we will find the river and—"

Stanley cut him off with a groan. A river of rage and resentment surged inside him. Stanley clenched his fists as he started shaking. "I hate the dark!" he screamed into

Blabbermouth's face. "It's your fault! We should never have come into the woods." Overwhelmed with a surge of feelings he'd kept stuffed inside, Stanley grabbed Blabbermouth by the throat and squeezed.

Confused, Blabbermouth tried to wriggle free as the light of the dumbnut tree started to fade, and Stanley's voice seemed further away.

"It's all your fault. It's all your fault," he heard Stanley say.

Stanley's hand squeezed tighter. Then, in the spirit of survival, Blabbermouth whipped his tail in a small arc, striking Stanley on the chin.

Stunned, Stanley let go. Blabbermouth sank his single, yellow front-tooth into Stanley's hand and released a nervous burst of bog-gas that sent Stanley hurtling backwards, choking and gagging on the stench.

As if a casual observer in someone else's dream, Freeman sat and watched.

Stanley sat against the base of the dumbnut tree, clutching his bleeding hand, while Blabbermouth retreated to the other side with his tail tucked firmly between his legs.

Having forgotten the exact details of her agreement with Stanley, Esmerelda skipped around the tree and continued through the woods—completely unaware that something luminous with an enormous head followed just behind.

The alien flitted between the trees, doing an abysmal job of remaining unseen. Having followed Esmerelda for some time, it suddenly stopped. Not great with directions, the alien had resolved never to wander too far from its sunken spaceship. Aesthetics aside, the spaceship shaped like an after-dinner mint was a functional craft and a good way of getting around. That was until its navigation database expired. Unaware of the error and following explicit orders from Commander Aachoo, the alien became hopelessly lost, and if it weren't for the space-stop on the planet called "Sharon," things might have been far worse. Offering fuel, refreshments, and other unnecessary things to amuse bored space travellers, the planet Sharon orbited on the rim of a volatile corridor of space. Subject to frequent and violent meteor storms, Sharon resembled a large and battered round of Swiss cheese. And in the darkness of space, the luminous debris left from passing meteors made the planet Sharon glow.

Whilst waiting for its spaceship to refuel, the alien had collected a bag full of Sharon's glowing crystal stones. It placed the egg-shaped crystals on a neat triangular display in the cockpit of its ship. And feeling quite happy with itself, the alien followed Commander Aachoo's orders and programmed the coordinates of the small space portal into the ship's navigation computer. Little did it know that the directions given by the spaceport attendant were wrong, and technically, the alien was now a fugitive of one of the meanest, greenest, and angriest Commanders of interstellar war.

Trying to forget what happened with Blabbermouth, Stanley turned his attention back to the woods. He watched as nearby Freeman grunted with frustration at his failed attempts to focus and levitate above the ground. Stanley thought of Delia—his thoughts haunted by images of her strapped to a bed and battling against the competing voices inside her head.

I have to find Evil Eva or Delia will die.

A fist tightened around Stanley's heart. He bit his lip and tried not to cry.

Annoyed at having to sit on the cold ground, Freeman focussed his attention on Stanley. "You can only s-s-save yourself," Freeman said as if he knew Brightspark's message to Stanley at the Villa of the Stony Crag.

"That's not true," Stanley replied.

"S-S-Suit yourself," Freeman said, "but you're w-wasting your time."

"I promised to help her," Stanley said through a trickle of tears.

"That's the unfortunate th-th-thing about p-p-promises," Freeman replied.

Close by, Blabbermouth rearranged the fur around his throat and sniffed at the ground for dumbnuts, disregarding the possible side-effects of eating more than three. Biting into an old pod of six nuts, his mouth filled with a burst of sour cacao. Blabbermouth's thoughts slowed. His mind went numb and strange ideas and old memories flashed by. In an instant, he was floating. Unhinged and free.

Moments later, the large, luminous white head of the alien appeared from behind a nearby tree. It blurted the only words it had learned from Esmerelda years before (which was a high-pitched, shrieking "Eeeeeeeeeeeeeee!"). Mistaking the sound for something friendly, Blabbermouth wagged his tail. He opened his eyes wide and barked three times, which in bog meant, "Okay, I don't know what you are, but you don't appear to be a witch so let me introduce myself."

Eager to make new friends, Blabbermouth pushed a dumbnut along the ground with his paw. He stopped and looked up when the nut collided with one of the alien's bony and white webbed feet. The alien kicked the dumbnut along the ground, and Blabbermouth froze. It was then that his thoughts slowly caught up with what was going on.

It is the witches. It must be the witches.

Still not in his right mind, Blabbermouth knew that the best thing was just to look away. He tiptoed to the other side of the dumbnut tree where Stanley sat with his eyes closed and nursed his bleeding hand.

"Ah, master?" Blabbermouth mumbled. "There is something you need to see!"

Stanley opened his eyes and glanced at Blabbermouth before he lowered them again in guilt. He poked his head around the side of the tree, and the skinny white alien stared back. Stanley vomited inside his mouth. Of all the terrifying things that he imagined could hide in the dark, this was about as bad as it could be. A familiar fog drifted across his mind. Unable to think or move, Stanley stood still.

The alien didn't move. Curious and mildly amused, Freeman watched. He stared into the alien's black, beady eyes. For the longest time, neither of them blinked; the alien because it had no eyelids and Freeman because he wasn't sure if it was the same alien he had seen years before. The alien took a step towards Freeman and cocked its head to one side.

"W-we meet again," Freeman said, as he wondered if, in fact, there were other aliens in the woods.

179

The alien, who appeared to sense no imminent danger, walked to where Freeman was sitting. It disregarded Blabbermouth, who was intoxicated with dumbnut and licking where he had bitten Stanley's hand. Moonlight shone on the few silvery leaves of the dumbnut tree. The alien pointed the longest of its six fingers at the ground and drew what looked very much like a sunken spaceship shaped like an after-dinner mint. Beneath it, the alien drew a large question mark, which was the universal symbol for "I don't understand," or "what?" or "I need some help."

Despite the alien's not-so-pleasant behaviour towards Freeman years before, the practice of levitation had assisted Freeman in letting a lot of things go. Freeman bent down, and with a neatly manicured nail, drew an image of pulleys and vines that they could use to set the alien's spacecraft free.

The alien responded, drawing the outline of a man that was sitting with crossed legs and closed eyes. He was hovering at approximately four inches above the ground.

Freeman, feeling a rare connection in his otherwise lonely life, nodded, fighting tears.

The alien folded its arms and crossed its skinny legs. And slowly, it rose into the air and hovered just above the ground.

No magnets! Freeman clapped at the miracle of levitation.

At first, the alien hovered sideways and then moved forward, placing its bony hands on either side of Freeman's head. Along with a couple of other bits and pieces, Freeman's mind instantly uploaded the secret of levitation from the alien's hands. It occurred to him that the answer had been in front of him the whole time. And it was simple—he'd just been trying too hard. Suddenly, Freeman understood what the alien had done to him years before.

For without a certain amount of happiness in its life, the alien would have died. In return, the alien had given Freeman the gift of life. And so, understanding each other a little more, Freeman followed the alien as it turned and walked towards the lake.

Sometime later, using pulleys made from small logs and vines, Freeman and the alien hauled the spaceship shaped like an after-dinner mint from the bottom of the lake. Deceptively thin on the outside, the spaceship was a Mark IV, which meant that apart from being overly complicated, it was fast, manoeuvrable, and had lots of other features that nobody ever used. Through a stroke of genius, the engineers had made the interior of the Mark IV wider than a large field, with a maze of corridors and bearing no resemblance to an after-dinner mint at all.

The walls of the cockpit were windowless and bare. Controlled by a silver panel, the spaceship shaped like an after-dinner mint was activated by the pilot's thoughts. And in the centre of the room was a tall silver stool topped with a thick white cushion.

After dragging the spaceship from the lake, dripping with mud and moss, Freeman and the alien leaned it against a suitably sized tree.

Then, happier than it had been for some time, the alien stood tall and bowed before Freeman in a gesture of profound thanks. It slipped sideways in through the narrow front door of the ship. Inside, and using the power of its thoughts, the alien issued a series of commands. Crystal columns rose from the floor, screens appeared on the walls, and a three-dimensional model of the galaxy and all its stars appeared in front of the tall silver stool.

Behind the stool was the display of coloured crystals the alien collected from the planet Sharon. Deep in thought, the alien looked at the crystals and cocked its head to one side. With one finger across its mouth, it pulled one crystal from the display, and whilst reluctant to part with a piece of its collection, at the same time, it was grateful to have its spaceship back. The door of the spaceship opened, and the alien stepped out, and in the darkness of the woods, the crystal from the planet Sharon glowed in its hand.

No one who had witnessed the potency of crystal eggs ever underestimated their power. Rare—except on the planet Sharon because they were everywhere—the eggs were effective as both a power source and an object of inspiration (as some beings just liked to stare at their changing colours). Their versatility and usefulness were profound. Capable of long-range communication and an ability to interpret any alien tongue, the crystals had consistently ranked highly in new editions of the bestselling *Useful Things to Have in Space*.

Standing in front of the spaceship, the crystal egg pulsed in the alien's hand as it received a message. A hologram of a city on fire appeared in the centre of the egg. It was Mentoria. Citizens ran, screaming through the streets as burning buildings collapsed around them.

Unsure of its meaning, Freeman carried the egg to Stanley, where he sat beneath the dumbnut tree. The image changed to a young woman with messy blonde hair strapped to an infirmary bed. She stared into the distance with a blankness that went beyond her gaze. "Help me," she said. "I am running out of time. Help me."

It was Delia.

Desperate, Stanley ripped the crystal egg from Freeman's hands and scampered into the woods in search of Esmerelda. Blabbermouth trotted closely behind.

Further on, Esmerelda skipped through the woods, still singing the same fragmented verse of her song. Brightspark glowed blue in her hands, and as parts of her memory returned, she thought about the owls. Whilst they had never bothered her before, she realised that she had never really liked them at all.

Why would anyone like a bird with big eerie eyes? Especially when they spied on people from the tops of the trees.

Having never travelled so far from the dumbnut tree, it occurred to Esmerelda that she was lost. Technically, she had been lost in the woods for years, but this was different. Not far away, an owl hooted, and the cathedral-shaped canopy of the trees amplified the noise. Behind her, there came a swooping sound.

"Esmerelda," a watcher-owl said with a sinister tone in the owl-language of Hoot.

"What?" Esmerelda replied, having a basic grasp of their tongue.

On a thick branch, high up in a nearby tree, another owl, with bigger and altogether more frightening yellow eyes, cleared its throat. "Ha, hmmm." In a dramatic display, the owl unrolled a dirty scroll of bark with red writing that was signed with a letter "E" for Esmerelda.

"Esmerelda?" the owl asked in an ominous tone and pointed to the signature on the scroll. "Is this your mark?"

"E is for Esmerelda," she replied, quite happy with herself for knowing the first letter of her name.

"We have an agreement," the owl said.

Esmerelda was silent.

"Well? Cat got your tongue?"

"Cat?" Esmerelda asked.

"It's a figure of speech," the owl said condescendingly.

"Well, I don't remember," Esmerelda said.

"That's convenient," said the owl, holding a monocle over one eye. It ran a sharp claw beneath every word on the scroll, then continued.

"It says here you agree to share any information that might be relevant or useful or solve any outstanding problems in the woods. Furthermore, it states, in the interest of everybody, everywhere that you will share none of this information with anyone but the owls."

Other fragments of Esmerelda's memory returned. Holding the scroll, the owl jumped to a lower branch. Esmerelda flinched at the size of its yellow eyes.

"Is there something you're not telling us?" asked the owl.

"No," Esmerelda said. "If there were something, I would tell you. By the way, do I get anything in return?"

The owl let out a loud "tsskk" and then referred to the scroll. "It says here at the bottom that if you keep your side of the agreement, we will grant you free passage through the woods. And we will leave you alone."

"Yes," said Esmerelda.

"So, tell us," the owl continued, "Is there something... something reportable... that you might have missed? Something we should know?"

"I'm not sure," Esmerelda replied.

"A little crash, perhaps?"

Like a deck of cards, Esmerelda's mind shuffled backwards. She remembered the day she first saw the alien in the woods. She remembered the bees. "Ah, that's right," she said. "I remember..."

"Well, that's all very well," the owl cut in. "But according to this contract, the matter was reportable some time ago. So, as I see it, we have a problem."

"A problem?" Esmerelda asked.

"You didn't honour your end of the deal," the owl said. It paused for effect, then added, "Of course, there are penalties."

Esmerelda looked around. On the ground below the owl, she saw a set of bloodshot blue eyes hovering above a mouthful of sharp white teeth.

The owl noticed her gaze. "I'm not sure you've met our pet," it said, referring to the bony and sick-looking white panther with blue eyes and a chain around its neck.

Esmerelda tried to look away, but something in the panther's eyes stopped her.

"Now tell me. What is that you are holding in your hand?" asked the owl.

"Pretty, isn't it?" Esmerelda replied nervously.

"I suggest you hand it over, and perhaps we can forget about your minor lapse."

The panther's eyes seemed to glow brighter. It licked its lips and panted.

"I'm just holding it," Esmerelda said. "It's not mine to give away."

"That's right," said the owl. "It belongs to The Master."

"The Master?" Esmerelda asked, her eyes fixed on the bloodshot eyes of the panther.

"Yes, The Master," the owl repeated. "It's just business, and you have something that's his."

The owl gestured for two smaller owls to take Brightspark away.

"I really shouldn't give it away," Esmerelda said. "What will they say?"

"They?" asked the owl.

185

"My friends."

The owl hooted a barrage of commands to his legion of equally eerie, yellow-eyed owls. Wings flapped, branches shook, and the chain around the panther's neck strained. Two owls dropped Brightspark in a basket on the big cat's back, and the panther closed its eyes, turned, and walked away.

Alone again in the dark, Esmerelda stood with her hands placed neatly in front of her dress. Whilst she felt bad for letting Brightspark go, she realised it was more important to piece together the fragmented memories from her past. But no matter how hard she tried to connect the dots, it was no use—for the images that she remembered remained like loose marbles, rolling around inside her otherwise empty mind.

On the other side of the River E, The Master dispatched a platoon of guards in quiet silver ships powered by large metal fans. Wearing larger than usual helmets with black visors to protect them from the deadly rays of the sun, The Master's orders were simple. "Find the fugitive—Stanley Luka—dead or alive. And bring me Brightspark."

Concerned by their first voyage beyond Mindset, the guards moved about their ships equipped with two large, long-life nummers strapped to nummer-packs on their backs.

It was night, and as they approached the Woods of Calamity and Eternal Darkness, the captain of each silver ship ordered the lights be dimmed. As far as anyone who was looking was concerned, the ships disappeared. They descended through a small clearing in the canopy of the woods, undetectable except for the gentle whoosh and hum of the ships' fans. That was, until one of the guards, dressed in a tight one-piece silver suit with a white helmet and a large flashlight, tripped over a rope on the deck of the ship and gave their position away.

It was not long after the owls returned from their rendezvous with a young girl in a pretty, cream dress that they saw the flash of light from the silver ship. And taking their position in the tops of nearby trees, they squinted, so their eyes were no bigger than small yellow slits. They watched with an air of arrogance as the Mentorian Guards walked down the ramps of their ships.

The commander—who was much shorter than the other guards—wore a badge on the upper part of each sleeve with the letters "MI." Short for "Most Important," it was well known in Mentoria that many not-so-nice deeds had to be committed to qualify for such a badge. The commander with the "MI" badges on his sleeves walked with tiny steps. His voice, which broadcast from a small slit at the front of his helmet, was distinctly metallic and sounded more robotic than it really was.

"We didn't expect you," hooted the greeting owl as it opened its eyes at the top of a nearby tree.

"Where's the fat owl?" asked the guard.

"Busy," the greeting owl replied.

"Find him. We have a problem," the guard demanded.

The owl hooted and opened its eyes wide, which was quite off-putting for the guard. Moments later, and in a less than graceful descent, the fat owl requested by the guard whistled gracefully through the air and slammed into the branch on which the other owl stood. The branch snapped, and both birds fell, in a cloud of feathers, to the ground. Unfettered by its awkward arrival, the fat owl stood up, puffed out its chest, and spoke to the guard. "I am the fat owl."

"Where is the crystal?" asked the commander.

"The crystal?"

The commander mumbled something to the guard at his side and then turned slowly back to the owl. "Where is it?" asked the commander, a second time.

"It must be quite valuable, this crystal," the fat owl said, waving its wing in the air for effect.

The guard pulled a computer tablet from a pocket in the thigh of his shiny silver suit. He showed the fat owl the screen. The image was of a dirty bog, two men and a pretty young girl in a cream dress, holding Brightspark.

"We believe you are now in possession of the crystal," said the commander. "Brightspark," he said, referring to his computer screen.

The owl shrugged its wings.

"There's no time for games," the commander snapped. He turned and nodded to the guard at his side. The less important guard raised his gun, pulled the trigger, and shot a hot green ray of light up into the trees. The doorman owl was nibbling at its wing and chasing a flea when the full force of the green laser light smashed into its chest. A puff of feathers flew into the air, and the smouldering doorman owl fell backwards out of the tree.

The fat owl started shaking.

"We mean business," the commander said.

"We don't want any trouble," the fat owl replied, followed by three hoots. In front of the guards, the bushes rustled as the bony white panther with bloodshot blue eyes walked lazily from the undergrowth. With Brightspark strapped to its back, it cast an ethereal, flickering, blue shadow across the trees. The

188

guards, who had only ever read about cats in books, stepped back. They cocked their guns and pointed them at the beast.

"What's that?" the commander asked.

"Brightspark," said the fat owl.

"No, the white thing."

"The panther?" asked the owl, regaining its composure in the beast's presence.

"It looks hungry," the commander said.

"It's always hungry," said the fat owl.

"What does it eat?"

The fat owl paused, then replied, "Meat."

"Bring me the crystal," ordered the guard, trying not to look at the white panther.

"Very well," the fat owl said, blinking slowly, then nodding twice at the panther, which was the order to "sit." Two smaller owls untangled the vines that strapped Brightspark to the basket on the panther's back. The large white cat licked its lips.

"That brings us to payment," the fat owl said to the commander, who seemed enthralled by the white panther's teeth. Immediately, the commander called for a wriggling sack of fat rats to be brought to the owl. He stuffed Brightspark into the already stretched pocket of his pants before he keyed the mouthpiece of his radio.

"We have the crystal. Now get me out of here."

15. MEANWHILE, BACK IN MENTORIA

Far above the flames that ravaged Mentoria, The Master spun in circles on a white, high-backed leather chair. The mayhem in the city had spread. Suffering from feelings and visions of a black dog carrying a red rubber ball, the citizens ran wild through the streets. And to make matters worse, it was Juaneeto who delivered The Master another bout of bad news.

"We're running out of power," he said.

"Impossible!" The Master scolded Juaneeto.

"I have checked a couple of times," Juaneeto said. "And the needle on the meter is stuck between *not looking good* and *empty*."

The Master thought for a moment, and then in a statement of complete denial, concluded, "It's because of the fire trucks — they use too much power and are sucking the city dry."

The Master called for an emergency meeting of the Council of Necessity without delay. Assembled in a small chamber that overlooked even the tallest buildings of the city, the councillors stared out of the rectangular window and watched Mentoria burn. Too afraid to say anything at all and with a tentative show of hands, they finally agreed on a couple of points:

First, that Mentoria was on fire.

Second, they were running out of power.

Third, the people were going mad.

And finally, the exercise taxes were not being paid.

After another long and useless silence, there was another show of hands, and they resolved that if they didn't do something, Mindset, the city's protective shield, would fail.

The Master tapped his long fingernail on the large black marble table in the room. "Well," he said, "any suggestions?"

The councillors looked at each other and then back out across the burning city. In the absence of any new ideas, The Master ordered a handful of citizens to be plucked randomly from the streets. With black hoods over their heads, the prisoners' hands were tied behind their backs. One by one, they were dragged by their interrogators into small, dark rooms and called nasty names. Terrified, the prisoners sat in silence, and it was decided that the gentle approach would not work. Stripped bare, the guards sprayed the prisoners with freezing water and flashed bright lights in their eyes. It was then, shivering and naked, the prisoners started to talk. They spoke of people laughing and crying and running through the streets. They reported seeing a black dog in the streets that spoke to them in the language of thought and seemed to want to play a game of 'Fetch the Red Rubber Ball.'

When no one said anything about painting graffiti on the city walls, and no one mentioned anything about a conspiracy to take control of the city, the guards were unsure what to do. They tossed around a number of ideas, and the answer became clear. Within the hour, the guards filmed a handful of hooded prisoners, kicking and screaming as they were shoved into one of the nummer drains of the city. Sliding past the sharp fan, they disappeared into the dark sliver tube—and were gone.

Convinced a good day's work was done, The Master retired to the penthouse shaped like a pill. The headache that had been stalking him for most of the day gripped his head like a vice. Desperate for relief, The Master called for Juaneeto, who promptly took his master's head in his hands. Looking up into his physician's eyes, The Master's instructions were clear. "Do whatever it is you need to do—just take this pain away."

Slipping in and out of sleep, The Master was aware of Juaneeto's large black thumbs massaging his temples. His thoughts drifted like broken boats on a stormy sea. The spectre of a black dog carrying a red rubber ball lingered in the shadows of The Master's mind. It was sitting there. Silent. Waiting for something, as if when the time was right, it would pounce.

Later, The Master sat up in his chair with a start. Juaneeto was gone. He rubbed his eyes and noticed the distant sounds of shouting in the streets. Closing his eyes, The Master swallowed hard, fighting the familiar feeling that he was falling into a dark and bottomless hole.

In a daze, he walked to his bedchamber and bit down hard on the mouthpiece of the nummer that was beside his bed. When the current surged through The Master's teeth, he jumped—but anything was better than the feeling of falling. Gradually, the numbness spread, and he closed his eyes. And when a crack in his consciousness appeared, The Master tumbled into a deep and troubled sleep.

Just before lunch, there was a heavy knock on the door of the penthouse shaped like a pill. Wearing his obsidian terry towel robe, The Master shuffled to the door. A short guard with a shaking leg, nervous fingers, and a badge on his shoulder that read "MI" stood in the doorway. He reached into the pocket of his tight silver pants.

"Brightspark, Sir," he said, holding up the glowing crystal egg with both hands.

The Master clenched his teeth to stop his smile.

"Give it to me," he ordered the guard, and stepping backwards, The Master took hold of Brightspark and closed the door.

This is it?

He turned Brightspark slowly in his hand.

I wonder?

Upon hearing the door and dressed in his over-sized white surgeon's coat, Juaneeto appeared at The Master's side. "My apologies, Master. Was that the door?"

"Yes," The Master said. "It doesn't matter because my headache is gone."

"You think it's because of the crystal?" Juaneeto asked, referring to Brightspark.

"It's the only explanation," The Master said. "Now the Sanitis-Or will have its day!"

"Yes," replied Juaneeto with a smile. "One way or another, things always have their way."

News of the announcement travelled fast, and the Council of Necessity assembled right away. From the end of the long black marble table, The Master sat staring at the silver-framed portraits of dead scientists that were hanging on the wall.

If only you could speak. What would you have to say?

He paused for a moment and stretched out his arms. Leaning forward, he took hold of the sides of the big black table. "We will stop this madness once and for all," he declared.

Each of the councillors looked at each other from the corners of their eyes.

"What do you have in mind?" asked a skinny, old grey-haired councillor.

"I have a plan," The Master said, standing up.

"The city is in chaos," said the skinny old councillor. He turned to face the others in the room. "If Mindset fails, we will all lose our minds."

Nodding their heads, the other councillors agreed.

"So, tell us," said the skinny old councillor. "What exactly is your plan?"

A rush of blood surged into The Master's face, and he started shaking.

"Well?" asked the councillor.

The Master nodded at the guard closest to the skinny old councillor and pulled him from his seat. At the far end of the room, another guard wheeled-in a large black obelisk with a hole in its side. Whilst several other councillors gasped, the skinny old councillor started laughing.

"And what's that? I suppose we're going to destroy the virus with a big black pointy crystal?" he asked.

Peeved, The Master tapped his finger on the table. "My latest invention," he roared. "The Sanitis-Or."

"The Sanitis-Or?" said the skinny old councillor. "So, what, we're going to clean the virus away?"

"Enough!" The Master bellowed. He nodded at a guard who then placed Brightspark into the hole in the side of the Sanitis-Or. At first, nothing happened. But when the crystal started to hum, a blue beam of light shot out from the Sanitis-Or. It struck the skinny old councillor in the face, and his scream echoed around the room, stopping only when his head slammed against the wall. Delighted, The Master looked around the room. The other councillors looked away.

"I think Plan A speaks for itself," The Master said proudly. "Any questions?" he asked.

No one uttered a word, except for the technician with large, black-rimmed glasses who rushed in from another room. He handed The Master a piece of paper, and keeping his eyes to the ground, scurried away.

According to the technician's report, the Sanitis-Or lacked the power to do anything very useful at all. Whilst it could melt the skin from a person's face at close range, it wasn't capable of firing far. Furthermore, because the first victim was already dead, there was no way of knowing whether the Sanitis-Or had successfully eradicated his feelings or, even better still, erased his mind.

The Master crumpled the piece of paper. Raising his small skinny arms in the air, he said what he needed to say. "Exactly as I thought. The Sanitis-Or will save our city. It will take the madness away."

The issue with the sedation of the scientist called Delia was that she was asleep most of the time. So, after discussing it with Juaneeto, The Master ordered her medications be halved.

"But she keeps shouting and singing and rambling about the black dog beside her bed," protested the physician in charge.

"Then triple her dose of pills marked with the letter P," The Master said, pointing at the patient's head. "Somewhere in there, in between the visions and the madness, is the information the city needs."

An hour later, Delia opened her eyes. She squinted, just enough to let in a sliver of light. The room wobbled, and when The Master entered, Delia's eyes flew open.

"Well?" The Master asked.

"Well, what?" Delia said.

"I need answers."

Delia turned her head away, and The Master ordered the physician to leave the room. He circled the bed, irritated at not immediately getting his way. "Perhaps there is something that you need?" he asked.

"Like what?" Delia said sarcastically.

"Well, I need advice on my device," The Master demanded.

Delia looked up. "Of course you do."

"Tell me," The Master said, "Luka–that's your brother's name, isn't it? Stanley Luka?"

"My what?"

"You wouldn't want him to come to any harm?"

"Where is he?" Delia asked.

"In Happysad," The Master smirked. "Safe… for now. But it won't be long before exposure to the sun will drive him mad. He'll start to choke on all those feelings buried deep inside."

Delia pulled hard at the cuffs holding her to the steel bed. She was about to scream but stopped herself when, on the other side of the room, something stirred. She looked past The Master at the black dog that was sitting in the corner the whole time. It seemed to be looking at something under the bed.

"What are you staring at?" The Master asked, looking across the room.

Delia smiled.

"You think this is funny?" said the Master sneered.

Delia's smile widened.

It's the red ball. The dog wants me to reach under the bed and throw the ball.

Ignoring the fact that Delia didn't answer, The Master handed her the report.

Delia thumbed through the pages, then laughed.

"What?" the Master asked, exasperated.

"It's simple maths," she said. "Your Sanitis-Or's never going to work."

The citizens of Mentoria ran wild through the city streets. In the Plaza of Logical Thought, a group of children watched the black dog slide in a slow circle while itching its buttocks on the chequered tiles. The dog's eyes were closed, and its face stretched into what had to be a smile. Every now and then, the dog grunted, unfurling more of its pink tongue that dangled from the corner of its mouth. In the gardens just below the city wall, a small boy sat in a fountain, scratching nervously at his skin.

On street corners, fires burned. The doors to the Great Hall of Power were closed. And far above the tops of the tallest buildings, Mindset's red halo thinned.

The Master handed Delia a small computer. "You'll need this."

"No," she replied. "It's simple—you need more power. Then you can charge the city's batteries."

197

"Batteries? Who said anything about batteries? This is far more important," The Master said. "With the Sanitis-Or we can expand… to Happysad. With the Sanitis-Or, I can clear the people's minds. I can engineer Mindset to fill the skies and protect everyone from the virus of feelings sent by the sun."

"Clear their minds? A shield that big?" Delia said.

"Impressive, isn't it," The Master said with a conceited smile.

"Look at the sky," Delia said. "Mindset uses too much power. It will never work in Happysad."

It was then that the solution dawned on The Master. He looked back quickly through the numbers on the report. "So that's it? All it needs is more power. Then it will work?"

Delia nodded.

"Well, good!" The Master said, motioning to one of the guards. "Tie her up, turn off the lights, and lock the door."

"What about Stanley?" Delia screamed.

"What about Stanley?" The Master mocked her as he walked out of the room.

The lift door opened at the top of the penthouse shaped like a pill, and The Master called for Juaneeto to make sure he was alone. When there was no reply, The Master pulled Brightspark from the box beneath his bed.

I wonder if what they say is true?

Closing his eyes and wanting more than ever for someone to advise him on what to do, The Master raised his hands in the air. The crystal glowed blue. He looked nervously around the room, and then focusing on the crystal, he asked, "Where can I get more power? Tell me what I need to do."

Inside The Master's head, a new voice—which happened to be a woman with a pompous tone—cleared her throat.

"Well, it's about time you paid attention," the voice said. "There is a space traveller in Happysad who collects powerful crystal stones."

The Master's stomach somersaulted.

Space traveller? In Happysad?

"A space traveller?" The Master asked aloud, but it was too late. The woman's voice was gone.

Juaneeto called from the other side of the room, "Master?"

Keeping his back turned, The Master lowered his arms and placed Brightspark back in its box.

"Who were you talking to?" Juaneeto asked.

"No one," The Master snapped. "Assemble the guards and load my skyship with extra nummers."

"What for?" Juaneeto asked.

"It's time to get more power," the Master replied.

On a small brown planet far away, the band of little blue beings stood in a circle. They watched the hologram of the blue-green planet. Seeming particularly interested in The Master's skyship as it left Mentoria, they followed its path upwards and into the night. When the skyship descended on the plantations on the other side of the River E, the little blue beings shuffled from side to side. They looked at each other with wide and excited eyes. Then all at once, they stopped shuffling. One by one, they turned to their right and said what, in their language, amounted to an animated "OOOOoooooooooooo."

16. THE SMALL WHITE DUCK THAT WENT QUACK

Blabbermouth wandered around the forest of Calamity and Eternal Darkness for hours. His mind, expanded by the effects of the dumbnut, had taken a particular interest in the brown colour of dead leaves. One by one, he picked them up and rubbed them against his face. That was until he was distracted by a nearby quacking sound.

Might it be a duck?

He imagined the duck, fat and white, waddling in circles and probably lost. And made hungrier by the dumbnut, the thought of the duck roasting over a fire put a quick stop to his fascination with the leaves.

Blabbermouth followed the "quacking" sound further through the woods, oblivious to the fact that each time he got close enough to see the duck, it seemed to be both invisible and moving further away.

The Master leaned back on the plastic chair of his skyship and sucked hard on the mouthpiece of a nummer. As he tried to remember his last time in Happysad, the numbness spread, and his old fears—witches, black dogs with red rubber balls and bogs—seemed to slip away. The comforting sound of two large mosquitoriums calmed his nerves enough so he could close his eyes.

According to Juaneeto, the mosquitoriums were filled with a specific species of blood-sucking gnat whose buzzing produced a soothing and hypnotic harmonic. Slowly, The Master's mind rose above the trestle of grave concern. That was until, contrary to an express order to be left alone, he was interrupted by the polite voice of a woman that said, "It's never too late to run away."

The Master sat up with a start. "Who's there?" he demanded, looking around. There was no answer. "Who's there?" he asked again. Then, doing his best not to think about the woman's words—which only seemed to make things worse—he sat back and closed his eyes.

When the skyship landed with a gentle thud, The Master opened his eyes. Wiping a stream of dribble from the corner of his mouth, he got up from his chair and pushed through the line of guards to be the first one down the ramp. The guards from the leading skyship had already tied red string between the trees and made a perimeter that was supposed to make everyone feel safe. In the centre was a folding chair marked with a golden capital letter "M," for "Master." Beside the chair was a table with a computer and a big bowl of white pills marked with the letter "P."

"Won't be long now, sir," said one of the guards in a metallic voice as The Master sat in his chair. Juaneeto sat on the ground at The Master's feet and seemed temporarily distracted by a white flower he had picked. A guard positioned the two bell-shaped glass jars—The Master's mosquitoriums—on the table. And The Master placed his hands behind his head, sat back, and waited.

It would have been difficult for Blabbermouth to convey the depth of his disappointment with what happened next. Fooled by his less than adequate tracking skills, Blabbermouth walked in ever-decreasing circles. Already, he could taste the duck, buttery and rich in his mouth. And when the quacking stopped, Blabbermouth looked around. Stepping back, he trod on a spring-loaded, spiked metal cuff that snapped closed around his furry foot.

"We have him!" a metallic voice exclaimed in the dark. The rope attached to the cuff pulled tight, dragging Blabbermouth backwards through the woods. When he reached the bright lights, the pulling stopped. Four gloved hands rolled Blabbermouth on his side, and in front of him was a small, bald man leaning back on a plastic chair with his hands behind his head.

"Ugh..." The Master grunted. "A bog...question the creature," he ordered Juaneeto, who had a greater understanding of the language of Bog.

"What are you doing in the woods?" Juaneeto asked.

And not knowing what to say, Blabbermouth looked at The Master and said the first thing that came into his head, "What happened to all your hair?"

Juaneeto ignored him and asked his question again.

"I was following a duck," Blabbermouth answered dismissively. "Have you seen it?"

The Master slammed his fist on the folding table. "I need answers," he said to Juaneeto. "What's the bog really doing in the woods?"

Even as a boy in Happysad, The Master had decided it was wrong for an animal to be bits of this and bits of that. For this reason, domesticated bogs became the focus of his early experiments on animals involving sticks, knives, and sap from poisonous trees.

"I was following the duck," Blabbermouth said to Juaneeto. "I promise."

Disgusted, The Master dismissed the animal with his hand. And as the guards led him away, Blabbermouth turned back to The Master.

"Where are they taking me?" he called out, his eyes still darting over the dimensions of The Master's head.

It's too big for his body—it looks more like a big egg than a head.

Blabbermouth's attention shifted when he suddenly noticed the two bell-shaped glass jars resting at The Master's side.

Taking a deep breath, The Master stood up. "Stop!" he ordered the guards. Already feeling the effects of Happysad, The Master's lack of patience turned to rage. He swallowed hard, and with his hands behind his back, walked a slow circle around the bog. Juaneeto followed two steps behind.

"I will ask you one last time," The Master said, with Juaneeto translating. "What business do you have in the woods?"

"I was chasing the duck," Blabbermouth said.

"And before that?"

"Dumbnuts, I was eating dumbnuts, and I had an argument with Stanley, and I bit him on the hand, and I don't know where

Esmerelda's gone because she skipped too far ahead into the woods. Stanley said she could carry Brightspark."

"Brightspark?" The Master asked.

"Yes, the crystal that glows in the dark," the bog blabbered.

A wave of not-so-nice feelings bubbled up and attached themselves to thoughts in The Master's mind. Dizziness came in waves, and he could feel himself starting to sway.

"Juaneeto?" he said, confused.

Juaneeto took The Master's arm and rifled through the large white pocket in his surgeon's coat for a pill marked with the letter "P."

"Guard, bring me a nummer!" he ordered, leading The Master away from the bright lights.

In the safety of his skyship, The Master's dizziness started to clear. Electricity pulsed from the mouthpiece of the nummer, sending strong currents through his teeth.

"We don't have a lot of time," Juaneeto said softly. "The nummers will only last for so long without the protection of Mindset."

"The animal's hiding something," The Master said. "Do what you have to and find out what it is."

When Juaneeto returned, Blabbermouth was sitting with his head in his hands.

"Bring me the decoy duck," Juaneeto ordered one of the guards.

"Is this the duck?" he asked Blabbermouth, winding the key in the duck's back.

"It sounds the same," Blabbermouth said.

"You must be hungry?"

"Starving, in fact," Blabbermouth said. "Those dumbnuts make you hungry, and that's why I was following the duck."

"Forget about the duck," Juaneeto said. "What would you like to eat?"

"I like meat, especially if it's slow-roasted. Any kind of bird will do, as long as it's not spatchcock because no one really likes spatchcock. After all, there are too many bones, and there's not much meat, and the bits get caught in your teeth."

Juaneeto handed Blabbermouth the carcasses of two singed owls.

"Eat, eat," he said, motioning with his hand. "And tell me...you said you were not in the woods alone?"

Blabbermouth nodded and spat out some tiny bones.

"Tell me, might you have seen a skinny white creature with big eyes and a bald head?"

"The alien, you mean?" Blabbermouth blurted.

"Ha...hmm," Juaneeto cleared his throat. "Yes, the alien."

"He's quite nice, really," Blabbermouth said. "At first, I was put off by its looks...those big black eyes and skinny legs. Thing is, it doesn't say much. Apparently, it's on a mission, and it's writing a book."

"Anything else?" Juaneeto asked.

"No, not really," Blabbermouth said.

"Did it mention anything about crystals?" Juaneeto asked.

"No, but it had one that was pretty and glowing, just like Brightspark."

"Interesting," Juaneeto said. "So, where would we find this alien?"

"First, I need something else to eat," Blabbermouth said. "The owls were nice, but I'm still hungry. You wouldn't happen to have any cheese?"

Juaneeto grunted, rubbed his chin and turned around. He placed The Master's two mosquitoriums on the table. Blabbermouth froze, paralysed with fear.

For Blabbermouth, his fear of mosquitos never made much sense. He was completely unaware that once upon a time and in another life, he was a black stallion with a shiny coat named Leopold. He had been the horse of a king and the proud wearer of a bejewelled purple saddle that he wore whilst hunting in the woods. His rider, the king, loved Leopold more than he loved his eleven wives. In return, Leopold loved his king more than apples or oats. The trouble started one morning when Leopold and the king were out on a ride. Confronted by a band of murderous thieves, Leopold stopped in a large stagnant pool of water on the path. It happened that the pool of muddy water was home to a particularly ravenous swarm of blood-sucking mosquitos that started biting him right away. Preoccupied with the mosquitos that stung his eyes, Leopold didn't hear the king when he commanded his stallion to bolt. But it was too late, because the king was already dead from the arrow that landed in the middle of his back.

Doing the only thing he could, Leopold whinnied and reared up, accidently dropping his beloved but dead king in the pool of muddy water. And not knowing what else to do, he ran for his life. From that day on, smeared with shame, Leopold hid in the shadows and never left the forest. And when eventually he died, it was not from the diseases carried by the mosquitos. Instead, Leopold died from the shame and agony of his broken heart.

Because of this, his fear of mosquitos had never gone away. Leopold, now Blabbermouth, cowered beneath his interrogator's halo of bright white lights. Slowly, Juaneeto removed the cork from one of the glass jars. The buzzing grew louder as the angry mosquitos started spiralling up and out.

"Stop!" Blabbermouth yelled.

"Very well," Juaneeto said, placing the cork back on the top of the jar. "Just between you and I, where can I find this alien who collects these glowing crystal rocks?"

Under threat of mosquitos, Blabbermouth told Juaneeto what he needed to know. Without thinking, and to make his story complete, he added the part about Stanley and the river that flowed out from the other side of the woods. Then he stopped. Something heavy shifted in Blabbermouth's chest. It moved downwards like a sinking stone.

With a chain around his neck, Blabbermouth led the Mentorian Guard away from the lights. He walked further into the woods and stopped at the clearing where years earlier, the alien's ship, shaped like an after-dinner mint, had crashed into the lake.

Reclining on a stretcher with the pose of a king, The Master kept his eyes closed as the guards carried him, following the bog. Juaneeto walked by his side, and everything seemed to be okay until the hoot of a lone owl made The Master sit up with a start. He looked sideways, left then right. The guards lowered the stretcher to the ground and reached for their guns.

The alien, who also heard the hoot of the owl, did not blink. Firstly, because it had no eyelids, and second because it sensed no need for alarm. It watched as the guards lifted the stretcher with the big-headed and bald, small-bodied man up in the air. Intrigued, the alien watched as the tall figure with the big white coat placed a gadget into the small man's mouth. But when a pair of white-gloved hands reached out from the darkness and grabbed it by the neck, the alien wriggled and struggled to break free.

"We have it," a metallic and trembling voice announced over the radio.

At first, The Master refused to open his eyes. He removed the mouthpiece of his nummer and whispered in Juaneeto's ear, "Tell me it's not a clown." It happened that, of all the horrors The Master remembered from his youth, it was the clowns of Happysad that had spread the dark veil of fear across his mind. Employed to attend the asylums and make people laugh, the clown-project had failed when they accidentally spread terror instead of joy. Unfortunately, and through no fault of their own, it was in the afternoon sun that caused the clowns' white make-up to melt, transforming their red painted mouths into hideous upside-down smiles.

Repeating his question, The Master said to Juaneeto, "Tell me it's not a clown?"

Juaneeto shook his head and answered, "No master, I can assure you, it's not a clown. All I know is that it is the same creature that was looking at you earlier, from behind a tree."

The Master opened his eyes and was both curious and repulsed at the shape and size of the alien's head, even though it was similar to his own. A shiver rippled up his spine.

I could be looking in a mirror.

On the other side of the lake, the spaceship shaped like an after-dinner mint was covered in moss and reeds and leaning against a tree.

"Is that yours?" The Master asked, pointing to the skinny craft. The alien did not reply.

The Master stared at it, lost in thought.

Somehow it looks familiar.

"It's a spaceship, and together they pulled it from the lake," Blabbermouth blurted.

"Shhh," The Master ordered.

Juaneeto turned to the guard who was holding Blabbermouth's lead. "Release the bog," he said, and with the chain clanking around his neck, Blabbermouth scampered off into the shadows of the woods in search of Stanley.

Not far away, a skinny and mostly naked man sat with his eyes closed and hovering approximately four inches above the ground. Beside him, a spaceship was leaning against a tree.

"Put the alien over there," The Master ordered the guards while pointing to a nearby log. He climbed down from his stretcher and walked slowly towards the skinny and hovering man. "Well, what have we here?" he said in a deeper than usual voice.

"W-what do you think?" Freeman said, opening his eyes.

"You?" The Master gasped, recognising him right away.

"Yes," Freeman said. "M-me."

The Master's fascination for the hovering man quickly changed to alarm. "Stop your hovering," he commanded.

"A-as you wish," Freeman replied, and he sank slowly to the ground.

Behind The Master, the guards stood in a neat line.

"I thought you were dead?" The Master stated.

"Y-you mean you h-hoped I was dead," Freeman replied.

Ten years older than The Master and much smarter when it came to electricity, Freeman was once a prominent practitioner of the healing arts. A long time ago and when he was just a boy, The Master had attended his clinic in Happysad. Afflicted with feelings that cluttered and confused his mind, Freeman had tried but offered The Master no relief. Like a fragile twig the following day, The Master's mind snapped. He was committed to an asylum, and it was beneath the shade of a grove of tall, leafy trees that he understood he had to leave Happysad. For good.

"Y-you don't look well," Freeman said as he wriggled to find a comfortable position on the ground.

"No thanks to you," The Master scoffed.

Freeman shrugged his shoulders.

"Have you seen this creature before?" The Master changed the subject and pointed to the alien who was sitting on a nearby log.

Freeman nodded.

"Does it speak?" The Master asked, placing his hand across his mouth. And as if telling a secret, he added, "It has no eyelids!"

"Th-that's why it doesn't b-blink," Freeman said. "And no, it d-doesn't speak."

"Well, there's something that I need," The Master said.

"No d-doubt," Freeman replied.

Juaneeto picked up a stick. He drew a circle—which was meant to look like Mindset—in the sand. Suddenly animated, the alien responded by drawing a series of wiggly lines.

Freeman chuckled.

"What's funny?" The Master asked. "And how do you know what it said?"

"Pictograms," Juaneeto said. "The alien thinks it's funny that you have no hair."

The Master stood tall and puffed out his chest. "You are our prisoner," he said to the alien.

Juaneeto drew a stick figure enclosed by a large square in the sand.

The alien looked at the image and cocked its head to one side.

"Tell it I am the ruler of Mentoria," The Master said.

The alien responded, drawing a large question mark in the sand.

"What does that mean?" asked The Master.

"It's a question mark," Juaneeto replied. "I think it means, *so what*?"

The Master folded his arms across his chest. "Well? Ask if it knows anything about glowing crystal rocks."

"Yes," Freeman said, looking at the alien's reply. "It happens to be a keen collector of all kinds of galactic rocks and stones."

The alien drew a few extra squiggles in the sand, indicating how proud it was of its collection, and added that it was only too happy to show it to them before it was ready to leave.

"Leave?" The Master said. "Leave?"

The alien scratched its big bald head.

"Freedom has a price," The Master declared, and Juaneeto translated his words by drawing in the sand.

211

"For the fair price of three glowing crystal eggs, you can leave," The Master said.

Confused, the alien stood up from the mossy log. The guards stepped back, and when they pointed their guns at the creature from outer space, the alien sat back down and drew a shape in the sand.

"A mushroom?" The Master asked.

"No," Freeman interrupted. "It's Mindset. The problem is with Mindset. The alien says Mindset is to be blamed for the electromagnetic anomalies occurring in this part of space. Wormholes have shifted slightly to the left, and lots of people have ended up a long way from where they are supposed to be. Computers are scrambled, spaceships have crashed."

"How do you know all of this?" The Master peered at him.

Freeman held the alien's gaze and kept on talking.

"Worst of all, Mindset's interference has mostly affected the older space tourists who have blown their life savings on the one trip of their lives. Travelling in circles, they have never been to see the four million, six hundred and forty-seven thousandth wonder of the universe—which happens to be a small seahorse living in a pool of dirty water on a radioactive and otherwise uninhabited planet. Aliens everywhere are furious. Not the least, Commander Aachoo of the fleet of warring starships, who is adamant about impressing his girlfriend for the first and last time."

The alien nodded slowly to itself as the skinny-looking man recounted his story for him.

What's a few crystal eggs? My grandfather's not getting any younger, and surely there's nothing more absurd than a city surrounded in a mushroom of light to stop them from feeling anything at all?

212

The alien traced an outline of three crystal eggs in the sand and a large intergalactic question mark beneath that. The Master stepped back, scowling as though irritated at the thought of not getting his way. He blinked quickly and placed his shaking hands behind his back.

Fastening the top button of his white physician's coat, Juaneeto stepped forward, "You have a question?"

The alien drew a line through its drawing of Mindset in the sand. This was accompanied by what looked like a larger and fatter alien with big teeth and lumps all over its body.

"It wants you to shut Mindset down," Freeman said.

"What?" said Juaneeto.

"For one hour every day."

"Nonsense!" The Master said.

Freeman levitated to a height of approximately four inches above the ground to clear his mind and with his legs crossed.

"I would advise you to agree to the alien's request," he said. "Apparently, Mindset has upset a certain Commander Aachoo, who it appears, likes blowing things up."

"Master?" Juaneeto asked.

Grunting, The Master replied, "We will do what we have to do."

Then, sensing The Master would not honour his word, Freeman traced a large fat cross in the sand.

The alien, despite wanting to see its grandfather again, certainly wanted no trouble from Commander Aachoo. So, with a blend of gullibility and denial, it nodded, and flanked by the guards, walked slowly backwards to the entrance of its spacecraft that was leaning against a tree. Waving its small hand in a circle, the alien watched as the spaceship's door slid open. It went inside and, moments later, returned carrying three glowing crystal eggs.

"I'll take those," Juaneeto said, reaching out with his arms.

"It's a trick," Freeman said, aware of an unexpected rush of blood to his head.

The alien walked up to where Freeman was hovering four inches above the ground. And leaning forward, it placed its hand on Freeman's head. Thoughts and feelings passed silently between the two until Freeman opened his eyes with a sense of peace. With a new resolve to do exactly what he needed to do, Freeman uncrossed his legs and placed his two feet firmly on the ground. "I, too, will leave today," he said.

"Come with me," the alien said in the language of its thoughts.

"No," Freeman said. "My place is in the Fields of Crying Babies, where I can teach the mothers how to rise above their sadness and their fears."

Uninterested in anything but himself, The Master turned and walked away from the lake. Juaneeto followed, carrying the three crystal eggs in his hands. When he turned back to look at the lake for one last time, Juaneeto watched as the spaceship shaped like an after-dinner mint lifted off and wobbled in the sky. It turned a couple of times slowly and then vanished in a halo of brilliant amber light.

It was not long before The Master's skyship rose above the Woods of Calamity and Eternal Darkness. With his seatbelt fastened tight, The Master sat on his hands so no one could see them shake. Beside him, Juaneeto sat with a box containing three crystal eggs beneath his feet. The Master lay back and hummed to the buzz of his mosquitoriums. The future seemed suddenly clear. And it was as if, just for a moment, The Master smiled.

17. THE LAKE OF THE ALMOST NAKED MAIDENS

Far from the centre of the woods, Stanley darted between the white limbs of the twisted trees. He was following a posse of fireflies that bobbed up and down as if they dangled from the ends of a puppeteer's string. Ahead came the sound of running water, while behind him, the darkness closed in. And his concerns about Brightspark were replaced by an image in his mind of Delia sobbing in the shadows of her cell. Then it vanished almost as quickly as it appeared, replaced by the first spears of morning light that stabbed at the edge of the woods.

On reaching the stream, Stanley followed its twists and turns until he reached the plain. In the distance, he could see the foothills of the far-away mountains that rose up to the pools of the Crystal Springs. Overhead, the remnants of a waning moon cut an eerie figure in the sky. Stanley sensed a jostling crowd of old and ugly shadows deep down inside himself, trying to break free. Then, without any reason at all, he dropped to his knees and started sobbing.

Shortly after his blubbers and sniffles stopped, Stanley sensed something approaching from behind. The combination of clumsy feet and panting and sucking sounds was strangely familiar, and Stanley stood up, slowly looking around. The shadow of something large bulged from the bottom of a distant tree.

Best be on my way.

Stanley ran as fast as his legs would carry him until he reached the other side of the narrow plain, and yet, the panting sound drew closer. The rumble of a waterfall smashing onto stones echoed from up ahead. As he started up the foothills, small pools of water appeared around him. He climbed up through a layer of fog, stopping to drink from a shallow pool. Looking through his reflection, he watched two small orange fish swimming in circles.

"There you are, master. I've been looking for you everywhere!"

Stanley toppled backwards in surprise and found himself gazing up at Blabbermouth.

Not one to hold a grudge for any longer than he should, Blabbermouth pounced onto Stanley's chest and licked his face.

Stanley pushed him away and wiped his mouth.

"I was worried, master," Blabbermouth said, "But I can see you are safe and all the things that could have happened to you didn't. So, it's okay. I'm here now, and I can protect you, and there is no need to worry about anything anymore."

"No need to worry?" Stanley said.

"That's right, master, you're safe now I am here." Blabbermouth pulled Stanley up off the ground. "Come on, master. We'd best be off. The clock is ticking, you know. There's no time to lose."

"Why the sudden hurry?" Stanley asked, suspicious.

"Delia. You've got to get back to Delia," Blabbermouth said, swallowing his lie as he tried not to think about all the things he shouldn't have told the guards.

What's done is done. If I think about something else, maybe everything will be okay.

"So, let's go," Blabbermouth said.

Stanley nodded and continued to climb the mossy stone cliff up towards the crystal springs. A band of grey clouds drifted across the sky. At the top of the cliff, a large field of red poppies opened onto a silent and shimmering lake. On the far side, black stone cliffs dove beneath the dark waters.

Blabbermouth, both anxious and hungry, sucked on the nectar of handfuls of red flowers he plucked from the fields.

Stanley walked without saying a word. In the distance, a single willow tree leaned out across the black waters of the sparkling lake. Captivated by the flotilla of tiny wooden boats drifting in large circles on the lake, Stanley stopped to rest as he stared at the figures wearing brown hooded cloaks and steering the boats with long staffs.

Through a mouthful of flowers, Blabbermouth broke the silence. "Strange, don't you think, master? Why would anyone be floating around in circles on a lake like this?"

Stanley shrugged.

"I say we just let them be," Blabbermouth said, "Don't want to be distracted. Best be on our way."

Stanley didn't move.

"Come, master. We have to go," Blabbermouth insisted, pointing to the trail that followed the edge of the lake.

"Okay," Stanley said, distracted.

Blabbermouth looked back across the field of red poppies.

It won't be long, he thought. They'll be coming.

"Quick," he said to Stanley. "Or it'll be too late."

Looking down, Blabbermouth noticed a large blue mushroom with grey flecks that was far too pretty not to eat. When he swallowed the fungus, he knew right away it was a bad idea. Blabbermouth's stomach contracted like a fist, sending spasms back upwards into his mouth, and he vomited blue-grey mushroom and carrots all over his feet.

Struggling to breathe, Blabbermouth fell on the ground, started shaking, and curled into a tight ball.

In the underworld of his feverish dreams, Blabbermouth sat at a small wooden table opposite a large jar filled with buzzing and angry mosquitos. Despite his fear, he picked up the jar and smashed it on the ground. The mosquitos started biting. Blabbermouth stood still, and as the poison took hold, he realised he was no longer afraid. And only then, taking advantage of a passing gust of wind, did the mosquitos spiral upwards and fly away, leaving Blabbermouth in a dark, dreamless sleep.

Distracted, Stanley stared at the figure dressed in a white cloak that stood by the edge of the lake. With a narrow wooden boat to their side, the figure appeared to be waiting for someone to arrive. When Stanley walked closer, the figure turned around.

"Come with me across the still waters of the lake," said the soft woman's voice. With two hands, she reached up and pulled back the hood of her cloak. The maiden's hair was wild and red and wavy and long.

Stanley moved closer, captivated by the maiden's innocence and beauty. He felt himself sinking into the depths of her large brown eyes, and he held his breath and started to count. Suddenly, it felt as though a knife twisted inside Stanley's chest. He wanted to run away. He wanted to stay.

Out across the lake, Stanley saw the other wooden boats continue in their slow circles as the sun slipped behind the clouds. Looking back at the girl, he noticed the emblem on her forehead.

A small golden star.

"Stanley," the maiden whispered.

"You know my name?"

The woman brushed her teeth across her lower lip, and she reached out her hand. "Come," she said. "It's time. The clouds have dimmed the light."

The mist of desire spread across Stanley's mind, and at the same time, the pain in his chest continued to spread.

I'm drowning.

The maiden looked at him and smiled. "Come with me across the waters of the dark lake."

Stanley took the maiden's hand. Her skin was soft, like silk. He stepped onto the small wooden boat and shuddered, sensing he was leaving something behind.

The maiden took hold of her staff and pushed gently at the shore. Already adrift, Stanley reclined on a bed of red velvet blankets and closed his eyes.

"Feel the magic of the lake," the maiden murmured.

Stanley pressed his fingers into his thighs.

"Open your eyes," she whispered.

Hypnotised, Stanley drank in her porcelain skin and the curve of her spine. At the centre of the lake, the other wooden boats moved away. The maiden lay down her staff, and untying the knot around her neck, her white cloak fell away. A copper-coloured under-robe hugged the maiden's body and fell midway down her breasts.

Stanley gasped.

Reaching forward, the maiden cupped her hands beneath his jaw. She started to sing. Stanley closed his eyes, feeling her moving closer, her breath on his cheek. She smelled like the woods. Earth and flowers.

"What is this place?" Stanley asked.

"It's whatever you want it to be," she said, her chin brushing his cheek.

The image of a serpent flashed across Stanley's mind. He flinched and pulled away. The maiden reached out and caressed his chin. Pulling him close, she kissed his lips. Then, with his eyes closed, Stanley surrendered to the maiden's whispers in his ear.

"Together, we are free."

A bolt of sunlight shot through the clouds and shimmered across the lake. Stanley leaned forward, his head against the maiden's chest as she ran her fingers through his hair. At the edge of the lake, the other maidens stepped from their wooden boats and onto the shore.

"I have waited for you," the maiden said to Stanley.

"Who are you?" Stanley asked.

"I am a maiden on a boat on a lake," she said. And standing up, she pulled at the cords of her copper-coloured under-robe. Almost naked, the maiden stood over him, her breasts heaving in the glimmering light. She moved slowly down.

Stanley ran his fingers along her neck and surrendered to his desire. The wooden boat bobbed on the lake, sending ripples to the shore, and at the edge of the water, the other maidens bowed their heads and started to sing.

Such was the blissful fate of many men who, chasing the white rabbit of happiness, happened to drown in the lake of the Almost Naked Maidens. Supposedly the stuff of myth, the maidens veiled their voluptuous and naked bodies beneath brown coloured cloaks. They hummed hypnotic melodies and lured men who were vulnerable and the unwitting slaves to their desire.

What began as a group of nature-loving girls eating berries and running almost naked through the woods had become something else. As their motivations had been completely misunderstood, the maidens were outcasts and labelled as whores because most of the time, they enjoyed taking off almost all their clothes.

And so, under the protection of Evil Eva—who lived in the nearby Amethyst Cave—the maidens spent most of their time almost naked, making daisy chains, floating in circles on the lake, and talking in song to the black birds that made their nests in the tops of the trees.

At the far edge of the lake was the entrance to the Amethyst Cave. Covered in vines and a garland of purple flowers, the mouth of the cave was hidden behind a gigantic white shell that Eva's dogs had dragged from the shores of an ancient sea.

Inside, and under the flickering light of candles, Eva toiled night and day. At any cost, she was determined to discover the remedy that would heal the agony of her separation from Salieri and her two beloved sons. In return for allowing the almost naked maidens to float around the lake, Eva laid claim to the bodies of their lovers. After drowning in the waters of their own desire, the bodies of the men were untangled from the reeds and delivered by the maidens to the mouth of the Amethyst Cave.

With smiles still hanging on their lips, the corpses were sprinkled with rosewater and laid to rest on small beds of little yellow flowers. At night, and after cleansing them of their desire in the purifying flames, Eva offered up the dead men's souls to the night. She whispered incantations to the invisible beings of other worlds, and she waited for what she hoped would one day be the divine gift of mercy to heal her broken heart.

In the middle of the lake, the Almost Naked Maiden brushed her nose across Stanley's lips. She whispered in his ear.

Stanley tried to think of Delia. He tried to pull away.

"Let yourself go," the maiden said, brushing her tongue across Stanley's lips. A wave of nausea washed over him. It was then that Stanley remembered his dream as if the Almost Naked Maiden was suddenly like the avalanche of ice and snow that threatened to swallow him whole. He was fighting and falling and pedalling into the darkness of his dream. Then it stopped. Stanley surrendered. Everything went white. The last thing he remembered was the wave of his desire spiralling up from between his legs and the vaulting in his stomach as the small wooden boat rolled onto its side, capsized, and started to sink.

Suddenly, the Almost Naked Maiden was gone. Stanley drifted downwards, like the countless corpses that had gone before. He sank to the bottom of the deep, dark lake. Alone and drowning in his desire.

18. PLAN B

It could be said that once the riots began, the downfall of Mentoria was just a matter of time. Outside the Great Hall of Power, a short fat man in a tight, white exercise suit argued with a guard. Despite having refused to go inside to pay his taxes, the guard nudged him, with the butt of his gun, towards the door. That was when the trouble really began. Tormented by recent visions of a black dog carrying a red rubber ball, the fat man turned and kicked the guard in the groin. With his finger on the trigger of his gun, the guard collapsed and accidentally shot himself in the face. A group of other guards, having witnessed everything, ran to the Great Hall. Mercilessly, they beat the fat man in the tight white exercise suit until he no longer moved. And inside the Great Hall, other exhausted citizens stepped off their cyclotrons and walked out the door.

An unexpected announcement came over the loudspeakers of the city. In a recorded message, The Master denied all the rumours of feelings, claiming that everything was under control. He insisted the safest thing for all the citizens of Mentoria was to stay inside their homes. But when the alarm on the rooftop of the largest infirmary of the city wailed, and red emergency lights everywhere started to flash, the citizens stopped listening.

On the journey back to Mentoria, Juaneeto realised the true state of The Master's mind. As the Mentorian skyship slipped through the cold dark night, Juaneeto listened to The Master crying out for his mother in his sleep. Immediately, Juaneeto gave The Master a handful of pills marked with the letter "P." For despite the risk of death from an overdose, in Juaneeto's mind, it was a reasonable risk to take.

He must make good decisions, and if the pills don't kill him, they just might set him free.

When the skyship landed in Mentoria, The Master awoke exhausted. Having trouble talking, he retired to his bedchamber in the penthouse shaped like a pill. Hours later, when he stirred, The Master opened his eyes to find a reluctant-looking Juaneeto tugging at his feet. He sat up, wiping the dribble from his chin. "What? What is it?" he asked out loud.

Juaneeto pointed at the screen on the bedchamber wall. Citizens with sticks fought against a small regiment of guards outside the Great Hall of Power. Beside the screen, a large, round lock with black numbers was ticking loudly and counting down. "17 hours, 52 minutes, 41 seconds. 40 seconds, 39…"

"Do we really need that clock?" The Master asked. "It hurts my head."

"It's the timer, Master. Remember your agreement with the alien?"

"I don't do business with aliens," The Master sneered.

"Yes," Juaneeto said, placating him. "But what about the other alien who likes to blow things up?"

The Master ignored the question. "I'm as likely to turn Mindset off as I am to get rid of all my nummers. Now tell me, how are things progressing with Plan B?" he asked.

"The Sanitis-Or?" Juaneeto asked.

"Well, that is Plan B, is it not?" The Master said sarcastically.

"They're running some final tests," Juaneeto said. "The city's power reserves are low. And there's no telling the damage the Sanitis-Or may cause if it bounces off Mindset and shoots back our way."

"Tests? There's no time for tests," the Master scoffed. "Take a good look outside. And besides, if there is a big angry alien headed our way, we'll use the Sanitis-Or on it too."

The alarms in the infirmaries of Mentoria continued to wail. And given The Master's fragile state of mind, it was the last straw when he watched footage of Delia—his physicist-prisoner—escape. His hands balled into tight fists as he watched her crash through the doors of her cell. Dressed in nothing but a white sheet, Delia ran through the city streets. The Master tracked her progress until she climbed onto an overturned truck and stood with her arms outstretched, repeating the same word over and over again.

"What's she saying?" The Master asked with a scowl.

"What does it matter?" Juaneeto said before quickly correcting himself beneath The Master's angry stare. "Stanley. She's saying Stanley."

"Order!" The Master yelled, in a rage, "We must restore order! Alien or no alien, I will not allow Mindset to fail!"

"We must stop the riots in the streets," Juaneeto said. "We need to remind the people of their fears."

"Yes…yes," The Master declared, slurring his words. "Find the physicist. Then, with everybody watching, we will erase her mind."

The simple task of pulling a girl dressed in a dirty white sheet from the roof of an overturned truck proved much more difficult than expected. And in the end, blood was spilled, shots were fired, and onlookers ran away.

The holographic image of Delia's head connected with wires to a power point on the wall was broadcast across the city. Dressed in a shiny red suit—because it was the only thing the guards could find—Delia sat oddly still. With the first bolt of electricity, her eyes rolled back into her head. A thin ribbon of smoke drifted from her ears. When it stopped, Delia opened her eyes. A single tear rolled down her cheek. And behind her, a small shadow of something, seemingly chasing its tail, danced across the wall.

The Master shuddered. On his command, the guard flicked the switch. Lights in the city streets flickered on and off, and when Delia slumped, motionless in the chair, the shadow on the wall disappeared.

Almost immediately, the riots stopped. Citizens, who had been whispering about the black dog with the red rubber ball, returned to their homes. Inside their hearts, feelings, forgotten and numbed, started to stir. And like lava, it started to rise.

19. GUNS BLAZING, BOOTS STOMPING IN TIME

Eva's dogs dragged Stanley's shiny, wet body into the Amethyst Cave. All that day, she had been visited by strange premonitions of change. The dogs were unusually restless and spent the afternoon fighting over the carcass of a bat that had fallen from its upside-down sleep on the ceiling of the cave. Obeying their orders, the dogs left Stanley's body beside Eva's big black pot before sitting tall on their hind legs and waiting for something to eat.

Appearing from behind the big black pot, Eva raised her hand in the air. "Go!" she said, dismissing the dogs. They pulled back and retreated to the corners of the cave. Eva untied the laces on Stanley's shoes and slipped them from his feet. Removing the red silk cloth from around her neck, Eva stroked Stanley's limbs with the care of a mother cleaning a newborn child. She doused him with a tonic of rosemary and mint, which according to a book of spells, increased the chances of returning life to the dead.

Unfastening Stanley's shirt, Eva gasped when she saw the small glass prism tied around his neck. And pressing her fist against her chest, she felt a small spark inside her heart for the first time in years.

Taking a deep breath, Eva reached out and touched the clear crystal prism around Stanley's neck. She noticed it was punctured with a small round hole that was sealed with a tiny cork.

"Impossible," Eva said out loud, her voice bouncing around the cave.

Each of the dogs cocked their heads to one side, following the echo of Eva's voice. They whimpered because even after all those years, it was Eva's voice that cast the long shadow inside their hearts.

Eva tugged at the leather strap that held the prism around Stanley's neck. When it snapped, she held it up to the flickering light. A small drop of liquid rolled around inside. "It couldn't be," she said, turning and rummaging around the discarded glass bottles on the floor of the cave. The dogs followed Eva with their eyes as she started singing the song that long ago she had sung to Salieri on the shores of the River E.

"Ha!" Eva exclaimed, holding an old, dirty, and cracked glass prism into the light. Looking back at Stanley's body, she knew exactly what to do.

And as she sharpened her blade and hummed the old tune, she stopped as it suddenly became glaringly obvious that for all those years she'd repeated the same mistake.

The remedy for my sadness is with the living. I have no business seeking answers from the dead.

Both happy and sad, Eva got to her feet and paced in circles, waving her knife through the air as she walked. Nervously, the dogs sat still, their eyes darting around the cave.

In a flurry of excitement, Eva held the prism up to her mouth and popped the cork with her teeth. She poured the single stale tear of a martyr into her mouth. In her heart, she somehow knew it held the essence of Salieri and the essence of her beloved sons. Eva's heart swelled with pain, and she collapsed to her knees. Her heart pounded with frantic desperation, and as though it might make some kind of difference, she leaned over and kissed Stanley on the lips. Then wondering where he had been, she kissed Stanley's silent heart.

Had he seen Salieri? Had he walked with her cherished sons?

As she sat back, Eva recalled a tale from her childhood. As the story went, there was once, in a foreign land, a man who possessed magical powers. With kind eyes and a short beard, he had walked among the people dressed in sandals and a robe. It was said he raised a man from the dead, and in the secret chamber of Eva's frozen heart, she always believed the story to be true. So, when Stanley spluttered, choked, and spat a mouthful of stale water from the lake, Eva fell back, horrified and almost amused.

Stanley lay still on the cold, stone table. He moved his eyes from side to side, his mind searching for something to grab hold of. The memory of the voluptuous breasts of the Almost Naked Maiden came to mind, quickly followed by the feeling of sinking slowly into the cold, dark depths of the lake.

Eva stepped closer and stroked Stanley's head. His foot twitched. The dogs, who hadn't moved from the corners of the cave, howled.

"Shhh," Eva said, raising her right hand in the air.

"Who are you?" Stanley asked.

"My name is Eva, and these are my dogs," she said, gesturing to the hounds that snorted with discontent.

"Evil Eva?" Stanley said. "The witch?"

Eva chuckled. "It depends."

"There is a Virus," Stanley said. "A black dog. It causes people to have feelings, and then they lose their mind." He tried to sit up, but Eva placed her hand across his head, gently holding him down.

"I need to find a cure," Stanley said.

"For feelings?" Eva asked.

"Yes."

Eva laughed, and the sound reverberated around the cave, making it sound like the collective voice of a crowd. Stanley shuddered as he realised he was speaking with a witch. He rubbed his chest.   The glass prism was gone.

"Looking for this?" Eva said, holding up the empty glass pendant.

"Give it to me," Stanley said. "It's mine."

"Tell me where you got it, then it's yours," Eva said.

"First, I need the cure for feelings," Stanley said. "For the virus, the black dog."

Annoyed, Eva placed the pendant behind her back. "No," she said. "Because if it weren't for me, you would still be dead."

Sensing their mistress was annoyed, the dogs sat to attention and growled from across the cave. When Eva whistled, the largest of her black dogs appeared at her side, its lips peeled back, exposing sharp, white teeth.

"So," Eva said, stroking her hound. "Tell me where you have been, and I'll see what I can do."

"The pendants, they sell them in the Valley of the Martyrs," Stanley said.

"The Valley of the Martyrs," Eva repeated as she caught a drop of rainwater from the roof of the cave. It was then that she sang the lullaby that had once sent her beloved sons to sleep.

"Why are you singing?" Stanley asked.

"Because songs can heal even the most troubled heart," Eva said.

"But what about the visions?" Stanley said. "The black dog with the red rubber ball. It drives people mad, and they lose their minds."

"It's not madness," Eva said as she continued to sing and collect more rainwater from the roof of the cave. "The feelings are locked and trapped inside their hearts," she said. "This song will set them free."

"But what about the dog?"

"That's something else altogether," Eva said, laughing again.

"I don't understand," Stanley said. "And how do I know you're telling the truth?"

"Because you have no choice, and I would not lie," Eva said.

Slowly, Eva filled her flask with the enchanted rainwater, only to be interrupted when two of her dogs entered the cave, barking and dragging a bleeding and wet Blabbermouth behind them.

"Quiet," Eva yelled.

"Master?" Blabbermouth said, looking up at Stanley. "I couldn't find you, so I swam across the lake. But then there were the dogs." Blabbermouth winced in pain, revealing a gaping wound in his side. He panted and unfurled his long pink tongue, and in a show of exhaustion typical to bogs, he bared his yellow front tooth. At first, the dogs stepped back, then seemingly terrorised by the site of the bog's single yellow tooth, they pounced. They tore at Blabbermouth's flesh until Eva screamed for them to stop, but by then, it was too late. Blabbermouth closed his eyes. "Sorry, master."

Stanley rolled off the table and crouched by Blabbermouth's side. A tsunami of feelings and shadows filled with pain flooded his mind. Helpless and not knowing what to do, Stanley vomited on the cave floor. "What have they done?"

Eva cursed at her dogs and placed a cork in the flask's top.

Stanley nursed Blabbermouth's head in his lap. Inside, he felt something fragile and old and hidden away, crack. Old tears spilled down his cheeks.

"It's because of the mosquitos," Blabbermouth murmured.

"What?" said Stanley.

"The mosquitos," Blabbermouth said with a wet cough, causing thick blood to ooze from the corners from his mouth.

Stanley stroked his head, trying to reassure him. "It's going to be okay."

No one saw the pinprick of light from the red laser as it flashed across the back of the cave. But the alarm was raised when Eva's dogs barked as they heard something that, moments later, became the sound of marching boots.

Blabbermouth opened one of his bloodshot eyes. "It's my fault, master," he said. "If it weren't for the mosquitos, I never would have told them about you. The guards followed me here. I led them to you."

In the commotion of dogs barking and boots marching, bullets ripped around the cave. And Blabbermouth, in the act of bravery he had sought for many lives, stretched out and protected Stanley with his dirty orange fur.

The Mentorian Guards entered the cave with guns blazing and boots stomping in time. Horrified, Eva filled her lungs with air and screamed a piercing note of "E." It reverberated off the walls, and the guards dropped their guns and covered their ears. Eva closed her eyes and sang louder. At that moment,

234

Eva's psychic abilities, long absent from her life, returned. There was a valley with crucifixes scattered across rolling hills and suffocating beneath clouds of dread and guilt in her vision.

Seizing the moment, and despite the pain in their ears, three of the guards lunged at Eva and took hold of her hands.

"You're the witch," one of them said.

Eva looked through him and allowed her anger to build. The other guard fastened a silver metal cuff to Stanley's wrists.

"It's all your fault. You and that girl—the physicist," the guard said. "But soon, it'll all be over."

"What do you mean?" Stanley asked.

The guard pulled a small, black, rectangular transmitting device from inside his jacket. He pushed a white button, and an image appeared on the screen.

Stanley swallowed hard. He watched as the electricity shot through Delia, and her body shuddered and froth formed at her mouth. He yelled at the guard and pulled at the silver cuffs. Realising he was trapped, Stanley screamed. The other guard, still holding Eva, kicked Stanley in the chest, knocking him down to the wet floor of the cave before turning his attention to Eva.

"Give me the antidote to the Virus Called Dog, and you will live," he said, mustering his bravest tone.

Eva chuckled, a steely determination in her eyes. "Do you really think you can tell me what to do?" she asked the guard.

Confused, the guard looked around, wondering what it was he had missed.

"Now untie my hands, and we shall see," Eva said.

As though mesmerised by the fact that he was talking to a witch who had done a lot of bad things by all reports—the guard obeyed Eva's command and untied her hands. Eva pointed to the pendant she had reattached around Stanley's neck. "The solution to your problem is right there," she said.

"What? That's it?" the guard said.

"Yes," Eva said. "One drop in the water supply is all that you will need."

No one really understood what happened next. Reacting to a flash of golden light, the guards screamed and started shooting around the cave. Later, it was said that Eva rose on the wings of an evil bird and flew through the air, shrieking and laughing in the key of "C." Others said that Eva just disappeared in the flash of golden light. But one thing was for certain. When the smoke cleared and the guards shone their torches around the cave, Eva and her surviving dogs were gone, and Stanley was floating, face down in the narrow stream that cut its way through the cave. With his hands cuffed behind his back, Stanley's body floated away. And terrorised by their exposure to dark magic, the guards grabbed their guns, turned, and ran.

Stanley passed through the passage worn by the river and out of the cave. The rumbling sound of the waterfall drew closer. Blabbermouth was gone, and he was sure Delia was dead. The glass prism bobbed loosely around Stanley's neck. And when he took a deep breath, the water rushed in. Everything sped up. The thundering of the dark falls grew louder, and the current sucked him down, so he was suddenly weightless, like a white bird falling through a black sky.

Falling, flying, choking, crying.

At the same time, and still suffering from a lifetime of indigestion, Heinrich, the whale, swam through the dark pool at the bottom of the falls. Distressed that he had not found anything nice to eat, he had accidentally led the pod astray. Convinced that he was a good leader after all, Heinrich was determined to fight the good fight and, no matter what, find the younger whale's krill or something else to eat.

Heinrich was halfway through a yawn when something plummeted from the black night of the cave and landed in his mouth. At first, he gagged, then he swallowed.

I hope that was not a bat.

PART THREE

RETURN TO MENTORIA

20. CLEAN HANDS AND RUSTY NAILS

Upon the wings of intuition, Eva travelled night and day. It was just after dark when she arrived at the Valley of the Martyrs. At the gates on the top of the hill, the centurion, wearing a shiny helmet with a red-feathered crest, paced up and down. He had tried to look busy for some time, and now and then—and mostly for something to do, he stopped and jabbed his long spear into the ground. Already, the evening mist had formed like a lid on the valley, trapping the melancholy air. During her descent, Eva flew past the guard. His back was turned, but even if he had been doing his job, even if he had paid attention to the fleeting scent of rosemary and mint, there were too many reasons for him to look the other way. Trailing a pack of wild dogs, Eva slipped into the Valley of the Martyrs, hidden by the first long shadows of the night.

The lights of campfires flickered in the village of the tents. Small figures in black cloaks huddled together, comforting each

240

other with sobs and dreary stories of everything that was wrong with their lives. Just before dark, the martyrs had lowered themselves from their crosses and hopped, barefoot and mostly naked, to the village. They walked with their heads down and held up their wooden begging bowls in the hope of scraps from passers-by.

Too busy feeling bad, no one noticed Eva as she moved between the campfires. It started to rain. In the distance, dark clouds gathered, and forks of lightning ripped across the sky. Eva followed the narrow and winding path that led away from the village of the tents with her destination away from the crowds. She walked toward the lone martyr who was still hanging on his cross, despite the approaching darkness and rain.

Eva glided slowly up the mount as the heavy rain cut holes in the ground. Puddles overflowed. Nailed to a large black cross, the lone martyr's head was tilted slightly down, and he looked into the distance through an open brown eye. A flock of black birds circled overhead.

Having decided to walk up the hill, Eva squelched in the mud. The pain in her stomach started even before she saw the lone martyr for the first time. Rain lashed Eva's face, and the wind washed away her tears. At the base of the cross, she knelt and kissed the ground, repeatedly whispering unspoken old words. Then she stood up and raised her hands to the sky.

Rivers of dried mud and old blood covered the lone martyr's body. His feet were infected where the rusty nails pierced his skin. Eva pulled a small ceramic pot of green paste from beneath her cloak and stroked his feet. The lone martyr flinched.

"I never stopped searching for you," Eva said. "I had to leave, so you and your brother could live."

The lone martyr raised his head. "Nobody comes here," he said. "Who are you? You don't know me. I might as well be dead. Go away and let me be."

But when Eva started humming an old tune, something in him softened. Instantly overcome with a rush of grief, the lone martyr started to weep.

"I know your tears," Eva said, kissing his feet.

The lone martyr opened his other eye, which was green. Eva's black robe billowed in the wind and rain, and as if he believed her to be the angel of death, the lone martyr whispered, "I am ready, black bird. Take me."

"Come with me," Eva said.

"Set me free," he said, closing his eyes.

"I have waited for this my whole life," Eva said, dropping to her knees. "My son. Come with me."

Shocked, the lone martyr looked down. "If you loved me, why did you leave?"

Eva wept, and unable to find any words, she started to sing.

The lone martyr looked down at his mother through the rain. Eva beckoned him with her hands. Overcome with the power of her love, she lifted from the ground, her black robes spread to the side, giving her wings. Drawing closer, Eva placed her son's head on her breast.

The lone martyr sobbed. "Why did you leave me?"

Eva kissed his face and stroked his head but remained silent.

"Is it true you are a witch?"

"I am your mother," she said. "The only real magic is the love for you I have inside my heart."

The lone martyr cried harder and pulled at the nails in his ankles and wrists until he started to bleed.

"It's time," Eva said.

"But there is nowhere for me to go," the lone martyr sobbed.

242

"Come," Eva said. "We shall see."

Stroking her son's head, Eva hummed softly until he fell asleep. With the help of a little magic, Eva pulled the nails from his hands and feet and cleaned his wounds whilst he slept.

It was almost dawn when he woke. The rain stopped, and together they sat in silence, waiting for the morning light.

Despite the disappointments in his life, things changed for Salieri the day he discovered the simple pleasure of washing his hands. For as long as he could remember, twice a day, Salieri washed with perfumed soaps left by pilgrims as gifts. His ritual became a habit that helped him relax and set his mind adrift.

With his back to the front of his tent, Salieri sensed Eva was near, like a dark and beautiful cloud across a lonely sky. Invisible to Salieri's guards, she entered his tent and stood in silence behind the man she loved. Paralysed by her presence, Salieri didn't move. Eva placed her hand on his shoulder, and he instantly felt a lifetime of sadness melt away. And when he turned to see Eva's pale and beautiful face, Salieri's heart opened and thundered so loudly, he could hear it inside his head.

"You are beautiful as the last time I saw you," he said.

Eva reached up and brushed the grey hair from his face. "My love. My sweet love. Forgive me."

Years of tears welled in Salieri's eyes, but their reunion was interrupted as a thin dark shadow appeared at the entrance to the tent.

"Centurion?" Salieri asked, but there was no answer. "Stranger, name yourself," he demanded.

"Shhh," Eva said, stroking Salieri's face. She turned to the entrance of the tent. "Come," she said, holding out her arm.

"Salieri, my love... it's our son."

The candles in the tent flickered. Tall and wasted, the lone martyr hobbled into the light. Dirty, bleeding, and bruised, he addressed Salieri.

"Father?"

Salieri tried to look away, but Eva held his chin. "You knew?" Eva asked, surprised.

"There was nothing I could do," Salieri said.

"Our son. You left him out there to die."

Salieri stared at the holes in his son's ankles and hands, and he clutched at his head as though a piece of his mind was splintering away. There was nothing for him to say.

"Why?" asked Eva.

"It's not his fault," interrupted the martyr-son. "My suffering is my own. I made him promise to leave me. But now it's perfect because both of you are here."

With a quick hand, the martyr-son pulled a curved and rusty blade from behind his back. He searched his parents' eyes and saw the one thing that was absent all his life. Love. Overwhelmed, the martyr-son jabbed the rusty blade into his side. Eva lunged and tried to grab the handle of the knife, but it was too late. Screaming, she collapsed to the ground beside her son, pressing her fingers against his fatal wound. And rocking back and forth, she wailed beneath the light of a menacing and half-full moon.

"Perhaps now he will find peace," Salieri said, looking away.

"No... not like this," Eva wailed as she looked at him.

"It was not the blade that killed him," Salieri said. "He died because love was too much for his weak and broken heart."

"What of our other son?" Eva sobbed.

"He left long ago," Salieri said.

"Where is he?" Eva screamed, "How could you let him go?"

"Mentoria," Salieri said. "The dark city on the other side of the River E."

With blood-stained hands and a hole in her heart, Eva flew away. As she sped through the night, the witch pulled two dumbnuts from a small leather pouch, and one by one, placed them in her mouth. Immediately, the clouds seemed to clear, and a memory streamed across her mind—an image of Salieri, lying by her side, naked on the banks of the River E. It was Autumn. And they were holding hands and sleeping soundly on a bed of golden leaves.

Thunder clapped, and lightning ripped across the sky. It was almost morning when over the Fields of Crying Babies, howling winds forced Eva to the ground. When she touched down, the wind stopped, and all around, the gentle sound of sucking and whimpering rose from the rows of cribs. Eva watched as the weeping women dressed in black moved between them, offering reassuring hands.

Reaching down, Eva lifted a baby girl from the closest crib. The child was sobbing and rubbing the side of her face with a sheet. But when the child looked into Eva's eyes, her crying stopped. That was when it happened—for, despite Eva's grief, the ice that filled the hole in her heart melted away. And at that moment, Eva once again felt the wonder and love that illuminated the child's tiny eyes.

The rain continued to fall. At first light, Eva rallied the weeping women dressed in black. "Your sadness is too much to bear," she said." From this day, I will stay with you, and we will love these children as our own."

Confused, the mourning women looked around.

"Now stop crying," Eva said, with her hand raised in the air. "What these children need is love, not pity or the poison of your despair."

21. A GIGGLE OR TWO

If ever there was anything that could lighten Heinrich the whale's mood, it was the ability to have a little laugh. One afternoon years ago, accompanied by his pod of itinerant whales, he was grazing along a bank of seaweed when he bit off more than he could chew. Unaware they were nibbling at the edge of a meteorite that had crashed into the sea, Heinrich forgot about whatever he had swallowed until the following night when the rapturous sound of a giggling child yanked him from sleep.

Nestled in Heinrich's stomach, the small metal disc could fit neatly into the palm of an average-sized hand and had been a universal project to make people laugh. Unfortunately, it had failed as everyone seemed to be too busy wishing they were somewhere else or doing other things. The 'giggle,' as the device was called, produced the simple sound of a baby laughing, giggling, and captivated in a rapture of its own delight. Because it always made Heinrich smile, he had come to rely on the device that elevated his spirits to a state of unabashed bliss in moments of despair.

And a laugh was precisely what Heinrich needed after swallowing the foreign object that fell from the roof of the crystal caves. A short time later, the giggle giggled. And despite being a vegetarian, Heinrich's concerns about what he had swallowed lifted.

It was when the giggling stopped that Heinrich first heard the moaning sound.

"Shh," he said to the younger whales because he was sure he recognised the voice.

"Ugh, it stinks in here," the voice complained.

"Who's there?" Heinrich asked, lurching from side to side.

"Shh," Stanley said.

"Not you again!" Heinrich said. "What are you doing in my stomach this time?"

"Stop talking," Stanley said. "It stinks in here, and I want to be sick!"

"Well, what do you expect?" Heinrich said, not taking offence. "And while you're there, you might do me a favour. Just before you groaned, there was a laughing sound. It's something I swallowed some time ago, and I'd like to know what it is."

Distracted from his misery, Stanley kicked at the barnacled metal sphere that was vibrating beneath his foot. As he picked it up, the disc hummed in his hand. The giggling started again. Slow at first, then with greater urgency and speed. Moment by moment, the sound of the giggling baby became louder and more excited.

Stupid toy.

Yet Stanley found he couldn't stop the smile from spreading across his face. After a brief silence, the giggle buzzed, then started again. The sound of the giggling child echoed around Heinrich's gut. And when Stanley began laughing along with it, he couldn't stop. He laughed so hard tears rolled down his cheeks. He coughed, and he laughed until the urgent bubble of joy that was buried on the day he was born, popped. It was the bubble of happiness, the memory of being cradled in his mother's arms, of her wiggling his tiny his fingers and tickling him as she counted to five. Stanley bent forwards and clutched at his stomach as he fell to his knees, hysterical. Then his laughter turned to tears. After years of nummers and pills marked with the letter "P," it was as if inside him, the small white bird of joy remembered it had wings and decided to fly. The haze of Stanley's sadness thinned, and he ran around Heinrich's stomach, bouncing off the putrid walls, and in a moment of weightlessness and laughter and tears, he screamed out, "That's it!"

"What's what?" asked Heinrich.

"Feelings," Stanley said, and he laughed some more. "I'm not mad. And they're not a virus at all. I have to return to Mentoria."

"What for?" Heinrich asked.

"Because Mindset was one big lie," Stanley said. "I feel happy. I'm not mad! And it has nothing to do with the rays of the sun."

"Happy to help," Heinrich said as he started swimming upstream. Later, after hyperventilating for quite some time, Heinrich took a massive breath and shot Stanley up through his spout. Flying through the air, Stanley caught hold of the skinny and rusted ladder on the spindle that kept Mentoria suspended far above the River E. And with the remnants of a smile and one hand in front of the other, Stanley climbed up through the clouds.

Hours had passed when he reached the city and squeezed past the broken fan of the nummer drain. Overhead, pods of fluorescent lights drifted in circles as Mindset crackled and hummed and cast its duller than usual red dome across the sky. The streets were empty, and Stanley kept to the shadows cast by the city walls. He moved toward the small blue light that pulsed on top of the penthouse shaped like a pill.

Because he was sure that was where The Master would be.

22. AN EXPLOSION FOR A MORNING KISS

The greatest problem for Commander Aachoo—who was adept at blowing things apart—was that he was unlucky in love. Nursing a fragmented and lonely heart, the commander had never figured out how to stop his lovers from running away. Because of this, and through no fault of his own, Commander Aachoo suffered from a constant bad mood. His girlfriend of the moment happened to have two heads and was perpetually confused, as each head wanted different things. On the left, her calculating head was masterful at fulfilling her desires. Her other head (on the right) was the ruler of her heart and had, in recent times, shown signs of boredom and cast a wandering eye over males half her age.

Her difficulty was that younger males were boring and broke and spent all their money trying to pick up desperate females in smoky, neon-lit bars. And it was this idea that the commander's girlfriend had done battle with since before dawn. Beside her, Commander Aachoo slept between snorts and bouts of sleep-apnoea. It was just light when Aachoo woke, and he lurched across the bed to kiss the lips of his girlfriend's left head. But met by the cool winds of indifference, he groaned and then consoled himself with the thought that his girlfriend was probably still asleep. Unable to get back to sleep, the commander turned on his computer in search of a distraction. A message, in the form of a large envelope titled "URGENT," flashed across the middle of the screen. Aachoo scrolled through the text and was relieved to learn that the skinny white alien with the large head, whom he had not heard from for some time, was returning home. The bad news was that the portal whose entrance hovered in space far above the amethyst cave in Happysad remained closed.

The commander slammed his fist on the desk.

Why can't anyone do as they are told?

It then occurred to him that his girlfriend may never see the strange little seahorse on the red and otherwise uninhabited planet.

Serves her right.

But on second thought, the commander realised that time wasn't really on his side and that if he were ever going to be successful in love, he would have to take matters into his own hands.

For despite her wandering heart, she is my sun.

Commander Aachoo tapped at the keyboard and replied to the message from the alien on the screen. "I order you to open the portal right away!" And with what seemed to be an afterthought, he added, "Or I will destroy you... and the book deal will go away." The commander pushed "send."

To distract himself from the realisation that he would likely always be alone, he opened the file attached to the alien's message. Sitting back in an uncomfortable plastic chair with his arms folded behind his head, he started to read.

In another part of the same galaxy, a spaceship shaped like an after-dinner mint slipped silently through space. The skinny alien with the big bald head sat at the controls, consumed by its thoughts.

Sometimes things worked out for the best.

That was before a new message appeared on its computer screen. Commander Aachoo's orders were uncompromising and clear. With its arms behind its back, the alien paced back and forth. Yet before it could come up with a solution or a reasonable excuse, it was distracted by a passing and unusually pretty constellation of stars. On the panel overhead, large numbers on a small clock counted down.

What would Freeman do?

With a pang of loneliness, the alien thought about Freeman, wondering if he was still hovering somewhere in Happysad, approximately four inches above the ground.

Following a breakfast of six black eggs stolen from a captive fire-breathing bird, Commander Aachoo returned to his computer to check on the alien's reply. Not quite grasping the irony in *The Chronicles of the Absurd—Volume 1*, Aachoo was overcome with a sense of nostalgia—as it occurred to him that, after all, space really was a big place. He felt suddenly small but was comforted by the unexpected touch of his girlfriend's bony blue hand on his shoulder. Each of her heads curled slowly around his, and she placed, right in the centre of each of his green cheeks, an obligatory morning kiss.

Suddenly inspired, Commander Aachoo got out of his chair and stretched his old arms around her waist. With the enthusiasm of someone half his age, he whispered into one of her ears, "My sun. All of this is for you."

The commander's girlfriend grinned and nestled her two heads against his neck.

Then, with the impulsive optimism of youth, Commander Aachoo issued orders to the general in charge of blowing things up.

For what could be better than the demolition of a planet to remember our journey together to distant stars?

"I'll give you fireworks," the commander said to each of his girlfriend's heads.

Distracted, she smiled.

Not quite getting the affection he deserved, Commander Aachoo sat and watched his girlfriend painting her nails. He was suddenly bothered by the thought that things between them were about as good as they were ever going to be.

What's the point?

Unexpectedly, his focus shifted to a pain in his bowel, caused by an obstinate bubble of gas. And it was then that he knew it was going to be a difficult day.

23. THE EWOM

The Master paced around the penthouse shaped like a pill. He called for Juaneeto, unsure whether he should return to bed, hide beneath his sheets, or continue walking around the room. Juaneeto placed two mosquitoriums on the small tables beside The Master's red plastic chair. But when the hum of the glass jars offered him no relief, The Master stood up and waved his arms in the air. The mosquitoriums smashed, freeing two swarms of angry gnats that spiralled upwards and mercilessly bit The Master on his hands and neck and face.

Despite his growing despair, Juaneeto did the only thing that was left for him to do. He rushed from the penthouse shaped like a pill and returned holding a large syringe filled with a near-lethal dose of dumbnut mixed with water. Juaneeto jabbed the needle into The Master's thigh, and his patient howled in pain. Stepping back, Juaneeto waited for the side effects of the dose, the worst of which would be a quick and painful death. Moments later, The Master jolted as though having a fit, then stood up and started singing a chorus of old songs. Then, pointing to his toes, The Master began to dance. He pirouetted around the penthouse shaped like a pill and pushed the Sanitis-Or, covered in a purple felt cloth, quickly out the door.

The meeting of the Council of Necessity started some time before the Master arrived. With a unanimous vote for the Virus Called Dog to be contained, their orders rang from loudspeakers around the city. "Citizens of Mentoria. Leave your homes without your belongings. And assemble in the streets."

The Master entered the meeting room with small steps on the tips of his toes, pushing the trolley with a strange-shaped object draped in purple cloth. Clearing his throat, he took a deep breath. "Councillors, the time to act is now." The Master meandered behind each of the councillors, running his fingers along the backs of their chairs. "Everything is under control," he advised.

"Really?" one of the councillors asked, standing up and pointing towards the window that looked upon the mayhem in the streets.

The Master clicked his tongue. "Soon, that will be solved," he said, "but first things first." And making no mention of the fact that Mentoria was about to be destroyed by a violent, green, and wart-covered alien—who, because of The Master, had not been given his own way—The Master shared his vision.

"I built this city," he said, waving his arms. "And I will not see it destroyed."

Nodding, the councillors agreed.

Slowly, The Master's sense of authority returned, and a projector shone a light on the wall. "The future of Mentoria…" he said, "is in our hands."

The image was of the Fields of Crying Babies on the other side of the River E. The rows of babies in their cots had been replaced by tall buildings made from steel and glass. There were gardens with fountains and statues of The Master with his large head, standing between the trees. Distracted by the drama, the councillors clapped.

"We must expand to survive," The Master said.

'In Happysad?" a councillor asked. "What about the virus and feelings sent from the sun?"

The Master turned around and pulled at the purple cloth. "The Sanitis-Or," he said, revealing the black crystal, which he'd modified to house several illuminated crystal eggs.

"Not that again?" one councillor said.

"Yes, with a few adjustments," The Master said. Then, completely losing the track he was following in his mind, The Master told them a story about aliens and the psychic power of glowing crystal eggs. He finished with a few words on the apparent benefits of levitation.

With their eyebrows raised, the councillors looked around the room. "We've decided to go another way," one of the older councillors said sheepishly.

It was then that it dawned on The Master why his thoughts were not his own.

It's dumbnut! Juaneeto gave me dumbnut!

He took a deep breath and asked, "And, which way is that?"

"The EWOM," the councillor replied.

The EWOM (Emergency Waters of Mentoria) was originally designed as the city's last line of defence. But despite the cleverness of its design, the inventors gave little thought to the EWOM's effect on the city's power supply. Hidden around the city were a series of gigantic pumps and pipes, and when the EWOM was activated, it sucked water from the River E and flushed away everything in its path.

"There's another way," objected The Master. "You'll destroy the city, the plaza, the parks."

"The decision has been made," the councillor confirmed.

When The Master broke into the side-splitting laugh of a madman, the councillor lifted the plastic guard from a shiny blue button on the control panel where he sat. Trying to stop him, The Master lunged forward, missed, and fell on the floor. And the word "flush" flashed in large letters across the screen.

Red lights blinked on and off throughout the city. Sirens wailed. Following orders, people assembled in the streets. Children ran in circles while adults tried to ignore the black dog with the red rubber ball that always seemed to be lurking, just out of the corner of their eye. The guards retreated. In the chamber where the Council of Necessity met, The Master was tied to a chair.

When the sucking sounds started, the city shook. Large circular holes opened like gaping mouths in the streets. A loud clunk, followed by several other mechanical whirs, delivered the first drop of water from the River E. The pumps gathered speed, sucking harder until a powerful wave of water surged through the city streets. Overhead, the fluorescent pods of red light flickered and went out.

Mindset failed.

Downstream from where the water smashed through the glass and washed people away, Stanley stepped from the shadows. With the guards gone, he climbed onto an abandoned patrol car of the Mentorian Guard. Clearing his throat, he called out to the crowd, who seemed confused at the sound of water coming their way.

"It's all a lie," Stanley called out. Then louder and with his fist in the air. "It's all one big lie!"

Distracted, the crowd turned around.

"A lie?" asked a man.

"Yes," Stanley said, pointing to the sky. "Look, stars."

Through the smoke and far above where Mindset was supposed to be, stars shimmered in the sky. The crowd gasped.

"We have a machine," Stanley said. "That can power the city with the light of the stars."

Confused, people started calling out.

"What about the virus?"

"What about the dog?"

But before Stanley could answer, a large wave of brown water ripped around the corner and exploded onto the street. In the Plaza of Logical Thought, statues smashed, glass shattered, and people screamed as the water washed them away.

"Run," Stanley screamed. "There is no virus. The dog is just a dog. And feelings are just feelings – they come, and then they go."

The councillors watched as the EWOM surged through the city, washing everything away. Gripping a broken statue of The Master's head, Stanley rode the waters through the streets. The levels continued to rise, and Stanley came to a sudden stop as he crashed through the glass windows of The Great Hall of Power.

24. THE BIG BRIGHT YELLOW RAY OF LIGHT

Clueless as to what she was about to do, the two-headed girlfriend of Commander Aachoo pushed the red "Fire" button. The big bright and destructive yellow ray of light shot into space. Commander Aachoo stood by her side with his hands loosely behind his back. He grunted, vexed by his girlfriend, who seemed more concerned with how she looked in safety goggles than she was with the spectacle of blowing something to pieces.

Deep in a dense asteroid belt, the skinny alien with the large head stood poised at the controls of its spaceship, shaped like an after-dinner mint. Unable to decide what to say or do, it did nothing. The alien stared out at the stars with a sense of regret. Overwhelmed by the threat of Commander Aachoo, it pondered the fact that its writing career had never really begun. Twiddling an old metallic probe that looked something like a scalpel or a pen, the alien marvelled at the sudden, big bright ray of yellow light that passed from left to right and travelled towards the strange land called Happysad.

"Hmm," the alien said in its native tongue.

All things considered, it's not a bad way to go.

The alien—who wasn't really a selfish creature after all—dismissed any idea it might have had of putting itself in harm's way. And with a firm destination clearly in its mind and a navigation database that was well out of date, the alien steered its spaceship towards a wormhole and zoomed away.

25. IN THE END...

With a good part of the city destroyed, and substantial numbers of the population washed away, The Master stood up. Under the influence of dumbnut, he wriggled loose and addressed the councillors. "You have made a grave mistake. Now there's only one thing for me to do..."

Meanwhile, in space, a big, bright yellow ray of light gathered speed, vaporised small satellites, and moved closer—to Happysad.

When the waters started draining from Mentoria's streets, the councillors sheepishly rubbed their chins with their hands.

"Satisfied?" The Master asked as he continued to wriggle free.

"Yes," said one of the councillors, shocked at the realisation of what they had done. Warily, he looked to The Master, who it seemed had regained some control of his mind. "What do we do now?" the councillor asked.

"Untie me, and we will see," the Master declared.

The councillor nodded to the guard.

With his hands free, The Master rubbed his wrists. Looking down through the smashed dome of The Great Hall of Power, he saw Stanley clinging to a broken statue of The Master's head.

"I have just the thing," The Master said, gritting his teeth and taking hold of the small joystick on the table in front of where he sat.

Outside, a mechanical claw telescoped through the air and plucked Stanley from the ruins of The Great Hall of Power.

"Think you could outsmart me, did you?" The Master said into the microphone. "Think you could ruin everything I have done for this city? Everything I have done for you?"

"You murdered my sister!" Stanley yelled back. "And now the people know about your lie."

"Ahh," the Master said. "That." He pushed a button on the console, and the mechanical claw squeezed tighter.

Stanley yelped, like a dog yelps when someone steps on its tail. "Mindset has failed," Stanley said. And the survivors have seen the stars. There is no Virus."

The Master looked perplexed. "Is too," he said, like a child, and he pushed the button, making the claw squeeze Stanley tighter. "This is all your fault," The Master said. "You and your sister."

"I have been to Happysad and didn't lose my mind," Stanley said.

"Yes, but you had feelings," The Master said. "Fe-e-l-i-n-g-s," he said again with disgust. "They've corrupted your mind."

Perplexed, the councillors looked around the room.

"And now a little something before you die," The Master said.

Confused and unsure how else to respond, the councillors clapped. The Master spun around and pointed the eye of the Sanitis-Or toward the Fields of Crying Babies.

"This will stop those whining babies once and for all," he said. The Master closed his eyes and pressed the "ERASE" button on the top of his machine.

A ray of red light shot out from the device and tore through space. Looking up together, the councillors inhaled in awe.

From The Great Hall of Power, Stanley watched the red ray of light as it flew as far as it could and then pointed downwards towards the target for the final stage of flight.

On the other side of the River E, Eva walked silently through the Fields of Crying Babies. It was raining. She knelt between the cribs amidst the small sucking sounds of sleep.

Far above the clouds, the Sanitis-Or's red ray converged with Commander Aachoo's big, bright yellow beam of light. They collided with a cataclysmic flash and an enormous bang. The shock wave knocked the women in the Fields of Crying Babies from their feet. The sleeping stopped, and in unison, the babies opened their eyes.

The interstellar impact sent ripples through space. Electrical things stopped working, and as the smoke in Mentoria cleared, it bathed the city in an aura of orange and yellow light. The claw that held Stanley seized and dropped him on the street.

Far above the city, the Council of Necessity demanded some kind of explanation for what went wrong.

"Was that supposed to happen?" a councillor asked.

"It's all part of the plan," The Master said, keeping his back to the room to hide his confusion.

"Did it work?" asked another.

The Master replied, "Just wait, and you will see."

In the report handed to Commander Aachoo, the brilliant flash of light was a good indication of destruction. On the bridge of his spaceship, the commander turned to his girlfriend and smiled. Always fond of fireworks, she blushed, "For me, Archie?"

"Yes," Aachoo said. "It's all for you."

Moments later, a message appeared on the commander's computer screen. It was from the skinny alien with the large bald head in his spaceship shaped like an after-dinner mint.

The electromagnetic pulse has opened the space portal. It's safe to proceed.

Later, the surviving children were the first to return to Mentoria's streets. With Mindset gone, they ran after each other in the afternoon sun. Stanley stood up and watching the children, he smiled. The giggle in his pocket started to laugh. Slowly, others joined the children in the streets. Some of them laughed. Others cried. And for the first time in years—they allowed themselves to feel.

All was quiet in the Fields of Crying Babies. Having just finished their afternoon bottles, the babies napped. When Freeman arrived, he didn't bother speaking to the women. Instead, he walked to the centre of the fields and sat down. Crossing his legs, he closed his eyes. Slowly, a smile stretched across his face, and he rose to approximately four inches above the ground.

"What's he doing?" one woman asked.

"He's defying gravity," Eva replied. "He's teaching these small souls how to fly."

Later that day, the rain stopped, and the heaviness that always hovered across the fields lifted. One by one, the babies woke and spat out their dummies. Then they smiled.

Using the power of his thoughts, Freeman passed the instructions for levitation to the babies on the evening breeze. The gentle sounds of "goos" and "gaas" floated across the fields. Giggling and with the flapping of tiny hands, the babies lifted above the ground. As they climbed higher in the sky, their sadness disappeared. It was then that the armada of abandoned babies floated across the valleys and plains to the shores of the River E. Over the skies of Mentoria, they appeared as a flotilla of tiny dots, slightly bigger than birds. Then, one by one, they flew to their mothers and returned home.

Far above the city, the Council of Necessity peered through a rectangular window. At the entrance to the building, Mentorians banged on the doors, demanding to see The Master right away. The guards had fled, so when Stanley and several Mentorian men barged their way inside, the councillors backed away. They pointed to The Master, blaming him for everything.

Two men picked The Master up, and despite his kicks and screams, they carried him away.

When he called for Juaneeto, The Master's personal physician was nowhere to be seen. As though seeing the writing on the wall, Juaneeto had overdosed on dumbnut and then, thinking he was a bird, stepped from the penthouse shaped like a pill and failed to fly.

All alone, The Master laughed a nervous laugh and was suddenly aware that he needed to pee.

Later, it would be said that The Master lost his mind—much like a man can lose his hat. But it was more than that, for after the near-lethal dose of dumbnut wore off, The Master's paranoia set in. He was convinced he was being followed by an angry green alien with lots of warts. Not to mention the black dog with a red rubber ball that was always right there, lurking just beyond the corners of his eyes. At night he hid his head beneath a sheet for fear of a band of little blue creatures from a small brown planet far away. Because if there was one thing he was absolutely sure—it was that they were there for one reason. To play with his mind.

Orders were given that as punishment for his crimes, The Master be locked away in a small cell on a cliff far above the River E—that is, without a nummer or pills marked with the letter "P." He was left alone to think things through for a while. Mostly he spent his days sitting on a red plastic chair. He rocked back and forth, saying nothing while staring at the walls. In Mentoria, the exercise tax was abolished immediately. For perpetuating The Master's lies, the Councillors of Necessity found themselves shackled and sentenced to a life of hard labour, constructing solar panels to capture energy from the Great and Central Sun.

Stanley, who, it was discovered, was not so stupid after all, started work on the production of small disc-shaped giggles right away. Even though Delia's invention never really worked, her name was added to the city's List of Excellent Minds on the plaque in the Great Hall.

Once every year, a single Mentorian was celebrated for having a good idea. Starting with Stanley—and his discovery of the "giggle" in the stomach of a whale—the crowd gathered in the Great Hall. With a giggle in his pocket, he looked out across the sea of faces and felt no fear at all. The crowd clapped. And when he was asked to make a speech, despite the tear in his eye, he stood tall and smiled. Basking in the silence, he had nothing to say. But most importantly, he didn't run away.

In the mornings that followed, Stanley stood in line and waited for the shiny silver train. He counted slowly inside his head as the carriages passed by. The doors opened, and he watched as the smart people of the city boarded the train. Standing on the platform, he watched the doors close. He watched the shiny silver carriages disappear into the distance.

Deep inside Stanley, fear came like a wind rippling across the waters of his heart. Then it was gone. Small bubbles of sadness surfaced slowly, then popped and disappeared. The big white bird of joy spread its wings.

Stanley shifted his weight and rocked ever so slightly from side to side. Feelings came and feelings went. With the sun upon his face, Stanley smiled. Behind him, the shadow of a dog rested on the wall.

But there was not madness.

No.

None at all.

Time passed in Mentoria. At times, the citizens laughed, and at other times, they cried. They thought a lot about many things. Sometimes they were happy, and sometimes they were sad. But one thing was for sure, despite their feelings, they were never mad.

Years later, and mostly in the afternoons, a woman visited the surviving prisoners of Mentoria. In a saffron-coloured robe with a pointed hood, she glided between the cells. In her basket, she carried bundles of dried herbs and small glass bottles that clinked as she walked.

"For you," she whispered to each inmate. Mostly, the old councillors, too busy arguing with the riddles and cranky voices in their minds, turned away. When she came to the last cell, The Master sat on a red plastic chair with his back to the bars. He had sensed her arrival even before she was there.

"For you," she whispered.

The Master nodded, but didn't say a word.

"Of course," she replied as she pulled out a bottle of water infused with rosemary and mint. As with each time before, she would hand him the bottle, and he would squeeze her hand for longer than he should.

If only for a moment, her son's mind was still, his eyes open wide. The Master hummed a short and happy tune, his left foot tapping unconsciously in time.

When he let go of her hand, Eva bowed. Something shifted as if at that moment, her life returned to the serenity of her old healing ways. She left without another word.

With her back to Mentoria, Eva walked towards the River E. A gentle wind flicked crystals of light across the water. The scent of rosemary and mint lingered on her fingers, and with a smile, she whispered the words to the second son she'd always loved, "To take away your fears."

EPILOGUE

Every now and then, the alien with the spaceship shaped like an after-dinner mint would visit the skies of Happysad. It would wave at Freeman, who seemed to spend most of his time in what used to be the Fields of Crying Babies, hovering exactly four inches above the ground. But mostly, the alien seemed interested in Esmerelda, who it planned to include in *The Chronicles of the Absurd–Volume Two*. For Esmerelda, acting on Freeman's advice had taken to walking around backwards in circles, hoping she might uncover more fragments of her memory and learn a little more about her past.

Far away on a small brown planet, a group of little blue beings continued to watch. Standing in a circle, they held hands and shifted vigorously, foot to foot, side to side. They smiled and laughed a strange laugh. On a beam of light, they sent forth an image, a gift of their perpetual delight—a black dog chasing a butterfly, jumping, and then, distracted by the tip of its own tail, running in circles. Barking and filled with joy.

For no good reason at all.

ABOUT THE AUTHOR

Warwick Renton is the author of "A Virus Called Dog" - a humorous science fiction/fantasy novel. Born and raised in Sydney, Australia, he has studied law, driven buses, cleaned toilets, been an airline pilot, managed a union, produced entertainment events and written a book.

Warwick has three amazing children and lives in Geelong, Australia. When he's not with his kids, working or writing, you can find him in the ocean on his surf ski, hiking or simply contemplating the mysteries and absurdities of life.

For more information visit: www.warwickrenton.com

Instagram: warwickrenton_author

Twitter: @dog_virus

Facebook: https://www.facebook.com/warwick.renton

www.ingramcontent.com/pod-product-compliance
Lightning Source LLC
Chambersburg PA
CBHW021953170626
46808CB00001B/138